Novelmania

My Ticket to Crazy Town

By Bardi Rosman Koodrin

Novelmania: My Ticket to Crazy Town
© 2017 by Bardi Rosman Koodrin

Published by Sand Hill Review Press, LLC
All rights reserved
www.sandhillreviewpress.com,
P.O. Box 1275, San Mateo, CA 94401
(415) 297-3571

ISBN: 978-1-937818-59-3 paperback
ISBN: 978-1-937818-60-9 case laminate
ISBN: 978-1-937818-69-2 ebook
Library of Congress Control Number: 2017940092

Graphics by Backspace Ink
Art Direction by Tory Hartmann

SHRP
Sand Hill Review Press

For Boris

What can I say about my high school sweetheart fifty years after the fact? We still really, really like one another. We cherish our son, his wife, and their two sons with the fiery pride of the elders we have become. Boris Koodrin has earned this dedication for his decades of editorial support as I wrote countless versions of my saga *The Mud Eater's Apprentice* while struggling to reach the core essence of the story. Burning that book sparked a new epoch and *Novelmania* was born. Boris should receive a medal for calmly witnessing my meltdown that blazing September day when I scooped up hundreds of pages, shoved them into our fireplace, struck a match, and then gawked as droves of black ash floated around me. The flue was closed.

CHAPTER 1

The End

Day 1 —

Kings Mountain, Woodside
San Francisco Peninsula
Wednesday, September 21, 1983

I'M SO BUSY cremating ten-year old Helice Polansky in my backyard I hadn't noticed two intruders creeping behind me. So much for Mary standing guard or, God forbid, protecting me.

I'm stuffing more of that annoying kid Helice into her eternal flames when the snarkier of the two men taps me on the shoulder. Like I said, I'm focused on the task at hand.

I let out a loud "AAAAGGHHHHEY" from the shock of being touched from the rear by God only knows who, after I'd made sure I was completely alone and free to kill the kid. The tap makes me toss a bit of said kid into the air as I'm twisting myself around to see what's going on. That's when I see the two men who've trespassed onto my property.

I lock eyes with a total cliché of a burley Mick cop. He's got the vivid blue eyes of Erin yore, along with a short pug nose that's freckled from decades of sun and—

oh, he's talking. What's he saying?

"We spotted smoke a half-mile away." Officer brawn is panting like there's a heart attack brewing in his future. He wipes his dripping brow with a handkerchief. He demands of me, "Who are you, and whaddya think you're doing?"

He's avoiding looking at me, I'm starting to notice. Yum, his young stud-muffin partner isn't shy with his eyes.

"Um, I'm burning trash?" I glower over at Mary, who's under the gazebo. She hates the heat, which is why she's staying put. Normally she'd be all over something like this.

He points to my crumpled clothes in a heap next to a burning fire pit. "Do you usually burn trash in your underwear?"

I glance down. Oops, I'd forgotten I'd stripped to my bra and panties. It gets so bloody hot incinerating a life.

He tells his partner, "Check her clothing."

Being clad only in black lace Victoria's Secrets and red four inch heels might come across as the wrong impression to two public servants on a service call. Making sure to sound like the fine upstanding citizen I am, I say, "Hey, Officer, you don't need to poke around my things like that, I don't have anything to hide in my pants."

I flash a smile at this twenty-something cop, a tender rookie by the looks of him. In fact, I like the look of him so much I take a leisurely stroll along his body.

He is directed to pat the clothing down. Then the other guy tells me, "Put your clothes on, ma'am."

The hunky rookie's face reddens adorably when he hands them over. We share a moment as our eyes meet, and our fingers touch during the transfer. Kismet, I'm in love! They both look away while I squeeze into my black leggings and pull on a slouchy top.

Visibly relieved, the older cop gets down to business. "Let's start with your name."

6

"Oh, okay." I stick out my right hand. "Hi, I'm Trez Evans." My hand gradually drops.

He starts to write my name but he seems confused. His pen stops midway.

I tell him, "My name's Teresa Rose Evans. Trez is my nickname." Total silence makes me nervous; it makes me run off at the mouth. "I was the third daughter born, which makes me, you know, three? Uno, dos, tres? Teresa, Tres, Trez? Get it? Ahh... so anyway, I thought it was kinda catchy, a lot better than Teresa. Blah. Or Terry. It's all so common it's sickening. Name's spelled T-r-e-z, by the way."

"Is it Mrs. Evans or Miss?"

"*Ms.* Evans. I worked hard back in the day for women's rights. What's your name?"

"Officer O'Doul," he says out of the side of his mouth. He doesn't introduce his partner, who stays mum. "This a typical day for you, *Miz* Evans? Burning trash in this heat, ten feet from high dry grass? Your place is halfway up Kings Mountain. Think nobody'd notice?"

"Well...I'm doing it here in the middle of my tennis court, which you see is not grass. I think it's clay. I took down the net, for safety's sake. There's the garden hose, of course."

O'Doul counts on pudgy fingers. "You got five portable fire pits all going full force. Why so many? They look new what with the price tags showing—no signs of weathering."

I say, "My paper shredder broke. There's no place close-by to get another, so I bought two fire pits when Mr. Olsen's hardware store opened at 7:00, and, and, the pits worked so well, I went back and got the other three to burn her up faster since I thought I was going to work but..."

"You got documents here?" He sweeps a hand over piles and piles of paper stacked around the tennis court. He is rather overdramatic and redundant, if you ask me, as he swipes at the black ashes floating above us.

"Exactly what are you destroying?"

"Um, it's not illegal to burn my own manuscript. *The Mud Eater's Apprentice*. I made it up, I wrote every crappy word. I have a right to kill the kid. Helice Polansky."

"What kid? She your daughter?" He steps closer. He is so close I take note of how his graying nose hairs flutter as his nostrils flair, not unlike a gelding I once owned.

"What? There's no child, Officer. She's, it's a character in my book. I was just trying for a little humor here. Ah, it's embarrassing to admit I'm a failed writer." The word *failed* makes me choke.

"A manuscript? Looks more like ten books worth here." He goes deadpan on me when he adds, "You're not in the middle of a *Shining* breakdown, are you?"

"Huh?" I can't figure him, until the image of a crazed Jack Nicholson comes to mind. "Oh, very funny, Officer. Trust me, there are 250 *different* words on each fricking page."

He's not buying my story, it's time to hype it up. "I wrote a gazillion versions over nine, ten years. Every page is pure crap. Look, I know this might seem ridiculous, crazy even, but I'm not hurting anyone. I'm burning my own freaking novel."

The cop shoves his finger too close to my face. That's when Mary decides to hop off the chaise lounge.

Eying her, he warns, "Watch that one, Marciano."

Yum, I love Italian. I allow my mind to drift deliciously away.

"Hey, is that a bottle of alcohol over there? Marciano, go get it, bring it over here."

The cutie gathers a knife, crushed coke cans, lime rind, and a drained fifth of Bacardi.

"So I've had a few drinks. I was up all night reading my stupid crappy novel."

"Uh-huh. It's..." He checks his watch. "It's not even noon. The news says it's the hottest September recorded since 1939." He wipes his brow again. "You're doing an illegal burn in a high-risk area during fire season. In redwood country, for crying out loud."

"You're right. Give me a ticket, I won't fight it."

"Maybe I should give you a sobriety test first."

"Is that necessary? On my own property. I'm just burning a little—"

"It's against the law if you were intoxicated when you drove into town for those fire pits."

He's gazing around. Uh oh, he's noticing evidence of my earlier attempts. He mumbles, "Why is smoke coming out all...?" He takes time to count the number of chimneys on his stubby fingers. "Smoke out of all four of them?"

"Look, I got fired yesterday because of my stupid book. As I was leaving the office in disgrace, I fell down a flight of stairs and whacked my head."

I rub my sore temple, hoping for a little compassion. He motions for me to continue.

"Um, okay, I couldn't go home and cry about it, last night I had to go to a celebrity chick's book launch at the Palace of Fine Arts. She booked the Palace for crying out loud! The most hoity-toity cocktail party of the season. Hardest thing I've done in a long time, asking her for party tickets but I was hoping publishers and agents might be there and—"

He interrupts with a gruff, "Who's this author you're talking about?"

My mouth bends and spasms it's so hard to say her name out loud. "Bethany Moraga."

He snorts, "Doesn't sound familiar."

"Oh, my God, you have got to be kidding. Everyone in San Francisco—and maybe the world—knows about Bethany Moraga."

His bloated face is blank, forcing me to talk even more about my bitch writer nemesis.

"She's made it onto the New York Times bestselling list. Twice! And she's only twenty-seven. Makes me feel even more of a failure since I'll be turning thirty thr...ah, never mind. Um, so you see, after I got fired, and fell down the stairs, after I suffered through this celebrity author's book launch instead of having my own, I came home and read through all my novel versions. There must have been a couple of cartons of paper, took me all night. Made me crazy. That's when I realized it was either her or me."

"Who you talking about? The other author?"

"Hell no. I don't want to think about Bethany."

"Who, then?"

"Helice, of course. My novel. I'd had a bad day and I was in major pain from hitting my head earlier. I'm still working through it by the way. A full-blown migraine where I'm seeing flashes of light in-between bouts of nausea."

He's pressing his fingers into the bridge of his nose, clearly not getting it.

It's best not to tell him those flashes of light turned into a shape that looks a little too familiar. My writing may not be top notch, but those lights are what made me burn everything. He doesn't need to know the real reason why—that the shape I saw turned into my character Helice Polansky. She followed me home. Plus, she was rude to me.

"Anyways, Officer, I was totally upset about everything that happened to me yesterday. Since I'll probably never get my novel published, I started feeding it page by page into the paper shredder. There was so much paper the damn thing jammed so I crumpled a page. I liked the feel, the sound of it.

"Oh, man, it felt so good I grabbed another. It was fun to punch holes with my fingernails. I actually bit a few of them into pieces. Before long, there was a big pile of crumpled and chewed novel pages on the floor. I liked seeing my story that way. Seeing Helice all smashed up. That's when I shoved a bunch of pages into my fireplace and lit a match. Whoosh!

"Watching Helice burn with the black ashes floating everywhere...well, it spoke to me."

The cop frowns. "You saying the fireplace talked to

you?"

"What? No, that's ridiculous. Pay attention, Officer. I had to exorcise Helice out of my life or she'd destroy me. You don't understand how long I've coped with her." My voice turns whiny. "That's why I burned my manuscript and everything I bought at thrift stores and auctions. Vintage clothing, shoes, books, and games. The story's set in 1953. She's from Detroit, a little polio victim. It's my angle. Everything had to be authentic, for the integrity of the...ah...piece..." My voice trails as I hear how lame this sounds.

"Detroit, you say. You got an address and phone number for this kid?"

"You're not listening to me! Helice had to go!"

"Oh, I'm hearing you, Ms. Evans. We both are." He mumbles an aside to my handsome rookie, "It's full moon time. That always brings out the crazies."

My lips pout. "Oh. Um, well...like I was saying, after the paper shredder jammed, I got the idea to shove her into the fireplace. I threw in chapters and props all at once. Felt so good to be free of her. Trouble is, the vent. Poof."

I wave my hand, flick my wrist. "Smoke everywhere. I tried each fireplace but the maintenance guy must'a tightened the flues. Every room is a mess. I went outside to burn her even if it is a thousand degrees today." I smile at my darling rookie, my newest future Saturday night date.

Burly guy tells him, "This lady keeps talking about a 'she,' a 'her.' Sounds like a person to me. It might be connected to the kid who went missing, what's her name?

Marciano prompts his superior officer, "Name's Analeese Loveland."

The old guy presses me. "Analeese? You been burning Analeese?"

"Who? I'm talking about *Heh-lease.* Helice Polansky."

"Names sound awful close," he says with squinted

eyes, as if he is literally thinking this out as he speaks.

Time to educate him. "I wanted my story to be accurate to the 1950s. So, I researched girl's names and when I found the name Helice, well, I got chills it was so perfect." He's flexing his neck like a dumb turkey so I go on. "Helice. The double Helix? Two intertwining spirals? The story's set in 1953, the same year that DNA was identified. Get it?"

The old cop groans, "Marciano, I got a bad feeling about this. Check out the fireplaces, sift through all the ashes."

Jeez, how long will this take? My bangs are uncurling from the sweat pouring down my face it's so hot. Raising both arms to twist my hair into a bun causes me to lose balance and stumble, which makes me look drunker. Despite having recently scored a fabulous black market drug made out of botulism that removes facial wrinkles, I feel myself frowning.

"Um, wouldn't you need a search warrant to do that?"

Marciano nods yes to me, while the other cop challenges, "You got anything to hide?"

"No, Officer," I sigh. "Go ahead."

I watch Tall-Dark-and-Italian run to my house. It's set a good distance away. Gives me time to check out his ass, nicely defined in his lightweight summer uniform. High and tight, the way I like 'em. His buttocks tense as he takes the stone steps four at a time. An athlete.

I hear a growl, low and long, the way Mary likes 'em.

The older cop takes a step back, while positioning his hand over his holstered gun.

"Ah, sir, I don't want this to get out of hand. Can I put her in the kitchen or something? I need to use the bathroom anyway. I'll take her inside and then I'll be right back."

"No. Stay where I can see you. You got a leash handy?" He goes to grab Mary's collar.

"Sir, I wouldn't do that if I were—" Shit. Too late.

Mary takes his feet out from under him.

"What the hell?" He's muttering this after landing on his butt.

Mary trots away, all one hundred and forty pounds of Rottweiler bad girl.

The cop's up again, brushing off his dusty pride. He grumbles, "How'd he do that?"

"She's a female," I quip, "and was professionally trained to flip over annoying men." Oops. That was probably one toke over the line. Maybe the rum will wear off soon.

"I've had enough of your smart mouth," the cop snarls. "Tie that thing up."

I look around. Except for a hose, there's not a rope or weed or anything long enough for Mary's twenty-six inch neck.

"How's 'bout we lock her in the tennis court and we stand outside?"

He wavers, as if he's thinking she'll eat the evidence. He finally says, "Tell her to stay."

Just then, we see my newest future boyfriend with the killer body, bounding up.

Delectably flushed and breathless in a sweet, little boy way, Marciano says, "You should see her house, Lou. It's a hunting lodge with animal heads. She's even got a real stuffed bear in her foyer. A grizzly. It's standing up, it's gotta be eight feet tall."

I lift my shoulders, then let them drop. "That's Woodside for you. Can you believe it was built for a few good ole boys just to play big bad hunter? It was a summer camp with guns."

My future lover-in-a-committed-live-in-relation-ship is still ogling my Victorian-era estate that's a skip and a jump away from a trail heading straight up Kings Mountain.

Bad cop doesn't care, he squares his shoulders and snipes, "You keep any guns in there?"

My yummy future husband answers for me, "I didn't see any, Lou."

"Was I asking you?" He turns to me. "Are there any guns anywhere on this property?"

"Not unless you count my nephew's plastic water pistol." I grin.

He tells his underling, "Quit your laughing, Marciano. Go back and check every room."

The father of our future adopted girl baby from China obeys.

O'Doul turns to me, "Who owns this spread?"

"I do. Technically it's still in litigation, has been for ten years. My late, first ex-husband's mother has made it her mission to fight his will, but she keeps losing—it's ironclad. She hates me, just because I was nineteen and her precious son was older than my dad when we eloped. He divorced me six weeks into it, and then," I snivel, "Lawton died a couple years later. He must have loved me. I was still in his will. So, his mother's just been blowing hot air. I figure at age ninety six, she doesn't have much air left."

I fiddle with a Band-Aid on the right side of my forehead. "Did I tell you that I fell leaving work yesterday?" Another tear escapes. "My head hurts. I didn't sleep a wink last night, I was so worked up about everything. But...but I simply couldn't go another day with Helice. Especially after she insulted me. She crossed the line."

I need to blow out a breath. What Helice said to me last night was brutal. I can't stop thinking about why she appeared to me out of thin air.

How she said, *I'm here to help her.*

I'm the stupid kid's creator, for crying out loud. Helice said she's here for someone else? Not me? Why can't I be number one to my own character?

Her! I'm just now realizing Helice has got to be talking about Bethany Moraga, with her big hair and shoulder pads as broad as a 49er linebacker.

A shiver runs through me. "Um, I still got ready for work today, to show my boss how much I wanted my job, but, but, I'd already started burning Helice in these pits and couldn't leave an active fire. I called him up to say I'd be late and that's when...that's when he fired me all over again."

An odd sound comes up out of my very soul–*a wail of desperate discontent*. Hmm, I like that analogy. Or is it a metaphor? Whatever. Think I'll use it in my next novel, if I ever decide to repeat the mental equivalent of flaying my own skin off inch-by-flabby-inch.

I have to blow my nose, and go potty too. Getting fired is so emotional. I know, since it happens to me often enough. I don't burn my life's work every day of the week, though.

"You got the deed for this property, Ms. Evans?"

"Why?" My sniffle turns into a sob. "D-Do I need to call my lawyer?"

Just then, Marciano returns. He's holding out a fire poker. Dangling from it is the smoldering remains of a child-sized, black and white saddle shoe.

O'Doul's brow furrows. He asks Marciano, "What's the name of that missing girl? The one from Redwood City?"

Marciano looks out into space like he's trying to remember something really difficult. "Analeese Loveland, remember?"

The old guy turns to me. "What's the name of the kid you've been burning?"

"Her name? It's not like she's real."

O'Doul's voice deepens. "I'm going to ask you again. Who is the girl you're talking about? What were you doing with her clothing? Why were you burning everything?"

"God." I blow out a loud sigh, which makes my migraine pound. "You are not listening to me. I made up a character, that's what authors do. My character is Helice Polansky."

The old guy enunciates, "Hel-*leese*. Ana-*leese*." His big furry eyebrows dance and he grins like a cat who just found a mouse. "Do you see any similarity?"

When I don't answer, he asks Marciano, "Think

that shoe would fit Analeese Loveland?"

Marciano shrugs. "It'd probably fit a ten year old."

It's got to be the migraine. And it's so damn hot. It's got to be why I can't think properly. Oh, and the rum, too. Why else would I pipe up, "Of course it fits a ten year old. That's how old Helice is."

He smiles for the first time. "Ms. Evans. Where were you between the hours of 6:45 and 8:30 earlier this morning?"

"Huh, what?" He repeats the question. "Oh. I was home and didn't leave." That is so not true but he doesn't need to know that.

"You sure about that, Ms. Evans?" I don't like this cop's tone. "Because didn't you admit driving into town to buy some fire pits? You said it was around 7:00 am, didn't you?"

"Um, I forgot about that. It was just a short ride into the village and then back home."

"Didn't you admit going back to the hardware store a second time to buy more fire pits?"

"It's a short ride. Give me a break."

"I don't think so, Ms. Evans."

I let out a moan because my left leg is bob-bob-bobbing I have to pee so bad. My desperation scares Mary, so she lunges at the source of my discontent. The cliché Mick cop whacks her with his baton, which pisses me off.

I whack him. Tall-Dark-and-Italian grabs me. He gets a handful of boob. Either he's scared or aroused; I can't tell if it's his member or his gun pressing on my full bladder.

Mary takes advantage of his faux pas to steal the shoe off the poker. I'm so scared they'll shoot her, I piddle.

It's not intentional, it just happens, but getting peed on pisses off both cops so they handcuff me to a gate before chasing Mary, who at a ripe old age of seventy dog years, bolts up Kings Mountain with Helice Polansky's burnt shoe in her mouth.

CHAPTER 2

The Beginning

I MAY HAVE CREATED a problem, what with being drunk and burning my novel and Helice's clothes and stuff. How could I have known that another little girl would go missing at the same freaking time? I can't move because I'm still handcuffed, but I can see Mary weaving through the underbrush, leading those cops on a goose chase. She grew up on this mountain; she knows it inside out. They probably won't catch her, but if they do, she'll surely bite them both. Oh no. Mary's already got two strikes against her for prior altercations she took care of in her own unique Rottweiler way. If she gets in trouble one more time, the county will...oh, dear. I have to do something, and fast. She's the love of my life.

The cops aren't making much headway, what with Mary's zigzagging. Clever girl. They're taking out their guns, so I scream, "You sonsofbitches, keep away from my dog!" I kick mounds of dirt their way but everything ends up sticking to my wet leggings because of the pee. They should have let me use my bathroom.

I yell at the top of my lungs, "Stop! I'll tell you everything!"

Marciano, my newest ex-boyfriend, is too far away to hear me. He is like a dog with a bone. He's out for blood, just because we broke up. Well, we never actually dated, we just met thirty minutes ago, but there *was* chemistry. The older cop stops in his tracks, though, like he wants to come back but he's wavering. I have to beef it up, grab his attention. Mary's life is on the line.

I yell, "Hey, O'Doul. I confess. I killed the little kid, okay? I killed Helice Polansky."

He's pivoting. He's returning to the scene of my alleged "crime."

As he approaches, I see his paunchy face is as scarlet as the bougainvillea growing on the iron gate I'm handcuffed to.

"You—" He's next to me now, huffing so hard he can't talk. We're so close, his eyes look like two cat's eye marbles.

He sprays salvia on me as he starts again, "You have the right." He tries to take in a deep breath, which only makes him gasp louder. "To an attorney. If you—"

That's when he falls. Facedown. His bulbous Irish head lands square on my foot with a considerable thud. I try kicking him off but he must tip the scale at two-deuces-and-a-half of dead weight. Oh, shit. Is he...? Oh, shit, shit, shit.

I scream, "Marciano, come quick. Your partner."

Marciano rushes back with the speed of a downhill racer. He's at his partner's side in a flash, takes one look, and bellows into his walkie-talkie, "Officer down. I repeat. I have an officer down." He starts CPR.

I'm screaming my guts out. It's not every day a cop, or anybody for that matter, drops at my feet. On my property. Marciano's working on him. Officer O'Doul stirs – finally. He lets out a moan. Thank God. Mary and I didn't kill a cop.

Marciano makes his partner as comfortable as possible. He turns to me, demanding, "Whaddya do to Lou?"

I look away.

My ex, Tall-Dark-and-Dazed, won't let up. "He say anything? Anything?"

"No, not a word."

Marciano yells into his talkie thing again. "I got O'Doul breathing but I have a situation: hostile dog running around the woods, and a suspect who appears to be drunk."

Tall-Dark-and-Stupid has some nerve. I am not drunk. Not that much.

I spot Mary hiding behind a California live oak. She'd doubled back around. The pink bow I'd Velcroed atop her head earlier is crooked; her tan, polka-dot eyebrows are dancing. Mary loves a good chase. Ask any of the food vendors in the village. Oh, I can see dirt on her snout. Looks like Mary buried the shoe. She's done away with the evidence. Good girl. She'll get an extra Coors with her dinner tonight, that's for sure.

Just then, I cock my head like a cute dog in a commercial "I hear sirens. What'd you say? They're coming for *me*?"

SOON THERE'S A BIG HULLABALOO at my place, cops are tearing up my household while I'm directed to sit outside on a garden bench. Thank heavens they let me leave the fence, but they won't take off the handcuffs, just rearrange them. I lift my tied together hands to shove my limp bangs aside; they are soaked from my head sweating so much. I don't adjust my drooping off-the-shoulder top since most of the cops are giving me the eye. It's nothing new; men regularly mistake me for that actress in Flashdance. Considering how smoking Jennifer Beals is, I accept the compliments even if I'm a head taller, don't look ethnic since my eyes aren't brown, my skin burns in the sun, and my hair's a lot lighter, especially now that it's streaked. I do have a dancer's body without ever taking a class. I can bend both legs behind my head and that is truly a gift from high, high Above.

Other cops are in my house, removing reams of paper I hadn't had time to burn. Whoa, there's a hot mess of static coming from a walkie-talkie, but I clearly detect the name Analeese Loveland. Oh, yeah, that's the name of the missing kid. I'm wondering what she's got to do with me when I hear one of the cops say, "We have zero leads. If we don't find that kid by tomorrow morning, do'ya think the FBI would want to head up the kidnapping search?"

Marciano mutters, "Yeah, right, like we'd ever let them muscle in on our case."

Uh oh. Do they think I had anything to do with that? I guess they do. They keep giving me the third degree.

It's time to explain my circumstances. Unfortunately, Marciano ignores my request to speak to him privately. Some other cop comes over instead.

"Um, Officer," I stammer, "I kinda went a little bonkers."

I do not admit my saga started yesterday afternoon after Bethany Moraga graded my latest story revision a big fat F. If that weren't enough, she wrote a big zero on my paper in red. *The plot of a paralyzed child in an iron lung during the 1950s polio epidemic is more boring than watching paint dry. The lousy writing makes it absolutely unbearable.*

Ouch. It hurt even more when some of the members sided with her. I've worked so hard to be part of that group.

I tell this new cop, "Bethany is court-mandated to conduct only twelve more writing sessions. Her second DUI was my saving grace." I can't stop the grin stretching across my face. "After hearing she'd be doing her community service out of the Chinatown YMCA, I ran down there chop-chop and signed right up. Been going for almost two months now. Trouble is, she doesn't recognize my talent. I go to every weekly session, even if she is mean to me."

It's depressing how much effort and time I've put in to that group. I let out a little moan. "My head hurts."

I'm attempting to pick up some pity points but this guy is a stone cold warrior. "Can you please take off the handcuffs?"

"No."

"All righty then." I continue my story, "I went to that writing group yesterday, just like every Tuesday from noon to two. The problem was, Bethany was more vicious than usual. She spent extra time criticizing my latest chapter. Did I already tell you this? When I got back to the office around three, I was fired. A girl can only take so much."

I feel my cheeks burning. Must be the sun beating down on me. I'm probably talking too much. Booze will do that.

"I tell you what, it killed me to watch Bethany act all sweet and witty at her book launch while she was being interviewed by the cutest ever TV reporter, while she totally ignored her guests. How rude is that? I hated her perfectly crimped hair and killer Armani power suit. I hated Bethany as she sat like a queen in the middle of her launch party. I hated that the reporter lobbed easy questions at her like she was a movie star on the red carpet. Not only is Tobey Vallencourt up and coming at KPIX, he's super sexy. Seeing Bethany basking under Tobey's *lights, camera, action.* spotlight threw me into a mega-rage. *That should have been me up on that stage!*"

The cop mutters, "Imagine that."

I go on, "It was even worse when they asked everyone to tune in to *People Are Talking* when it airs tomorrow, which is probably today. Oh shit, I guess I missed it." I soldier on. "Anyway, I was so mad it felt like a bomb exploded inside my brain. An atomic bomb. No wonder I'm still suffering from an epic migraine."

The cop asks, "Ma'am, are you all right?"

"Officer, between the fall down the stairs, the champagne at the book launch, and reading the thirty-freaking-eight versions of my novel plus a plethora of notes, mind you... I love that word, plethora." I burst into song to the tune of Groucho Marx's *Lidya, Oh Lidya*: "Plethora, oh plethora..."

One of the other newly arrived cops comes over and warns, "Shut your trap."

These cops are cranky, what with one of their own almost croaking. Officer O'Doul was taken away in the first of two ambulances. Dogcatchers are tracking Mary up and down the mountain, fighting dense scrub and light-blocking redwood trees. Good luck. She once punished me by hiding out for a week. Funny thing is, Mary came back even fatter, probably from raiding restaurant garbage cans in the village. Visualizing a net big enough for a hundred forty pound dog gives me a chuckle.

There's nothing worse than an ex-lover, or a guy who could have been if he was nicer to me. Marciano's busy talking to some bigwigs in suits, and they're all staring at me.

He's saying, "As you can see, she's acting strange. We need to keep her. She could be a suspect with that Redwood City girl gone missing this morning, but on what grounds?"

It's hard to believe Marciano has turned on me so viciously. After everything we could have had together.

One of the suits says, "Tell you what. Make this a 5150. There's cause, and it'll buy us three days to sort things out."

I turn to my very own entourage, a darling paramedic, and his trainee. "What's a 5150?" I give the medic my best combination Trez Evans smile and enticing eyebrow raise.

My medic and new potential love interest says, "Think of a spa, a nice place to rest. C'mon, I'll drive you."

I tilt my head, give him a little pout. "Really? I thought you guys were mad at me."

"We can tell you're stressed out," says the paramedic. "We want to help."

Something doesn't feel right. If I could think straight, maybe I'd figure it out but what the hell. Mary's proven she can be on her own for a while. I need some me time.

"Okay, although I don't want to go in an

ambulance. Call for a driver. I like Town Cars.”

“But I pulled some strings to get you in on such short notice. They’re expecting us.”

“Why, thank you...” I squint at his nametag. “Brad, is it?” I flash my dimples. “I deserve a treat. You see, it’s been a tough day. I haven’t slept.”

“Oh?” He’s encouraging me with a sympathetic nod. “Tell me more.”

I giggle like a schoolgirl. “Well, you see, Brad. A little girl named Helice Polansky has absolutely obsessed me. Stupid kid. I think about her day and night, which is why I haven’t been sleeping in...oh, I can’t even guess how long it’s been. I had to get rid of her, don’t you know? Before she ruined me. Survival of the fittest. Right, Brad? Right?”

I MUST SAY, riding inside an ambulance isn’t as fun as it looks. First off, I’m flat on my back on a stretcher that’s so bloody narrow my butt is hanging off the sides like two skins of rendered sausage my Slovenian grandma used to make. Worse, my four limbs are strapped down as if Brad thinks I’m a lunatic. Worst of all, the driver is a trainee and he’s been riding the brakes all the way down a very twisty Kings Mountain, which makes for a damn choppy ride.

At least the handcuffs are off and my circulation is slowly returning. Oh, crap. The rum and cokes with lime twists are catching up with me. They’re catching up with the Thorazine shot they gave me, just because I gave the cops some lip. Don’t they know Thorazine is for crazy people? But then again, I got the shot before my new best friend Brad, the darling paramedic, promised he’d take me to a spa. That’s all he needed to say. I was all sweetness and light after that, especially after thinking about getting a mud wrap. There is a small part of me that thinks a spa offer sounds too good to be true, but Marciano must feel guilty for being mean to me. Oh, and I want a massage. Definitely need a good massage.

Uh-oh. Sour taste in mouth. It's making me swallow over and over again. I'm...I'm...

As much as I hate to barf, it always makes me feel better.

"Aw," cries Brad, "why didn't you say you had to throw up? Jesus, what a mess."

Hmm. Brad is not the gentleman I took him for.

The trainee driver turns for a look-see. "Gross. Does she need a shot of Compazine?"

"Good call for nausea, Hanson. That's exactly what I'll give her."

"No, wait. I'm allergic to Compazine. It works the opposite on me. Seriously, Brad, listen to me."

The cute paramedic gives me a shot with the biggest needle I've ever seen.

I am not responsible for what happens next.

I warned Brad that Compazine makes me sicker instead of better. So, it's not my fault that I'm now spewing brown rum and coke plus orange cheez doodle remnants all over his speeding sickmobile.

Thank God. The blaring siren finally stops. Before we left my house, Brad had told me to picture a pastoral scene. So, I'm smiling as the rear double doors open. I can hardly wait to meet the personal attendant Brad promised me. I'm thinking someone will hand me a glass of chilled Chardonnay right away, before drawing me a nice bubble bath and—

The paramedics pull me out of the stinking ambulance and set my stretcher down in the parking lot. They just plop me on the ground as if I were cargo. Looking through dried weeds poking out of cracks in the concrete, I see the front of an ugly red brick building. I squint at a sign: *Peninsula Mental Health Facility*.

"What the hell?"

Four men dressed head-to-foot in white greet us. They are gigantic, the human equivalents of my Rottweiler dog.

They transfer me, none so gently I might add, from the stretcher to a gurney they'd rolled out to greet us.

The stretcher was narrower, not a great fit for my hips, but this gurney is a lot harder on the tush. Brad hands them some papers, then takes off in the ambulance. My unrequited love doesn't even say goodbye to me.

I fumble with the tight straps holding me onto the gurney. The largest man says, "Come on, Ms. Evans. Don't make this any harder on yourself."

"Did Brad tell you I need a loony bin? Just because I did away with a little girl I made up in the first place? I've had a bad day. A very, very bad day. All I did was burn my manuscript. It's my story, I can kill off any character I want. Helice is a little brat. I'm so much better off without her. Why don't you call me a cab and we can all forget about it?"

These guys aren't buying my earnest plea.

"Wait. Can I tell you a secret?" I look all around me and lower my voice to a raspy whisper. "So here's the thing. I was at a party last night when I first saw her."

One of them prompts, "Who?"

I shout, "Helice, my character, that's who! At first, I just saw a big flash of light. But then, when I looked really hard it was her. She came to life, I swear!"

"Yeah, lady, whatever you say."

I can't be certain she manifested into a real physical body. I was too afraid to touch her, but these guys don't need to know that. After all, the kid was half hidden in the shadows, no one else noticed her. It spooked me, though. No wonder I drank so much. I kept my distance from her. I tried to get with the party spirit and chat with my date and other writers from my group but Helice kept trailing me. I could see her out of the corner of my eye. She even talked to me, a real shocker I have to say. She asked me the darnest thing. She wanted a book on American Indians, as if the launch was held in a book store. Stupid kid.

I burst out, "I couldn't tell anybody that my character was harassing me, could I?"

The orderlies are milling around the gurney, staring hard at me. To convince them I say, "All of a sudden

Helice put her hand on *me*. I mean it, a fictional character I created came to life and touched me. I can't tell you how she did it but it happened. Believe you me, I let out a 'AAAAGGGGHHHHEY' from the shock of being touched by God only knows what."

One orderly startles from my outburst. Good, I'm getting to him. Three more to go.

I tell them, "You better believe I dropped my drink from that shock. The glass shattered. Everyone stopped talking and stared at me."

Funny, these guys are staring at me so intensely my cheeks are burning, just like last night at the party. Wide, unblinking eyes will do that. Good thing it's only four people compared to hundreds.

"So, you guys realize I had to get away from Helice, right? Right, guys?"

I wait until they nod in agreement before continuing, "I ran out of that party like a bat out of hell. She followed me home. Now she's back, haunting me even more. Can you believe that?"

I stop my story short to ensure my audience is fixated on me. "Bottom line, guys. I gotta tell you, she scared me and my dog too. That's why I burned Helice. To get rid of her."

"She dead." One of the orderlies cracks, "Hah, now you got yourself a Casper the Ghost."

His teammate corrects him, "Nah, it's a pretend ghost. She done made it up, remember?"

All four of them crack up they think they're so funny.

Hah, hah. Time to get serious. "Hold on, this building is so old, it sure doesn't look safe. We're in earthquake country, it could collapse any minute. Don't you worry about that? Hey, can you at least take me somewhere else 'til I fix this little misunderstanding? Nicer, more private? I have money."

They laugh. The cutest of them says to the others, "She a *rich* crazy bitch."

He then tells me, "Lady, you here for a 5150. You

don't got no choice."

There's that number: 5150. I swallow a lump in my throat. "What does that mean?"

All four of them pipe up at the same time: "Involuntary confinement for 72 hours."

"Hell, no. Wait. I'll give you each a hundred bucks if you let me go. I'll catch a taxi home. Well, if you'll loan me a twenty. But I'll get the money and—"

"Like we ain't never heard that before."

Shit. Four musclemen are each grabbing a limb and they don't seem to be too concerned for my ladyship. It's a good thing I'm double-jointed, what with being spread-eagled in my leggings that are wet from my bladder accident earlier. My legs are still covered with dirt from my stomping fit to be untied from the iron gate.

"This lady stink like a dead ho. We gotta put her in the tank. Ain't that right, Virgil."

Virgil, the biggest attendant, asserts, "It's my turn to use the sprayer hose."

I talk fast. "Hold on, guys. The cops got it wrong. All I did was burn my story about a little girl. I'm not supposed to be here, it's just a big mistake."

"Sure 'nough, lady. You right and we all wrong."

"Guys, listen to me. I really am rich. All you need to do is look the other way while I hop off this stretcher. All you have to do is slip me a twenty for a taxi and I'll go home, get my money. I'll come back, promise. I'll give each of you a thousand bucks. How's that sound? Guys? A thousand bucks each, no strings?"

They're laughing at me. At least three of them. Virgil unstraps my arm.

Oh, it feels so good to be free. I go to stretch but accidentally punch Virgil in the nose. That's not a good thing, judging by the crunching sound. Oops, it's already turning purple. Best not to mention my recent boxing lessons.

When Virgil gets out a stained white jacket thingy with long dangling straps, I shout, "No!"

Someone jabs me with a needle. My skin burns from whatever is injected. I try to fight as they shove my arms into the jacket that stinks of the worst imaginable BO, like a herd of camel jockeys. I attempt to defend my inalienable rights as they cross my arms in front of my chest and strap me in so tight I can't breathe. I manage to take in enough air to threaten them with my $400.00 an hour lawyer who, I tell them, "Eats chum for breakfast. He'll eat all...you."

They're unimpressed, so I must sweeten the pot. "If you let me go, I'll...he'll, swear to God, Jackson Milan, he's my lawyer, I promise he'll give you each $10,000 buckos. Cash in your pockets." I yawn. "Soon as—"

"Look on the bright side, lady. That kid, the one you kilt? She ain't here."

I glance all around me. "You're right." Suddenly things are indeed looking brighter.

"Helice has been haunting me but she couldn't have followed me here." I try to smile but it feels like I'm stretching a tight rubber mask across my face. "How great is...that, you guys. I did it! I created her, I wrote every word she ever said, and I damn well had the right to kill off her character. I had to. That girl got in so deep, right down to my very soul, know what I mean? Now she's dead and buried...well, the pages were burned, so her ashes are still around, it's not windy today. Glad she went, I ah... so very, very sleepy."

I stop, look up, stare at the sun overhead. "Oh, wow. I never...Hey, guys, ever notice how rays poke out from spongee yellow circle? I never knew. Whoa, I, it's dizzy. Who's shaking the stretcher?"

Virgil's voice sounds far, far away. "Man, check out her eyeballs rolling backwards."

Someone else says, "Damn, that look nasty."

My head drops, my eyes close. I'm going nighty-night. I'll finally be able to sleep, now that Helice is gone. Gone for good, out of my very soul. Sweet dreams to me...to me...to me.

Wait. What's that? A quick flash of a familiar red

buttoned up sweater puts me on alert. It can't be. Ten years old, pony-tailed, her freckled face all shiny with that perpetually annoying optimism of hers. Wearing one black and white saddle shoe, the cotton sock on her other foot slipping down on her heel.

I try to speak, but I can't get anything out.

CHAPTER 3

Now I Really Want to
Kill That Kid

CAN IT BE? A tongue seems to be gliding along my face as I slumber.

I *am* being licked. A master with a supple brush is painting me with lip's dew to arouse me from oblivion. As sleep vies to win me back, I think to ask, *exactly who is this lover?* The thought occurs, *does it matter?*

I straddle the edge of two worlds, the apex where dreams drop off and waking consciousness begins. He is real, isn't he? He has to be. Strands of his long silky hair cascade as if raining from the heavens above, gliding along the contours of my face. They are tinder for my lonely soul, striking a flame, igniting a path through my darkness.

Where am I, that I am being explored with copious abandon? Oh, to have such an earnest devotee upon me.

A moan escapes me...soft at first sound. My lips part, craving more of the passion fruit I am being fed. I inhale his milky, slightly sour taste. He presses his head against mine; his ear smells waxy. I hunt for familiarity, a sense of coming home to this man. And yet, my sensory memories are not aroused. There is nothing.

Wait. This is no dream. An overgrown moustache with spidery legs tickles my face as I struggle to wake up, force open my eyes.

Oh! He's turned into a ferocious animal devouring its prey. *Carnivore*, I demand, *who are you?* Struggling to focus, I zero in on a coarse black brow that is furrowed in single-mindedness. Brown eyes. Beady. Sweat dripping from a nose as long and obvious as an exclamation point. Weak chin. I spot yellowy, tobacco-stained teeth when his tongue slips off my cheek.

There is indeed a man behind my erotic encounter, a man dressed in an institutional blue top with matching pants who is hovering inches from my slobbered face.

I attempt to rise up, get away. My arms are useless, strapped tight across my chest in a stinky canvas contraption that maybe a million lunatics have worn before me. I want to scream for help but nothing comes out except a pitiful squeak no one could possibly hear.

Conjuring every bit of myself, I fill my lungs and yell loud and clear, "Help!"

"Your..." His bristly mustache brushes against my face as he whispers, "Light."

I jerk my head away but the little weasel is hot on my trail. I again scream for help. It scares me to think no one is around. Someone has to be in charge, right?

"The light," he says. "I feel it." He licks me. "Taste it."

"Leave me alone," I hiss, "or I'll 'taste' a chunk of your face."

Maybe my threat worked. He's edging away. But he turns back, gets even closer to me. My entire being clenches when he leans down with his mouth so wide open I see his uvula.

"I need." He leans down, slides his tongue along my jawbone. "So shiny."

"You're slobbering all over me."

He does the weirdest thing. Yammering about my light, he jams his thumb into my left ear. He does it so hard it makes me cry out, "Dude, what the hell?"

He mumbles, "Power," before stuffing his thumb into me again.

"Hey, leave me alone or I'll scream so bloody loud your eardrums will burst."

He removes his thumb to sniff. He seems pleased.

I have no clue why these particular words come out of my mouth. Perhaps it's primal, a female weapon against boy bullies when I burst out, "I'll tell your mother."

His lashes flutter against the plane of my right eye.

The abrupt, thunderous assertion of horror that follows isn't coming from me. The man is screaming like a little girl.

I add my voice to the fray, "Help—get this thing off me!"

Four guys dressed in white scrubs rush in. They crowd around my bed; it's set in a narrow space that looks to be curtained off from the main room. I think it's a holding area.

The leader says to the screaming man, "You all right, Roman?" That voice. I recognize it, but—from where?

The guy I can't quite remember glares at me. "What the hell's going on in here?"

"Oh, my God. I was sound asleep when I felt this guy licking my face like a dog."

One of his minions in white snickers, "She got Romanized." They slap one another's palms. The manly ritual continues when they high-five the joker and they feel the need to repeat, "She got Romanzied all over herself."

The leader, the one I can't put a name or a place to, sizes me up before saying, "Poor Roman. So what if he's a little different, what makes you think he'd want to touch you? Lady, you must'a lured him in here."

I look down at what I'm wearing under the straightjacket: a shapeless hospital gown. Pushing aside the trepidation as to who undressed me, I snort, "You're blaming me? I'm wrapped up like a cocoon. Plus, I was sleeping."

I glance over at my Roman lover, who is shaking like he's trying to get out of his skin. His wet, chapped lips are flapping but no words are coming out, he's still squawking like a loony bird.

Oh, crap. Now I remember. I'm locked up in the loony bin. This is all that kid Helice's fault. And she's not even real!

An orderly says, "Don't make Virgil lock you up again."

Virgil. His nose is a swollen mess. Someone must have slugged him hard. I'm struggling to remember but it's an effort, my brain feels so hazy. They must have drugged me.

A woman in a starched lab coat shows up. She is obviously in control. Virgil and the guys are quick to step aside, give her the floor. She snaps, "Why is Roman in here?"

Virgil is real slick. "He was coming from group therapy and he heard this new patient making a stink. You know Roman, he's a one-man welcoming committee." The woman is frowning so Virgil adds, "You weren't around, and I had my hands full with her."

"You know that's against protocol." She turns her back on the orderly and addresses the licker with a calm authority, "Roman, what have I told you about approaching new patients? You can't assume everyone is interested."

Roman hangs his head, cowed by this woman in high command. He looks to be one minute away from pissing himself. The woman folds her arms, crinkling her pristine white coat. "Roman, did she want you to help her?"

Roman, it appears, is a little worm. He squirms, but with her prodding, he nods his head.

"No. I did not."

All eyes turn to me, the lickee. The woman waits. I figure she wants me to continue, so I say, "Like I was telling Virgil, I was sound asleep. All of a sudden, I feel this guy licking me, all over my face. It was awful."

"I see." She tells Roman, "Go back to your room. I'll handle this later." He slinks away, but she doesn't notice that he's lingering just out of sight.

I plead my case, "I'm not supposed to be here, it's all a big mistake. And then...then I get attacked by a crazy man."

Okay, I guess that was a bit cruel, considering Roman is back. But he doesn't stop there. He bursts into tears, high-pitched wails that make me crunch up my face. Tensing my jaws hurts my head.

I raise my voice to be heard, "You see, I have a killer migraine. Plus, I definitely remember being drugged at my house by a paramedic, and then again here. Was it two times, three even, when they booked me into this place?"

Roman is still carrying on, so I yell at him to shut up. Judging from everyone's reactions, that is a mistake. Maybe he has an arrangement on the side with orderlies so he can lick unsuspecting patients? Roman is clearly the more popular of the two of us.

The doctor directs Virgil and the guys to calm down the squirming, shrieking, ferret-faced Roman.

Then she says to me, "This isn't the best way for you to begin your stay here, Ms. Evans."

I may be stuck in a straightjacket but that doesn't stop me from giving her some attitude. I cock my head, arch my left brow, and say to her, "And you are...?"

"I am Doctor Lively, head of this psychiatric floor."

"I want to call my lawyer. Jackson Milan is the best San Francisco shark there is. He'll be furious with the cops for dumping me here without any reason and—"

"I wasn't finished, Ms. Evans." She refers to a chart she's holding. "You'll be staying with us for the next few days under a 5150 enforced confinement order. Seventy-two hours at the very least."

Oh hell, I have shot my own foot. I decide to turn things around and give her a big Trez Evans smile. "I'm sorry, I'm a little upset, as you can surely understand. Ah, do you think we could start over?"

She nods, giving me a slight advantage I readily accept. I ask, "Um, could you get me out of this thing? I can't feel my arms anymore."

She motions to Virgil, who feels compelled to inform her, "She threw a punch at me earlier when she came in. Broke my nose."

She pauses to examine his nose. "It'll be fine. Release her."

"Doctor, I don't think—"

"Enough, Mr. Comstock." Her voice is steely. "We will discuss this incident later."

Lowering his brows to glare ferociously at me, he unbuckles the straps holding me down onto the gurney. He loosens the straightjacket and slides it off me.

"Thanks, Doctor, that's so much better." I flex and wave my numbed arms more than necessary. The doctor helps me to sit up. "And please, call me Trez."

Doctor Lively isn't buying my ploy. "I see you've had quite a day, Ms. Evans. Not only do you appear to be having a psychotic episode brought on by acute alcoholism, you—"

"Alcoholism? I was just having a bad day. Jeez, it's not a crime to have a few drinks." The doctor doesn't speak, which makes me run at the mouth and give her the recap on everything that's happened to me in the last crappy 24 hours. I give her my best smile. You can imagine how bad I felt, right? So I drank a little."

The doctor narrows her eyes. "It says here you're a person of interest regarding the kidnapping of a girl in Redwood City, plus your actions contributed to a police officer's heart attack." She continues reading, "Oh, and there may be evidence of your having murdered a child from Detroit—"

"Doctor, you have got to be kidding. I didn't kill anyone. It's just a figure of speech. I tried to explain all that to the two cops who, by the way, trespassed onto my private property. I'm a writer, not a murderer. I wrote a novel about a kid, a ten year old girl named Helice Polansky. I did tons of research, the story's set in Detroit during the 1950s polio epidemic. I put her in an iron lung, you see, I figured that would make her a more sympathetic protagonist."

"I fail to see how a book caused your errant behavior." She pauses, refers to my file again. "Or why you felt the need to burn reams of paper outdoors during high fire season."

Oh, I am so going to kill that kid Helice Polansky. This is all her fault. I slide my legs over the side of the gurney to face Dr. Lively.

"Helice makes me crazy. I've been obsessed with that stupid kid for over ten years. I write a chapter, then I rewrite it." I grip the gurney's thin mattress and dig my nails into it. "I rewrite it over and over again. I had to destroy my manuscript to get rid of her."

Lively isn't buying my excuse, so I throw in a therapeutic term to prove I understand the error of my actions. "I needed 'closure,' a figurative 'death.' That's why I was burning my novel when the cops came. Obviously, it wasn't the best idea I've ever had. I'm sorry, I really, really am."

Dr. Lively's voice softens. "Ms. Evans, as a writer you can take control of your story and redirect the plot any way you choose. Or, write an entirely different story. It's up to you."

"It's complicated. Helice goes into a coma and ends up in a different world where she doesn't have polio; she runs and jumps just fine there. Then she meets a naked Mud Eater named Magdalena who needs her."

I stop talking when Dr. Lively frowns in confusion. The Mud Eater character has baffled everyone in my writing group and now, even a shrink doesn't understand my story. No wonder I burned it. But she motions me to go on.

"Uh, so Helice doesn't want to go back to the iron lung. Who can blame her? But I...I don't know what to do with her now. It's best if I just move on, maybe write a comedy or something."

"Oh, so it's a fantasy. I hear there's quite a market for that genre."

"Don't you get it? Helice is *haunting me*. I had to kill her off."

Not only is Doctor Lively staring at me, so are the four guys in white scrubs. In the distance, Roman is too.

"Hey," I shout at him. "I'm not the freak who's licking people."

Roman goes into another tizzy. The doctor gives orders for Roman to be taken away, but when Virgil grabs hold of him, Roman screams so loud, I can't think. And when I can't think, I overreact. I overreact to Roman's drama with some deafening shrieks of my own. Trouble is, once I start, I can't seem to stop. Maybe it's because I'm drugged and locked up with crazy people. I can't stop screaming, not even when that no-nonsense doctor pulls a filled syringe out of her pocket and pokes me in the arm with it. Why she pokes me with it and not Roman, I'll never know.

She should have asked me. She could have taken a minute to learn that medication has an opposite effect on me. I tell her that medics already had loaded me with enough dope to kill a horse. Plus, I moan, "I'm so dizzy now, it feels like I'm floating away."

Doctor Lively mutters, mostly to herself, "Oh, dear."

I let out a dry, strangled sort of gasp. "W-What's that?" Everyone turns to where I'm pointing a finger, a bit unsteadily, at a spot near the corner. Where that damn kid Helice Polansky has shown up. She's grinning at me from across the room like she doesn't have a care in the world.

"Grab her Virgil," I yell. "Don't let her get away."

Virgil holds up his palms, acting like he doesn't know what I'm talking about. Doctor Lively is flicking a little flashlight across my eyes. It hurts like hell. I brush the flashlight out of her hands but I must be stronger than I think, because she topples over and lands on her hip with a shriek of her own.

Virgil and the guys are distracted with the groaning doctor, so I decide to erase Helice once and for all.

I want to reach for her ponytail, and pull it right out of her head. I can do that. I created her. It would feel so good to yank out her dark blonde hair in big tufts that would float through the air. I'd like to peel all the freckles off her pug-nosed face. I burned her in my manuscript, now I'll delete her from my memory banks. Oh, the joy.

I can hear myself laughing through the din of Roman crying, and the whimpering doctor, and Virgil shouting into the intercom system.

I jump off the gurney. The kid's grinning at me. It's pissing me off, so I decide to charge full speed ahead. I tackle her, only to end up empty-handed and worse, banging my forehead smack into the wall. Ow. Oh, there she is, over there. I try to get a hold of her but it's like grabbing air.

Helice is acting all wise and mature, like she's the grown-up, and I'm the naughty child. What? She's inviting me to follow her.

No way, I inform her. Rubbing my forehead, I can feel a thickening lump from banging into the wall.

Helice gestures for me to follow, as if it is indeed possible for the two of us to slip right through that solid wall.

A hallucination doesn't appear in flesh and bone, does it? I'm not sure, but she smiles just like a real girl. She wants me to come with her.

Really? I giggle like I'm the ten year old.

She gestures again, like it's just a matter of holding hands. She's got her hand out, encouraging me. I look over at Virgil and the guys. They are not happy with me, that is clear. I hear people coming down the hallway. They're going to blame everything on me.

Okay, I nod to Helice, I'm game. Where are we going?

I get the feeling I already know. Back to the Mud Eater's pond where it all began.

She's offering me her hand but I'm distracted by staff coming through the door. Instead, I rush the wall. Headfirst at full speed. Smack. The sheetrock cracks where my head hits it. I stagger, sway a bit, then collapse into a heap.

My right temple is gushing blood like a broken dike. The room is spinning and I'm close to losing consciousness. I can feel my eyes rolling back in my head but for some reason, I can clearly see Helice Polansky. She is kneeling on the floor next to me. I get the feeling she's annoyed, that I'm not listening and shouldn't have tried it on my own. Hmm. She didn't mean I could go with her in my *body*. I wrote the story, didn't I? Didn't I describe how some other part of Helice that wasn't paralyzed got up out of her iron lung? Didn't I create a way for her to pass through walls as easily as a breeze flows through a lace curtain?

Virgil lifts me onto the gurney. He straps me down. A medical team pushes it out the room and down a hallway. Someone shouts, "Take her to L-13," amid the rapid rolling screech of four rubber wheels along a red and black checkerboard linoleum floor.

I lift my head to see where they are taking me.

Oh, brother. It appears that I am once again straddling the edge of two worlds, the apex where waking consciousness drops off and the absolute freedom of my dream begins.

The team is taking me to get my head wound treated. There should be a doorway at the end of the hall, or a turn to keep going. And yet I can see that the typical walls, floor, and ceiling, as one would expect to find in the real world, have receded into a hazy white nothingness.

I should have done a better job of burning my manuscript, because the character I created is just a few yards away. She's waving at me.

The team obviously doesn't notice that Helice Polansky is standing thigh-high in a lush savannah nestled along the foothills of a coppery plateau, set against a lilac-tinged sky.

We are heading straight at her.

CHAPTER 4

The Red Eden

UH OH, THE FLOOR is merging with the rich soil of the Red Eden. We're so close to crossing over, the feathery tips of wild wheat growing at the very edge of the two worlds are tickling my face. There's no telling what will happen. The gurney I'm strapped onto could crash into the base of the granite plateau we're rapidly approaching.

I brace myself for impact.

A man shouts, "We're losing her." It's the last I'm aware of the team. I assume they took me to the ER.

My vision has switched off, making me blind in the midst of a black nothingness. Normally it would freak me out, yet I feel a mighty propulsion forward, as if someone has stuffed me into a canon and lit the fuse.

Funny thing is, it doesn't bother me to be traveling at hyper-speed to who-knows-where. Oh, I can see again. A brilliant white light is surrounding me.

Now that I've been shot out of my normal reality, I have a breathtaking aerial view of the Red Eden, like a giant hawk soaring over my personal fantasyland. It is a glorious place. The purpled blue mountain ranges and rolling valleys look just as I'd imagined them. It is so lusciously decadent to be here in my perfect version of paradise, I want to—

"Hey, lady, can you see me? I'm over here."

Helice's shrill interruption forces me to lose my lofty perspective. Dropping downward fast, I feel myself, or at least what I think of as my "self," landing hard in one of my artfully-crafted meadow scenes. Thump!

I'm sprawled out, face down on the ground described as blood red. Knowing the inside scoop about that particular soil, I scramble to get to my feet and dust myself off.

Helice skips over, oblivious to the jolting fall she caused me. "Told ya we'd get here."

I burst out, "It's amazing...but...how? Why'd you come get me? Oh, I am so confused. Talking to a character."

She says softly, "Too bad you didn't listen to me. Your head is bleeding awfully bad."

"That's imposs—" I touch my temple, only to pull away, my fingers wet and red. It takes me a moment to get orientated. Oh yeah, my banged up head.

You'd think I'd be my beautiful self in all my glory in my own damn dream. I touch my scalp again. "Oww."

Helice is staring at me, her nose crinkled with disgust. I can only imagine what my head wound looks like. Groping my face, I can feel blood oozing over my damaged right eye. Squinting, I glance around for the waterfall that should be close by but there are only cracked rocks. Everything looks parched and grimy. Where is the grove of trees set within the savannah to provide a welcoming shade? Where is the pond?

Helice kicks at a gnarled tumbleweed. "It's not pretty around here anymore."

"Don't worry about it," I tell her. "There must have been a storm or something."

Privately, I have to admit that the Red Eden has lost its luster. Haven't I written countless vivid descriptions of this world? The bark and leaves of my trees should be uniquely colored hues of lavender and turquoise, some bearing stripes, depending upon their placement within the verdant garden. Plants and shrubs should be masterpieces of pattern and texture. My insects and birds should sing with purpose.

Instead, clumps of charred bushes cower next to others that survived without a mark. Fallen trees are flanked by comrades standing tall. It reminds me of the fire pits I bought, where chunks of my novel pages were mixed in with sooty ashes. Talk about consequences. Did an impulsive act of setting fire to a manuscript in Woodside, California really torch this alternate reality? It's freaking amazing a temper tantrum could inflict such damage. My power is immense.

A satisfying superiority spreads through me as I say, "So, Helice, what do you think of this place now?"

Her lips twist into a scowl, her chin quivers. "It makes me so sad. Nothing's the same." She bites a fingernail. "I had to find you, lady. You need to fix this."

Lady? Oh, that's right. Even though she's been haunting me since last night, we haven't been officially introduced. I'd assumed she knew me, her Creator. This is so cool. Playing God will be a fun game, at least for me.

"Watch me." Helice is poised with feet spread and her palms raised above her head, readying herself to do a cartwheel. "I'm all set. Are you looking? Are you?"

I murmur, "Yeah, sure kid, go for it." Out of the corner of my eye, there's a blur of a red sweater amid a whirl of motion. There is a soft padding sound as she lands square on her feet.

"Did you see me?" She pipes, "Lady?"

"Don't call me lady. My name is Trez. Trez Evans."

"Pleased to meet you, *Trez*." True to her mid-century, middle America mores, the little girl is the model of proper behavior. She extends her right hand. How cute is this? She did the exact same thing when I had her first meet my character Magdalena, keeper of the mud pond.

We shake. I get straight to the point, "Tell me, why'd you show up last night? I gotta say, it was a shock to see you."

She gives me a grin. There it is, the adorable gap-toothed smile I'd bestowed upon her. Hanging out with my literary character in an alternate world of my making is a real trip.

I love her eyes, they practically twinkle. A gasp escapes me as I'm suddenly struck by their similarity to my mother. I'd specified Helice's eyes to be hazel, a combination of amber and green highlights on a mid-tone brown. I don't recall detailing Helice's iris to contain flecks of dark brown.

As a girl, I teased my mother about bits of "tobacco" floating about in her eyes. It was my childish effort to get her to quit smoking. There was never an intentional link to my deceased parent, but here it is. Helice has my mother's eyes.

When Helice appeared to me at Bethany's book launch, her image was blurry. I had to strain to see her. Now that we're in the Red Eden, I can see her more clearly. I'm noticing she also bears more than a casual resemblance to me. Well, not in her personality, body structure, or coloring. Her front teeth have gaps and mine don't. As a child, I refused to turn cartwheels but still, there's something similar between us.

I flash back to being ten years old. My favorite sweater was a red wool button-up cardigan just like Helice's. I can still recollect how my sweater smelled like wet sheep after getting caught in a rainstorm. My blue pedal pushers were striped like hers and we both refused to give them up long after the knees wore out.

I'm in awe walking through the world I've somehow torched. Helice doesn't speak until I ask, "If you didn't know who I was, how did you find me? Did Magdalena send you?"

She nods, "Yep. She's the Mud Eater. That makes her boss of the Red Eden. When did you meet her?"

"First off, *I'm the boss*, I made up this world. She 'met' me when I created her and wrote her into my book."

Helice's mouth pops open. "What book?"

"The book you're in. *The Mud Eater's Apprentice.*"

She lets out a shriek.

"Don't be so melodramatic. Surely you know you're my book character. A main character. It should make you happy, there are lots of references to Helice Basha Polansky."

The kid stammers, "W-why?"

To make her feel better I explain, "This book commemorates your life and death struggle with a dread disease." I add an aside, "Even though you were never born in this world, you'll live on in literary infamy. If I ever get the bloody thing published, that is."

"Did my parents say you could do that?"

I let out a hoot. "That's hysterical. They're not real either. None of you people are."

"But, but, we live in Detroit. Want our address and phone number?"

"Helice, I gave you those facts. That's what authors do. They compile complete profiles of characters along with their family backgrounds so their histories read true."

The kid looks completely lost.

I put a hand on her shoulder. "Let me explain. The readers know you from the details I give them. For instance, they know you're an average-sized ten-year old girl; not too tall, not short. They know you have light colored hair like your mom, while your pop and two brothers have dark curls. See what I mean? Characters come alive to the readers. They might think about a little girl they know, a real child, when they read about you. They might picture you in their minds differently than you look to me but that's their prerogative. Fiction allows readers to see what they want in a character."

"Huh?" Helice tilts her chin. I notice her ears are dirty, which upsets me. My great aunt Euphemia used to say kids who sprouted "potatoes in their ears" wouldn't grow up properly. Did I use that line in any of my novel versions? I designed her mother to be meticulous about hygiene, even if she has six little buggers with one on the way.

"Hmm, maybe it'll help if you know the novel

setting. In chapter one you babysat your siblings the night you came down with polio. You bathed your three little sisters and—"

"Katia and Natalia." Her voice catches. "Lucia too." She jabs at a tear running down her cheek.

"Yes, that's right. You put all five kids to bed moments before you became sick. Paralysis was overcoming you so drastically you could barely crawl to your bed."

"Para what?"

"It means your arms and legs didn't work, you couldn't move them. It's 1953. There's an epidemic."

Her face goes white as she cries, "Why?"

"It's called polio, a mid-twentieth century disease."

She bursts into heart wrenching sobs.

I plead, "Please, stop. Do you want to go home? Is that what you want?" She doesn't reply.

"Guess I could rewrite it, it wouldn't be the first revision. Please, let's sit on this log and we'll talk about it. Okay?"

She plops next to me and sighs, "I remember now. I have to stay in the hospital and live in an iron monster."

Poor Helice, existing within the confines of an iron lung. These obsolete artificial breathing machines were the size and shape of a small one-man submarine. They were noisy too, never ending. The patient's body was internally encased, with only the head exposed, propped up by a metal shelf with only an overhead mirror with which to view a hospital ward filled with other polio victims. I've been too hard on her.

I rub my hands together. "I'm the one who paralyzed you to increase the story's tension and drama. I can just as easily make you well. A real happy ending."

Oh, this disclosure does not go over well. Instead of thanking me profusely, her eyes again fill with tears as she wails, "*You* made me sick."

"Sorry." I reach out to her, but she recoils.

"Why would you do that to me? I'm just a little girl."

45

It's best not to mention my initial novel version when I added tension by creating simpleton mutants to stalk her. Gawd, I hate admitting I'd sunk that low. To my credit, they were deleted early on.

It's a tough call, but I have to tell her. "Ah, you need to know that in my world it's 1983."

Other than her puzzled expression, she doesn't react.

"C'mon, you've got to be surprised. Since you're coming from the year *1953*? And I live in California, not Detroit."

"I'm inside a book?" She moans, "I don't understand. How could I fit?"

Eager to change the subject, I sweep an arm toward the far off horizon. "So, what's going on here? Do the other characters, I mean people, know where you are?"

She smiles. I'm not supposed to tell you what's going on with the Adamah."

That gets my attention. Adamah. That's one of my monikers for the naked Mud Eater. Magdalena came from the red clay so it was logical to tie her in with the biblical first man, Adam.

I tell her, "You understand I'm confused, right? How am I supposed to react if I don't know the game plan?"

Helice grins. "That's the point. Maggalena says you need to stop...um..." She pauses. "Stop being *you* so much."

"What the hell does that mean?"

"Please don't yell. She said you'd get mad."

"Helice, you need to understand you surprised me big time." I pause, recalling how the champagne glass slipped out of my hand at first sight of her, how I let out a mortifying scream. Once my escort learned that my literary character had somehow materialized, he was keen to spot her in the banquet hall. Try as he might, he could not. Assessing the crowd, he was convinced nobody could see her. According to him, no one seemed even remotely aware of her presence. But I know what I saw.

I gaze at my little character. How much of the story does she remember? And what version?

"Do you remember Tirigan?"

"Nuh uh."

"Pria?"

"No," she says, calmly.

"Alastar?"

"He's a she, so I guess I can."

"Magdalena?"

"I miss Mother and Pop. But I have to stay here. I have an important job to do." She wipes her drippy nose on her sleeve and heads south. I follow. "The mud doesn't taste right," she complains. "Ever since the fire. We don't like eating it anymore."

"I only wrote one scene for you to taste the red clay."

"What are you talking about?" She bites off a fingernail and spits it out. "Maggalena and I ate mud every day."

Is this cool or what, the Mud Eater and her apprentice performed exactly as they'd been designed. And yet, I hadn't given Magdalena permission to go off script.

"Hey, wait a minute, you ate mud every *single* day?" I trot after her. Her ponytail bobs up and down in response. "Helice, how could that be? I had you taste mud, once, at a highly climatic moment, and then the chapter ended. End of story."

Helice is quick to argue, "Nuh uh, we kept going."

The slow shake of her head tells me otherwise. I'm almost afraid to ask, "What else did you guys do?"

She breaks into a toothy grin. "We took long walks and Maggalena told me stories about when she was a little girl."

"Hold on." I stop in my tracks. "I never gave that woman a back story. In fact, she's meant to be a total enigma."

Helice is scratching her head, she's sure to ask me

what that means but I'm on a roll. "Any author worth her salt knows the reader needs to keep guessing 'til the very end."

"What do you mean, salt?"

Using a cliché makes me cringe. Thank God my writing group won't know, they'd shame me into dropping out. The bottom line, though, is that I seem to have lost control of my character. She is not the one in charge. This is my story, for godsakes.

I'd designed the Red Eden to be my version of paradise but now that I've actually set foot upon the infamous blood-red clay, it sure feels like hell to me. Have I been had by a character?

As if that's not enough of a smack down, my ten-year-old protagonist is throwing me major attitude. Helice is giving me a look I swear reminds me of the face my mother made whenever she disciplined me.

Even the tone rings true as Helice nags, "Maggalena said you messed up. Now we have to make everything right."

Fisting both hands on my hips, I counter, "Oh, yeah, says who? I'm the creator of this story. I told you that makes me like a god to you. Hell, I made up this entire world. I can make it go away in a flash." Just for emphasis, I begin snapping my fingers like a hipster.

Helice's eyes bug, her mouth pops open so wide I see her back molars. The poor little kid breaks down sobbing before collapsing into a trembling heap on the parched ground.

She pleads, "Please don't set fire again, please."

I bend a knee and sweep her into my arms. She lays her head on my chest as we embrace one another tight. I rub her bony shoulders and back. My God, she feels like a real live girl.

Holding her is awkward. I typically avoid the younger set, but she's an innocent victim. She deserves comfort.

Snorting nose gunk, she pulls herself together. "Sorry, Trez. Maggalena told me to take charge, even though I'm just a kid."

I ask, "Feel better now?" Helice gives me a weak bob of the head. "Great." I stand and help her to her feet. Brushing dirt from her striped peddle pusher pants, I say, "All righty, kiddo, let's start over." To show compassion and unity, I keep hold of her hand as we proceed along the trail. "Let's talk about what brought you to that book launch."

We walk a ways but then she stops. "Um, Trez?" Letting go of my hand, she hedges. "Um. Can I ask you a question?"

"Sure."

"Why is Maggalena naked?" Helice's cheeks flame. "She's a nice lady but my mother wouldn't approve, not one bit."

I can't help laughing. "You're not the only one to ask me that. Sorry Helice, I honestly don't know."

"But, why?"

I throw up my hands. "I guess I wanted to give her a unique trait no other character would have."

Helice narrows her eyes. "She eats *mud.*"

"Yes, true, but...Tell you what. When I figure it all out, you'll be the first to know. Okay?"

From the looks of it, she's not convinced. Whatever. It's my turn. "Why did you show up at Bethany Moraga's book launch?"

She doesn't answer.

"Helice?" Nothing. My eyes hood, my voice tenses. *"How do you know Bethany?"*

"Who?"

"Bethany Moraga."

She shakes her head. There's that ponytail swinging back and forth again. As the adult in charge, I give her a warm smile and put my hand on her shoulder. "C'mon, help me understand why you came into my world."

My character looks at me with such trust, I am filled with awe, as befitting a mother seeing her baby for the first time.

I slouch when Helice says, "I came for *her.*"

Gasping mid-breath I snort, "Oh. My. God. It *is* Bethany. You're here for *her*."

"Who's that?"

"Listen, Helice, you're my character, not hers."

Looking around at the world I'd fashioned, it dawns on me. "Oh, crap. Is Bethany trying to keep you for herself?"

I put a hand to my rapidly beating heart. "I can't believe that thieving witch stealing my character right out from under me. No wonder she keeps slamming my story. Throwing me off track. She doesn't want me to know."

I have a new thought. "If she's ripping off my character, that means I'm a good writer." I raise a fist in triumph. "Her books have made it to the New York Times bestseller list. *Twice.* I must be a goddamn fantastic writer."

Helice's hazel eyes widen. "Eww, you swore. My mother would be mad at you."

I spread my arms as a benevolent gesture. "Tell me Bethany's plan."

Helice acts confused, but I think she's bullshitting me.

"C'mon, Helice, now that the cat's out of the bag, you need to tell me. I'm the one who thought all this up, not her. What's Bethany's plotline?" I stop. "Maybe she's plagiarizing the whole story! It's obviously good enough, and...*and* my story is so unique she could never have thought of it herself."

I snicker with self-righteousness, "The only thing she can write is gossipy nonfiction. Her so-called 'characters' already create the story in real life, she just puts it down on paper. She's probably figuring on getting her version of my novel published first. Hah. I will sic my shark lawyer on her so fast her head will spin. Jackson Milan, Esquire, will chew her up and spit her out on the witness stand. Bad publicity is better than no publicity—*we can work with this.* Wonder if we can get the trial televised."

Helice rudely butts into my musing, "Where's the cat? Can I play with it?"

"Huh? What?" It takes a second to figure it out. "There is no cat. Jesus. Pay attention. You showed up for *her*, but you're *my* character. You need to be loyal to *me*." I stamp my foot. "Tell me what you know, damn it to hell."

"You're mean. I'm just a kid." She bursts into tears but I think they're the crocodile kind. She's playing me for sure.

"Hey, Helice," I say with a fake cheeriness, "let's go find Magdalena." My motive is to dump the kid onto her. After all, Magdalena lives here. Let her deal with the little scamp.

Before long, the kid is skipping like she doesn't have a care. Wish I could say the same. I'm not happy with the changes around here. I grew up in a household stuffed with too many siblings and two overwhelmed parents. Is it any wonder I spent my childhood fantasizing about my own slice of heaven, and drew scores of pictures to work out exactly how it should look?

Somewhere along the fifth or sixth year of reworking this story, I changed the title to *The Mud Eater's Apprentice*, after I got the brilliant idea of having Magdalena eat the mud in the pond she is guarding because it is hiding a deeply rooted secret.

Why she is a *naked* Mud Eater has been my conundrum. I'm hoping someone around here will shed light on that.

Blood is still dripping onto my hospital gown from my head wound. Helice calls it "yucky." We've been on the lookout for water so I can clean up. Although I wrote copious references to water throughout the story, we have found neither a pool nor a puddle, not to mention Magdalena's pond.

Helice has been walking ahead of me. She's been turning her head this way and that, babbling nonstop like a caged parrot. After changing course a few times, she's led me into an unfamiliar valley. Hmm. It's not part of the scenes I created for my novel, nor has it suffered a burn like where we landed. This area is unspoiled, its moist red clay is teeming with life, its shrubbery a striking emerald hue. Songbirds flit through the azure sky. This valley is so picture perfect it looks as if Walt Disney drew the storyboard.

Helice walks to the middle of a grassy field, where she stops to sit upon a boulder. She pats the space next to her and asks me to sit down. Its crevices fit my butt perfectly.

She turns to me, "This is the place. For the story."

I smile, "It's pretty but, my story is finished. Is this in Bethany's story? If so, please tell me about it."

Helice snaps me back to the moment when she says, "I'm not talking about the one you burned. There's a better story."

She scoops up what looks to be a fluffy black caterpillar and tries to drop it into my hands.

"Hey now." I bolt up off the rock, my fingers curling protectively. "Don't touch that, it's dirty." She does it anyway. "I'm not kidding. Whatever it is could have mites."

Helice rolls her eyes. "Remember this." She stuffs the black thing into a crack. "This is the place for the story."

"Is that so, kiddo?" Attempting to be playful, I poke her in the ribs. She doesn't seem to like it so I say, "Who's the *we* in 'we have a story to tell'? You talking about Bethany?"

She gives me a funny look, but doesn't say a word.

Ah hah, it must be true. Helice has been sent to spy on me. She's out to glean the ins and outs of my plot. Let her think the Red Eden was ruined when I burned my manuscripts. Bethany doesn't need to know I have backup copies of all my versions tucked away in a safe place.

She points. "Look at that big, big tree branch over there. It's weird, don't cha think?" When I don't look up,

Helice says, "Do you see it, do you?"

She'll just keep nagging me, so I make a point of studying the tree. One of its largest limbs is oddly formed. It reminds me of an upside down V. This limb is colored a solid black as compared to the rest of the tree's mottled tan tones.

Helice glances down at her Mickey Mouse watch I had specified as part of her 1950s costume. She fiddles with its red vinyl strap. "We have to hurry, time is ticking." To make her point, she puts her wrist up to my ear. "Hear that? Tick tock, tick tock. Do you hear it, do you?"

When I don't acknowledge all the ticks and the tocks, she gets up with an exaggerated exhale. Sweeping her arm across the field, she says, "You gotta remember this place."

"Yeah, sure."

Helice walks south with purpose. We come across a stream burbling out of a blue granite outcrop. We stoop to drink. Its water is sweet and utterly refreshing. We feast on the berries Helice gathers. "Native people know how to do this," she tells me. "They live off the land."

"Yeah, sure, kid."

Then she picks wild grasses. She pounds them with a rock, drizzling water and mashing as she works. It turns into a moist poultice, which she applies gently to my head wound.

"Ahh, feels good, Helice. Where'd you learn to do this?"

"Alastar taught me."

Alastar used plants and herbs to heal her people. "So you remember her?"

"Yes," nods Helice. "Once you reminded me."

Helice leads the way to the mouth of a low-lying cave partially covered over with orange ferns. I'd featured a cave near Magdalena's mud pond, but this one is much prettier.

"You've killed a couple of us," Helice says as she glances sideways at me, her small voice echoing out of the cave. "Will you kill me, too, Trez?"

"No, absolutely not. Helice Basha Polansky is the main character. That's you. The entire story revolves around *you*."

"Then why'd you burn your book? To get rid of me?"

I shrug while Helice watches me intently

She inhales, holds it, then exhales. She turns her head to the right and stares straight ahead. "Yes, I feel it, too. Okay, I'll tell her." She refocuses on me. "Trez, it's time for you to go back now."

"What's going on? Who are you talking to?"

Helice hesitates. She looks straight ahead again, then says, "Yes, I understand why." She turns to me. "Tic tock. Time to go."

"No, wait, answer my questions." Uh oh. I feel a weird sensation, like I'm being lifted up and away against my will.

Helice yells, "Trez. You gotta remember this. Don't forget."

It feels like I'm floating farther away from her. Before Helice disappears completely from my field of vision, I shout back to her, "What the hell are you talking about?"

I HEAR MYSELF MOANING. Upon my drowsy return to consciousness, I am suffering the mother of all headaches. My right eye isn't cooperating but I manage to open the other one. Everything's blurry. It takes all my concentration to squint up at a nurse dressed in white standing over my hospital bed.

Obviously, I'm not in the Red Eden anymore. Damn, I wasn't finished grilling Helice. I'm no closer to discovering why she showed up. Oh, I have my suspicions, with that gossip-monger Bethany Moraga being at the top of my shit list. But, then again, it doesn't answer *why* my character came to life. What's Helice up to?

Not only are there no answers for Helice's appearance, I have no recollection of "coming back" to a locked mental facility in the suburbs of San Francisco. It's more than I can take, the pain, the confusion.

The nurse says to me, "There, there, honey, don't cry. I know it hurts. I added another dose of morphine to your IV drip. It should kick in shortly. You're in the ICU right now, it's routine. We'll transfer you to a room probably tomorrow. And please, don't move around so much. We need you to lie as still as possible. Can you do that for me?"

I try to ask what the hell she's talking about but my words come out all jumbled. "Auugg I byee roose?"

"That's the aphasia kicking in. Your speech might be affected now and again if you're tired or stressed, we don't think it's permanent. The main thing is, your head injury was more extensive than we thought. A substantial subdural hematoma on the right hemisphere of your brain. Dr. Watkins performed a craniotomy to relieve the swelling on your brain."

My hand flies up and hits a patch over my right eye. She explains, "You scratched it somehow. It'll be fine. Your left eye may be blurry for a few days as well because you have a concussion. Along with the hematoma."

My fingers probe beyond the eye patch, where my head feels like it was hit by a Mack truck. I scratch around a thick wad of padding at...oh, crap...my bald scalp.

The nurse gently takes my hand. "He only shaved a half of your head."

Visions of sporting a Mohawk make me scream, apparently out loud.

"If you calm down it won't hurt as much," she soothes.

Trying to sit up causes an intense pressure on my chest. "Your ribs are bruised."

I try anyway.

She makes a tisk tisk sound with her tongue. "Come

on now, don't make this worse."

I like my odds better in the fantasyland of my own making. Not like here in the real world where I have no say as to being locked up in a loony bin and enduring emergency brain surgery.

I'll be better off in the Red Eden. The only trouble is, how do I get back there?

CHAPTER 5

The Real World

Day 2—

I AWAKEN TO irritating slurping sounds. Drowsy from drugs, I remember they transferred me from the ICU to a tiny private room, so what, or who...? The curtains are drawn; the light is low to aid my recovery from the emergency brain surgery. It's not a nurse or doctor, they dress head-to-toe in white and practically glow in the dark. Besides, they don't plop in the chair next to my bed.

Oh, no, is it Roman, that loony bin patient with a long wet tongue? Has the ferret-faced Lothario snuck back into my room to lick me again?

I squint, but can't see who it is, what with a patch over one eye and nauseatingly blurry vision from the other.

I inhale. Thank God, I don't smell the sour milky odor mixed with earwax that is Roman. I can detect that this person, a man judging by the intoxicatingly musky after-shave wafting about, is munching on something crunchy.

I take a longer whiff. Fritos Corn Chips. Like a bloodhound nosing a track, I seek out confirming clues. The rustling of a suede jacket...no, it smells more like calfskin. It moves as he moves so easily it has to be a "summer" hide tanned so paper-thin it is practically weightless. Perfect for San Francisco's Indian Summer. September offers the best weather we have all year.

The man in question slurps again, followed by sounds of a straw being stirred through mushy ice. Ah hah. He's finishing up a Diet Pepsi, his preferred soft libation.

He zings the first line of what has been a lifelong, mutually satisfying quest of besting one another. "Jesus, Trez. You look like shit."

Ross Evans. I look up at my six-foot-two-inch, larger than life, little brother.

Shifting in his chair, he loses no time to tell his side of my story. "I talked to your surgeon last night. One minute I'm at the club schmoozing with record execs, the next my assistant tells me the San Mateo police are on the line." He frowns. "Jesus Christ, it's bad enough to hear you had emergency brain surgery. They said the surgeon needed to talk to a family member ASAP. Scared the bejesus out of me.

"Apparently it took them a while to find your next of kin. Damn it, what'd I tell you, Trez?" He gets preachy. "You need to take care of things like that."

My good eye tears up.

He softens. "Look, from now on you and me, we'll be one another's contact person. Okay?"

I manage to nod my head, even though it hurts to do so.

"The surgeon and I talked a long time. You sure did a number on yourself. Bleeding on the brain. He had to cut open a portion of your skull cap to get to the clot."

Ross puts down his soda cup. "What the hell?" He leans closer to investigate. "Do you know you have a goddamn drainage hose coming out your head? It's disgusting."

My hand flies up to investigate. I'd known that half my scalp was shaved but no one told me about a tube. My fingers trace along a thin rubbery piping to a...oh, shit, that's that?

"Aww, don't cry, Trez, don't cry. I'm sorry, I

shouldn't have...I...ah, I should have been cooler about telling you."

Ross is surprisingly gentle as he takes hold of my shaking hand. He guides my fingers along my shaved head to the right side above my ear. He says, "Feel that. It's a pretty elaborate drainage system. There's a tube extending from your skull where the hematoma was. It's draining into this..." He steers my hand to what feels like a plastic pouch. "Don't play with this, it could leak."

I immediately squash the gushy bag. "Akk."

"Hey, I told you not to do that. It could burst open. That would be really gross."

I can't help it. My tears are turning into full on sobs.

"Don't...come on, now." I feel his hand heavy on my shoulder. "The doctor, his name's Watson, he said you'll make a full recovery. It's just going to take awhile."

Crying makes my chest heave, which aggravates my ribs, so I stop. My nose must be full of mucus since he hands me a tissue and orders, "Blow."

He won't take the used tissue I'm now extending. I assume it drops to the floor.

After an awkward silence, he says, "Took me ten minutes to get into this joint." As is his custom, he makes everything about him. "You're not supposed to have visitors, but you know how that is, heh, heh."

Probably a pretty young thing at the reception desk, or a student nurse, is already dreaming of dating the current *SF City Magazine* pick for "San Francisco's Most Eligible Bachelor." Opening the first nightclub south of Market made his grade.

"Cheryl – she's really hot. She let me read the report. Confidentially, of course."

Of course she did.

Ross claps his hands. For some reason it makes me jump like a scared bunny, a reaction my cracked torso does not appreciate. Plus, now my head throbs even more.

"Damn, you're really hyper-reactive. One of the temporary effects of brain damage."

Brain damage?

He moves in close. "Can-you-comprehend-what-I-am-saying?" He laughs, delighted with himself. "Anyway, the police said you did this to yourself. A 5150. What were you thinking? They told me the medics were just trying to get you settled in and you went all postal on them."

Ross bugs his eyes, wiggles his fingers for effect. "By the way, that psychiatrist you knocked over? She broke her hip. She'll be out for six weeks." He pauses for effect. "Minimum. Cheryl says the rumor is that woman is royally pissed."

He leans over from his chair to tell me low and slow, "You're lucky. Staff can't sue their nutcase patients."

The doctor had explained that my brain is swollen right now. He said I might be slow to comprehend certain things, especially outside of my usual comfort zone. But Ross is making me feel on edge, like I got in big trouble at school and everyone knows about it.

The doctor told me my speech can be affected at times, such as right now since I feel cornered. Some of the words coming out of my mouth sound bizarre even to me, like Alice's jabberwocky.

I struggle to tell him, "Agggh it-it's not myyyyyy fault. Theeey drugged meeee."

"I can't understand what you're saying, but I'm assuming you're defending yourself, as usual. You can't deny you went on a bender. The arresting officer, name's Marcio, or something like that, he told me you were drunk out of your mind, half naked, burning a ton of paper and clothes and kid's toys. He said they didn't have any other choice but to commit you. What the hell were you thinking?"

He pauses. "Ah, yeah, that's right. You weren't thinking, were you? You gotta own this, Trez." Ross softens his voice, perhaps realizing the severity of my situation.

"Don't worry, Sis, you'll get well and everything will

work out." He sweeps his hand around my room, but I know what he means. The 5150 incarceration against my will.

My highest priority is all about my Rotti dog. I croak out, "MMMMMaryeeeeeeeeeee?"

"You saying Mary? Jackson and I caught up with her this morning way up Kings Mountain Road. She was practically at Huddart Park."

Imagining that wild goose chase makes me smile for the first time.

"We met for breakfast to discuss your..." His upper lip curls. "Your latest dilemma. Jackson took off right after we grabbed her. I found a new vet in Woodside who boards dogs. The good news is he's never heard of Mary so he took her in, no questions asked. He'll probably find out about her, ah, 'peculiarities' the hard way but so what, he'll just tack on more charges. Nothing you haven't had to take care of before. You'll get his bill when all this is done."

Ross brushes off a piece of lint from his pants. "Speaking of sending you bills, I had to get my BMW detailed. Mary took a retaliation dump on my backseat."

Mary, Mary, quite contrary.

Ross' eyes come alive as he says, "But the worst? Heh, heh, heh. She bit Jackson in the ass. Made a hole in his brand new suit. He ran home to change."

Picturing that scene makes me burst out laughing. It kills my ribs but I don't care.

"Heh, heh, heh. Wilkes Bashford is already making him a replacement. Wilkes has your billing address on file; he told me it's not the first time Mary's torn through Jackson's gabardined ass."

I'm laughing so hard it doesn't matter if it makes my head pound.

Speaking of the devil, my lawyer walks in. He snaps, "What are you doing here, Ross? Never mind, don't tell me."

Jackson is the fiercest attorney in the City. People in the know fear him. But since he won't come anywhere near me right now, it appears that I scare him more. He's pacing back and forth from one edge of the closet-sized room to the other. Judging from his gagging sounds, he seems to be fighting bile rising up his throat at the sight of me. Although Jackson "Shark" Milan is known for eating his opponents in court for breakfast, he can't look me in the eye. My one non-bandaged blurry eye. Specifically, he looks as if he's about to upchuck his cookies. I really should get a mirror; see for myself what brain surgery does to a girl.

"Trez, you are in deep, deep trouble," says Jackson. "The cops pegged you as a top suspect in a missing girl's case."

He can't believe this load of crap, can he? He should focus on the cops, they're using me as a...what's it called? A patsy? My protest is loud and to the point, "Imm innnnnnooscennnt."

The guys give one another a look like *I'm* the problem.

"Seriously, Trez, you need to cool the insanity," orders Ross. Jackson continues standing as far from me as possible. He smoothes his impeccably tailored suit, one of dozens in his closet, before addressing me. "Trez, my advice is to walk a middle line. Play the game well enough to stay in this place until all the kidnapping crap blows over. Just don't overdo it or I might not be able to get you out. Ever."

Jackson lets out a belch before he informs me, "Your original seventy-two hour confinement order will take effect as soon as you're released from the medical wing. But, I advise you to remain in this facility under voluntary psychological observation. Indefinitely."

He waves a finger when I start to protest. "I don't want to hear a word out of you, do you understand? Trez?"

"Ooooookaaaaaaaay, *Johnnnnnnnnnyyyyyyyy.*"

Johnny Miller. Ross' friend from one block down and three houses over. He's the older brother of Ross' classmate, albeit the Miller boy Ross liked better.

Despite the difference in age, they became fast friends. Johnny had just graduated law school and passed the bar first time around. To celebrate, he flew to Rome at the end of Ross' junior year of college. In a classic story of a young man finding himself in a classic city, Johnny Miller came home reborn as Jackson Milan.

Ross is enjoying himself. He loves a good zinger regardless of who happens to be the zingee.

My lawyer gruffs, "I mean it, Trez. Keep your mouth shut. The police want to talk to you as soon as the doctor gives the go-ahead. Could be as early as tomorrow. When they come, do not offer anything they haven't asked for. You got that? Answer only what they ask, briefly, succinctly. Don't go into any detail." He raises his voice, "Nothing."

Jackson thinks a minute, then opens his brief case. He pulls out a blank sheet of paper and a pen, which he hands to me. "Write something," he orders.

Um...? The pen is poised in my hand, the point pressed on the paper ready to go. A seemingly simple task, right?

Jackson dictates the classic typing class exercise, "The quick red fox jumped over...come on Trez," he pushes, "the fox jumped over the lazy brown dog."

I scribble jagged lines with no discernable words.

Ross weighs in, "Don't worry about the cops, nothing she says or does makes sense."

Jackson snaps, "You sure about that? As for right now, she's not herself. Obviously, I can't hear *anything* that might compromise this situation. It's serious. A little girl went missing in Redwood City the day you burned what police consider evidence. I'm saying it's a good thing the doctor thinks she's had a brief reactive psychosis."

Jackson points to my bandaged head. "Listen Trez, running into a wall could be construed by the district attorney as a ruse. I may be called to prove you didn't kidnap anyone. I'd have to establish you'd been incapacitated to accomplish such an intricate plan."

He's still pacing. "It's why you need to stay in Crazy Town until this gets sorted out."

Ross has been atypically quiet. "Stop being a drama queen, Jackson. At least have her transferred to Stanford hospital so she—"

"This is a lockdown facility. She stays put."

Ross does not object. This is not like my brother at all.

Jackson speaks to him as if I am not in the room. "It's good that she's deranged. I can use this to our advantage."

Excuse me? I want to set things straight with my asshole lawyer but my thoughts are muddling up from the stress, and my jittery body is telling me it's time for more pain meds.

I scowl at Jackson but decide not to talk. My words might come out sounding as unhinged as he thinks I am.

Ross stands, and my two visitors make ready to leave. When Ross leans over my bed to give me a kiss on the cheek, he provides me with a much needed dose of familial comfort.

Jackson strides out of the room without a goodbye.

Ross stalls. "Uh, was this really all about your book?"

I nod.

"You have to know how insane that sounds. Right?"

I nod again.

"Okay, long as you recognize that. So...you have to figure Janine's over-the-top worried."

Our eldest surviving sister appointed herself surrogate mother to us grown-up orphans. Good thing she's in Seattle.

"She's ready to fly down here," he says way too casually.

I squeeze the bed sheet with knuckle cracking intensity.

He continues, "But I told her no visitors."

I burst out with a loud, "Thank youuuuu." My voice

levels out when I ask about our youngest sibling. "Dddddddaaan-nee?"

"You know him. Danny's cool. Well, I gotta go." Ross makes his way to the door. I hear him rubbing his hands together. "Cheryl's getting off duty soon. I'm hoping she'll let me play with her gun."

She's a guard? Oh, brother.

Ross pauses on his way out. "You'll be fine."

YOU'LL BE FINE. It's been hours since Ross tried to reassure me with a platitude.

Funny thing is, I seem to recall saying that very thing to Helice when we were in the Red Eden I can't get that kid out of my mind. I mean, come on, she's a fictional character. And she might even have linked up with Bethany Moraga. Or was that a nightmare?

There's nothing worse than lying around helpless after brain surgery. What I can do for myself is roll over and beg Morpheus (or another god for that matter) for a nice deep slumber.

I'm game to meet with any or all novel characters who show up in my sleep. My eyes are droopy, the sleep god must be responding. I order myself to have a significant dream. Best to leave it open to interpretation, see what happens.

HELICE AND I ARE in a dream state somewhere, but I don't think we're in the Red Eden. There's no sky or ground wherever this is. She is crying so hard, it starts me bawling. Everything feels so chaotic. I try to speak, to question why she's haunting me. My lips are so rubbery the words fall out one by one. She does not offer the slightest clue.

Oh, here's a rush of movement in the shrubbery as a muscular, black haired boy around Helice's age flits by. At that moment, though, he stops, pivots, and faces forward, as if he's looking straight into the "camera lens" of my dream. It is eerie, as dreams can be. I wonder who he is, since he does not resemble any of my characters. Helice turns from me, and reaches out to put a protective arm around him.

There had been a little boy featured in the original version from ten years back. Tirigan. Alastar's son. I'd dropped him from the roster since coping with two kid characters doubled my annoyance quota. But he'd been a four-year-old towhead. So much in my story has changed without my knowledge, perhaps he's older now, and his white-blond hair darkened as he aged?

Before they leave, Helice makes a point of putting her lips along my ear to give me a message. *It's time. Tick tock. Wake up.*

Huh, what? My eyes won't open, as if they're glued shut. Nothing makes sense so I still must be dreaming.

Oh, crap. A tall lean figure is advancing at a quick pace. Pria. Of all my literary characters, it has to be her?

Pria is a spectacular six-foot platinum fem fatale who can overpower an adult male, disembowel, and dress him like a deer. Called a gutter, she collects souls and buries the bodily remains in the soil that has over time turned blood red.

Her character was developed as a startling vehicle with which to propel the story. A great villain. I am deathly afraid of her.

I'd designed the Red Eden as a way station for recently deceased people. Pria and her boyfriend round up straggling people who don't realize they've died. They're classic bad guys who gut souls and dump the bodies so folks can go on to heaven. That's why this Eden has turned blood red.

In my story, Pria had never encountered someone like the comatose Helice Polansky, though, someone who lingered between life and death.

Uh oh, Pria's getting closer. She's wearing the costume I'd specified: a full-length gown that has no sides. It is merely two narrow lengths of mauve silk front and back, joined only at the shoulders, the silky cloth clinging to her size D breasts.

Voluptuous hips curve out on either side of the twenty-five-inch wide panels, cinched at her impossibly tiny waist with a silver cord. There are no undergarments. As one can imagine, nothing is left to the imagination as she moves.

She's barreling right at me. I brace myself as we go down hard. She screams, "Murderer! You killed Egregor."

I'm on my back in the mud and she's on top of me. I should play possum, but my feisty self can't help itself. "You're crazy, I didn't kill anyone."

"He died in the fire." She springs up and hovers over me.

"There was no fire." I'm halfway sitting up now and really should shut up. "Listen, I'm the author. I say who lives and dies."

She kicks me in the gut with her purple stilettos. Then she leans over and jerks my arm at an impossible angle so my fingers are jammed deep into my head wound. Somehow, she wedges her pointy-shoed toe in between my fourth and fifth ribs. It hurts like holy hell.

She yells, "My lover's dead. It's your fault I'm a soul gutter. You made me into a monster. I hate eviscerating people. At least I had Egregor." Balling her fist, she punches me in the temple. "Why'd you ruin everything? Half this place burned down."

She socks me in the jaw; the blow is so powerful my head snaps back. She doesn't miss a beat. "You don't give a shit about the people who live here. People you created. Bitch."

It's a long shot but, what the hell, I ask her, "Do you know why Helice found me in the real world? Did Magdalena send her? And, where exactly *is* Magdalena?"

"How would I know?" She jeers, "You're asking me? After all your bragging about how *you* created *us*?"

I should leave it alone but I am an obsessed author in need of a perfect ending. "Has that catty bulimic

Bethany Moraga been here asking questions? If she is, you should—"

Pria head butts me with the force of a world-class soccer star. Oh, great, here comes Bethany riding on cop Marciano's broad shoulders. He lets her down and poof, he's gone. She's dressed in gold silk boxers and a wife-beater. Her surgically enhanced breasts are infuriatingly perky.

I'm in my hospital gown. Since this is nightmare, my gown is soiled and my naked rear end is exposed. The brain slop bag is attached to my head, this being a freaking nightmare. And it's fricking leaking all over me.

Bethany and Pria tag team. Bethany pries my mouth open. Pria clamps onto my tongue, repeatedly stabbing it with her razor's edge fingernail. Pria drags me along a rocky trail to the soul-gutting dungeon. I know what she is up to; after all, I conceived this psychopath.

She can't kill me. Technically, she isn't real. Right?

Bethany, who, even though I hate her, is the best writing teacher I've ever had, is in league with the she-devil of my own making. As for Marciano? What's his take? Can I trust my he-man rookie?

It's all too much. I can't take Marciano's rejection. I need a man to get me through this ordeal.

"Trez?" Hearing my name, I roll over, open my one good eye. It's a nurse. Thank God. I'm back in the hospital.

"You were screaming. You must have had some nightmare." She examines my mouth. "Oh, no wonder you're gushing blood. Your tongue has several deep bite marks."

No, not true. I didn't bite myself. My fictional character slashed me with a fingernail filed to a vicious point. So, it's obvious. Pria is in league with the viperous human plagiarist, Bethany, who I now know is after my story—and my rookie.

THE SURGEON, Dr. Watson, just left. He said I was crying during my nap so loud, the entire ward heard it. I don't remember much, but he said it took them awhile to calm me down. The word "hysterical" was used; one of the nurses wrote that and more on a clipboard. This won't bode well for my psych evaluation but then again, Jackson had advised me to remain here voluntarily. I might not have a choice now.

I did my best to convince them I'd had a nightmare. Or a daymare. There's no window, I can't tell if it's day or night. Dr. Watson told me some side effects of a "temporary brain trauma" are hallucinations and sleep disorders. He noted I've proven to be sensitive to medications, so he seemed to buy my story.

After I complained of chest pain, he discovered one of my ribs is cracked. He'd played it down, saying they must have missed it during their initial exam, but I know the truth. Pria broke my rib! It wasn't broken before, only bruised. By telling me I have a "touch" of epilepsy, which is normal for this trauma, he added his own epilogue to this story. Dr. Watson thinks I was pressed up against the bed's metal guardrail during my "touch of epilepsy" and the force cracked my rib.

Oh sure, and Pria wasn't going to town all over my body.

What was Helice crying about? Maybe she turns into a typical crybaby whenever she wants her own way?

Crap. Now I'm wide-awake. A nurse set up a radio turned low, my guess as a way to soothe me. *Every Breath You Take* is playing at the moment.

It's not calming me at all, considering my newly cracked rib causes every intake of air to feel like it will be my last. My throbbing head is keeping beat like a bongo player on speed.

You'd think they'd give me a shot, take me out of my misery. The doctor continued my epilepsy meds but decided to postpone my painkillers for at least two hours. He offered two lousy Tylenols.

They'd repeatedly told me to lie still since the

surgery, to not move much but now, without any opioids in my system, everything hurts.

There are tubes connected to various parts of my body. My left hand is already sore from the IV needle stuck into my vein; just flexing my fingers is cause to bite my lip. It's such an effort to turn over onto my side it feels like an elephant has taken up residence on my chest. It's my first attempt at moving around without anything to cut the edge.

Damn, that elephant is stomping on me as I try to sit up. My groans alert me that it hurts to take a deep breath. I want a nurse, but have rolled too far away from the call button.

Fighting a rising panic, I realize it's not just the physical ills bothering me right now. Something Ross said earlier has been haunting me.

I'd tried to make excuses for my berserk behavior.

He'd stopped me with a stern admonishment, *"You gotta own this, Trez."*

CHAPTER 6

The Gent Comes a'Calling

JUST WHEN I CALM myself down and start to nod off, I hear a loud voice call out, "Hi'ya Trez."

I open my one good eye to squint at a family friend sauntering into my hospital room. Phineas Warren McCool.

Phin is what my Gram called a long drink of water. He is a modern day Icabod Crane in royal blue bellbottoms and orange plastic flip flops. Almost six feet tall, his stick body probably weighs one twenty—tops.

He doesn't explain why he brought a boombox as he sets it down. As if comforting a widow at a funeral, he whispers, "Hey there."

"Heeeeeeyyyyyyyyy uuuuuuuuuself."

I can't help myself from giggling like a fool. I'm thinking if his body is a matchstick, his hair is its flame. Long pelts of mahogany red fur stick out from the sides and back, merging with a scraggly beard and mustache.

Here it comes, he's bending down to kiss me. Plumes of red ocher tip precariously on the upper edges of his undersized crown behind his short narrow brow.

"You poor thing," he coos softly. "Does your head hurt? It sure looks like it hurts."

Since he's bent over, I can't help but take in the bump on the tip of his peak. His is not a subtly misshapen pate, one that would only be noticeable when he grows into his golden years and loses his hair. No, this cranium seems to have been custom designed for him alone.

It is still a mystery to me as to why I allow this guy into my bed, however occasionally we couple. Hmm, maybe we hook up because I'm not the typical Barbie playhouse type?

Phin is no Ken doll. Although, once in a while he gets a sexy look in his eyes that melts me. He's polite, respectful, and a good listener, especially when I'm totally frazzled. He offers perfect advice most of the time. Plus he's amiable all of the time. Best of all, he doesn't try to dominate me like most of the guys I've been with. Phineas McCool knows better.

He's yammering about my situation. "So Trez, Ross told me what's been going on. Man oh man, it sure is weird to be here visiting you, I'm usually the one, don't you know?"

How could my fussy, methodical, left-brained brother have ever befriended Pluto?

Phin flashes me a muddled look. "What'd you say? It's hard to understand you. I could swear you called me Pluto."

Oops, didn't mean to say that out loud. He shouldn't look so hurt, though. Pluto is my favorite Walt Disney character. Walt designed Pluto after one of his Irish Setter dogs, who with their pronounced head bumps, are known for being hysterically funny, dumb as dirt creatures.

It's best to just move on. "Wyyyyyyyyyyyyy youuuuu herrrrrrrrrrrre?"

"I'm sorry, what'd you say?"

There is an uncomfortable silence before we manage to communicate through gestures, tilted heads, and eyebrows.

He works out my query. "Oh, got it. They have a strict no visitors policy, but me and the head orderly go way back. Virgil's his name. He lets me in whenever he's on duty."

I show my palms, mug a questioning expression.

He spins a hunk of red hair round his finger. "I've been an in and out patient for years. First time wasn't my idea, then later it was. It's like a diagnostic tune-up now and then, don't you know." He's back to playing with his hair.

Oh, yeah. Ross had told me about Phin's various meltdowns over the years. I hadn't paid much attention, who has time to track other peoples' problems? It doesn't seem so funny now. His parents have enough money to buy this place. Why hasn't he gone to a tony "spa" for treatment?

His mood turns on a dime, typical for Phin. "I can't believe you burned your novel. Leave it to you." He chuckles, "With all those versions it must have made a gigantic fire."

I may have made a big show of burning my novel, it sure felt good to kill that kid, but any author with half a brain would never destroy *all* the precious words. Phin's North Beach flat has been serving as a five-room safety deposit box for years without my having to worry about losing the key. Oh, it dawns on me to make certain that my lawyer doesn't know about this secret stash. Evidence. The cops think they have everything. Tee hee. Our little secret.

Phin is the only person who has read my entire novel—every single one of the too-numerous-to-count versions of Books One, Two, Three, and the incomplete Book Four. His obsessive-compulsiveness makes him an excellent editor, even if the said author in question often refuses to pore over his exhaustive suggestions written in a teeny weeny hand. Not to mention his taco stains all over my manuscripts.

My usual response is always, "Just tell me, already."

Truth be told, he's been instrumental in refining my vocabulary. Since I swear like a longshoreman, I'd sprinkled my spicy vernacular throughout the novel. He got me to recognize that one of my principle characters is a child living in the 1950s mores of Middle America. It's why he'd reacted to Ross' swearing. He worked hard to convince me to change. The bottom line is he challenged me to come up with creative avenues with which to follow the number one directive for writers. He kept telling me, "Don't tell 'em, Trez, *show* 'em."

"So anyways," Phin says, "getting back to your stay in this place. It can be scary, being dragged in here by cops. I wanted to give you support in your time of need."

Time of need? First, he sounded like a mortician, now he's acting like one.

He adds, "I know from experience how hard this can be, the psych evaluation and all..." His voice trails. "It can be tough, especially when you don't think you need it. And now, since you can't talk on top of it, I'm here to help."

He points to the boombox. Ever the techno geek, he says he wants to record my aphasia affected speech so he'll have an easier time deciphering my more "nuanced syntaxes."

I'm too exhausted to protest.

He sets up his machine. "Okay Trez, let's start. First off, say the Pledge of Allegiance. Because." He sighs. "It's more formal, that's why."

I oblige, but not without plenty of attitude.

He smiles. "Good. Now say the Our Father. Because it's poetic. Don't argue, just do it...please. Thank you. Now, tell me about your morning so I can get all your casual speech patterns.

"Great. Listen to this. I'll play the whole thing back."

He pushes a button. I can't understand a word I'm saying on tape, my words sound so warped.

He laughs, "Ross told me he can't make out much of anything you say. I'm sure he and Jackson have been polite, because of your brain damage, don't you know. They have no idea what you're talking about. But I..." He pats himself on his narrow, chicken breastbone of a chest. "I hear you, lady."

Enough. I want to know about the kid.

"Hhhhhhheeeeeeeeeeleeeeeeeeccccccce?"

"Man oh man, is she here? I'd love to meet her." Plopping into the chair next to my bed, he turns his head left then right. He looks up at the ceiling before kneeling down to check under the bed. "So, is she here? Is she?" Without waiting for my response, he exclaims, "Hi Helice."

Although it hurts to roll my good eye, I can't help it. He is such a dweeb. A manically annoying, albeit sweet, dweeb.

He sighs, "Oh, guess it means she's not around, huh? Think she'll ever show up again? We can only hope. You were so shocked when she popped up outta nowhere, you got yourself all flustered." Phin chuckles, "We had ourselves quite a time afterwards, heh Trez?"

My cheeks burn at the memory of our latest coupling. He is acting so innocent I reach up to grab his T-shirt at the neck. Freezing like Bambi in headlights, he lets out a high pitched squeal. I slowly release my chokehold so he'll give me details about the book launch. I don't remember much.

"Tellllllll meeeeeeee wwwwhaaaaatt happennnned."

He's sitting close by with his ears cocked at attention like a German shepherd. Is he straining to hear me?

I speak louder. He jumps back as if he's been hotwired.

"Hey, hey, Trez, calm down." He regains his composure. "Ahh, if you're asking about Helice, I didn't know what was going on during the book launch. I knew you were pissed off about getting fired, and then Bethany got all that attention. That was enough to irk you, but a character from your novel showing up in real life? Far out."

Phin smacks his thigh. "All of a sudden, you screamed and dropped your glass." He leans in close to emphasize, "Everyone turned your way. You freaked out big time. You were so drunk it took me forever to figure out what you were saying. Funny, just like now but it's from brain damage. Ow, Trez, don't pinch me. Okay,

okay, I'll get back to the story. I was dying to check out Helice. Too bad I didn't see a thing."

"Ddddiiiiiiiiiddd thhhhhat bbbitttchh Bethannnny seeeeeeee herrrrrrrrrrr?"

"Um, what are you saying? You asking about Bethany?"

Deciphering my rush of questions, he stresses if he couldn't see Helice, Bethany couldn't have either. He insists Bethany had no clue that my hallucination had come to life. "Helice is for you, Trez, only you."

He seems so sure of himself. He's swearing Bethany couldn't have stolen Helice since she wouldn't have known about the kid. Plus, KPIX roving reporter Tobey Vallencourt was interviewing Bethany live on camera while my dilemma was going on at the other end of the banquet hall.

Can't fold that easily. I insist Bethany snatched Helice.

"You're wrong. Why don't you believe that?"

I fold my arms tight around myself.

Phineas shakes his head. "She'd have stopped the show if she heard about a fictional character materializing. Even if it wasn't from a book she'd written. Don't forget, she hired a PR firm. They'd jump on something that fantastic, they'd put it out all over the media. From her point of view, of course."

He chuckles, mostly to himself. "Leave it to Trez Evans to bring her character to life. The ultimate show, don't tell."

My frown tells him he's failed to show me otherwise. Is Helice safe and unmolested by the bestselling gossipmonger?

He shrugs. "How would Bethany or anyone else know your character came to life unless you announced it?"

I reach for Phin's shirt again. Dodging me, he gets the hint. "You want to know what happened next, is that what you're asking? No can do. I wasn't paying attention to you."

I scowl at him. He surprises me by narrowing his eyes, contracting his lips. He's throwing attitude back at *me*?

Shaking his head he blurts, "You know what? You're not the only writer dreaming of fame. That indie publisher I was talking to might have been interested in my graphic novel but no, you pulled me away. You wanted to ditch Helice ASAP. You couldn't wait two minutes."

I wait, patiently, for him to get over his hissy fit. Oh, hell, enough is enough. I blast him, "I gggggoooooott the ticketsssssssss. Youuuuuuu weeeerrr there for meeeeeeeee."

His eyes darken. "I was there only for...you? Is that what you're saying?" I tilt my chin several times.

"Hah." He forces a laugh. "I go to Bethany's writing group too. All her students were invited."

Whatever.

Ignoring my flipped up finger, he manages to understand my next question. "No, I don't know how Helice found you after we left the party. You and I drove to your place but you said she wasn't in the car. Man oh man it was a mad hatter's wild ride. I was screaming you drove so fast."

He fiddles with the tape of my weird aphasia speech. He's taking too long. I want to know how Bethany managed to steal my character. I shout, "PPhhiiiiinnneeeeeASS."

"Okay, okay, don't be so impatient." He inhales, making a big deal about blowing out his air. "Hey, Trez, you want to meditate together? It'll calm you down."

How dare he. My eyes hood as he goes for the second breath. Seriously? He's a complete doofus if he thinks I'm unaware of what he's doing with the technique I conceived.

He frowns. "I can't figure how Helice knew where to go."

"Mmmmaaaaarrrrrrrrrreeeeeeeeeeeee?"

"Ah, yes, Mary." Phin smiles. "At first, Mary went

off the rails. I don't know if she could see Helice or not but that dog of yours sure sensed the kid's presence. I gotta tell ya, Mary was growling and carrying on something awful. Pretty far out, huh?" He gets a wistful look on his face before going on.

"The madder you got, the more Mary calmed down. At one point you were arguing with Helice but then you stopped to tell me that Mary sat down right on the kid's feet."

Hmm, I'd forgotten about that. My aloof dog's behavior tells me something positive about Helice. Mary rarely sits on anyone. Yet, she stayed put on Helice's feet all night. That unusual action not only means the person is accepted into the pack, Mary gives her personal rump of approval.

But, how could a dog sit on a hallucination?

Raising his hand, Phin waits for my nod before saying, "Why were you mad at Helice? You were so drunk by then I couldn't understand you."

I let out a loud snort and explain. It's unclear if he comprehends all of my rapid fire aphasic words. My point is Helice must have come here for a reason. The problem is, she didn't come for me. What does that say about me? *Me*. She's my character, damn it. I start to snivel.

Phin says, "After we got back to your house, I heard you carrying on about her showing up for Bethany. I couldn't see the kid so I don't know about her reactions. I couldn't hear her responses but I gotta tell the truth, I was embarrassed for you."

Ouch, that hurts. Honestly, I was such a cutthroat to an innocent child, I feel like a heel. But he mustn't know that. My two word retort leaves nothing to the imagination.

"Oh, nice one, Trez. Why do you have to be so mean?" He twists a chunk of his red hair around his finger, a nervous habit of his that drives me crazy.

"Commme onnnnnn." Rubbing my sore hand bruised by the IV needle, my voice turns to pure bellyaching. "Whooooo knows where Hhhheeeeeecccceee is?"

The doctor cut off my meds. I tell Phin the kid's gone and drugs are the key to hooking me back up with her.

"But I thought you wanted to get rid of her."

I push down my temper and explain that was then, this is now. I now need her. I repeat my request. Since Phin is keen to discover Helice's reason for being here, he needs to bring me his stash from home. I flash him an enticing Trez smile, which is fun, sexy, and flirty without promising anything.

He readily responds with a full mouth grin.

I flash him another smile, one that leaves nothing to his imagination. He stammers, "Ahh, I don't understand." He removes his jacket, turns around, and takes the time to hang it neatly along the back of his chair.

"Yessssss uuuuuuu do." My words come out like a stroke victim but my coyness is spot-on. It takes concentration on my part but eventually he gets the gist. His medicine cabinet at home is stuffed to the gills and I want some.

He counters, "Prescription medications. All legitimate." He pushes back his hair. "I only take what my doctors order." I hate his self-satisfying smirk.

Through gestures and pantomimed mugging, my motive unfolds. Come on, I tell him, let's be honest. You need drugs to cope. Now, so do I. He folds his arms tight over his *Keep Bob Marley Alive* T-shirt. "Then ask your doctor."

Time to pull out the big guns. My lower lip quivers, my good eye floods with tears. My damsel in distress comes across, with me imploring him for help since he's the only one who could do this for me.

His brow drops even lower on his face than usual as he sighs, "I know what you're doing."

Do you, Phin McCool? Do you know the full wrath of Teresa Rose Evans? I lean forward even though it hurts. I remind him of the time Ross sent him packing and he had nowhere to go but my place. I say things like you couldn't go back to Rome, could you? Huh, could you? He hangs his head. Your parents didn't want you to come home to Chicago, did they? I pound my mattress for emphasis. You had no place to go, did you, Phineas? I was the only one to take you in, wasn't I? You stayed in my guest house for an entire year, didn't you?

He lifts his head, takes in a deep breath, then expels it. "I haven't the faintest idea what you're saying, but I still won't give you drugs."

"Damnnnnnnniiiiiiiit."

"Man oh man." He takes in another breath, lets it out slow and easy. "Um, okay, I got this. Here's the way I see it."

He levels his gaze on me. It is truly unsettling. Hmm, I might be seeing something new in him. Breathing in and out a third time, he says, "Let's work this out together. Once upon a time, the entire premise of your novel was that Helice found herself in an idyllic setting she didn't want to leave. That's the Red Eden. Who could blame her? It was better than the real life she had being paralyzed in a hospital." His attitude grows more intense as he adds, "After all that, she left anyway. Why?"

He holds up his index finger. "Your novel spells out her reason quite clearly. She went back to the hospital when Magdalena got her to accept her fate. Helice learned to find joy in the worst situations. Man oh man, it's heavy stuff."

He stands to drive his point home. "Helice Polansky did ultimately leave paradise for the emotional climax of going home, of finding a purpose for herself despite the physical challenges the little girl knew she would face."

When did he get so wise? When he speaks, it's as if his face is being illuminated from an unseen source.

"Trez. You know you're amazing, right?" He waits for me to agree. "You're capable of accomplishing anything you set out to do. Right?" I nod again. He goes

80

on, "For some reason, Helice came to you, the author. You keep asking why. You've been crying over what to do with your story for ten years.

"Look at it in a different way." He studies me. "Before you do, take that first breath." He models it by inhaling a gulp, holding it in, and then exhaling slowly and deliberately.

As if I don't know anything about meditative techniques.

"I believe you have more control over this story than you realize, Trez. You just have to figure it out."

"WWWhhhat?" Figure it OUT? I scream so loud the entire ward must hear me. Positive thinking crap. Phin almost had me believing in that fricking bullshit. Some nerve, 'teaching' *me* to breathe. I wrote the goddamn book on breathing. I want to kill him, but first, there is a delicate subject to discuss. Exhaling, I relax, give him a smile.

This has to do with our...well, hate to call it a "relationship." Through my aphasia-stilted English and attempted pantomime, I warn Phin to never, ever, mention that we... um... we found comfort in one another's arms.

First off, if Ross heard of our coupling he would blow his top. I'm his sister, after all. Also, it would tarnish my A-lister reputation among all the women who look up to me, not to mention my gentlemen friends. The guys I know would never stoop to compete with Phin for my feminine favors. It'd drop them deep into the pits of the social status dump.

An involuntary quiver runs through me as I study this guy. Gawd. What was I thinking? Hmm, the reality is I was so drunk I couldn't possibly have thought it out. Phew.

Phin hangs his head. "Fine. I won't say anything."

I reward him with a smile. Just when I think we're in the clear, he has to ruin my moment by asking, "But why do you keep warning me not to tell after we sleep together? I mean, if it keeps happening, doesn't it mean that uh, that we...?"

He catches my evil eye and dodges my fist that's hovering by his chinless chin. He backs down. "Okay. I promise. Mum's the word." He makes his way to the door. "I'm not trying to piss you off, but it'd help if you meditate."

Phin figures out my diatribe. "Hey Trez, careful with the language. Helice might be here without us knowing it."

Flipping him off helps me get across my point. What a dipstick. It hurts me to admit that Helice isn't here anymore.

I burst out crying. Nurses swarm my bed. They explain I'd overtaxed myself; it was all too much too soon. They tuck me in and offer two white pills for my pain and suffering.

I swallow them greedily, yet nurses refuse to knock me out. They won't fill a syringe with magical elixirs so I can meet up with Helice again.

CHAPTER 7

Who's Who and What's What?

THE DOCTOR'S MORATORIUM against my drug cocktails is over. I've made up for lost time by begging prescription "treats" from the nurses. We're all getting along so well, I ask one of them to change the radio station. We go through a pantomime worthy of an Abbott and Costello *Who's on First?* routine. She eventually figures it out.

The new release *Maniac* is playing. I'm keeping beat with my fingers, singing, *"In the real time world no one sees her at all, they all say she's crazy."* There's no telling what alien sounds are coming out of my mouth.

A different nurse passes by. She cocks her head, gives me a sideways glance, and flips the radio dial to a classical station.

Oh, the music is lulling me. I'm lying in a satiated stupor when a dumpy nurse with droopy boobs walks in to announce, "It's time you get up and walk."

Is she nuts? I just had brain surgery.

I argue how Stanford hospital wouldn't make me walk this soon, why can't I go there? She can't understand me and probably doesn't care, so she lifts me out of bed and plants my feet on the floor. She orders me to walk around my tiny room. I am woozy but manage to stay upright.

Satisfied with that effort, she leads me into the hallway. "Go up to the nurses' station and back down here. Twice."

I'm exhausted by the time she guides me back into bed.

Cooing, "Nightie night, Ms. Evans," she takes off.

My eyelids are fluttering with the promise of a deep sleep as Marciano, the beefcake rookie cop, walks into my room.

"Hello, Ms. Evans. I'm Officer Marciano. Do you remember me from the other day?"

Instantly enlivened, I forgive him his trespasses. I flash a perfect Trez Evans come hither smile. Maybe we can become rebound lovers. There's nothing better than makeup sex.

Marciano takes a long look at me. He drops his gaze, fumbles to pull out a pocket handkerchief and gags into it. Despite my encouraging efforts, he refuses to look at me again. So much for us getting back together.

He's accompanied by another uniformed policeman who's so self-conscious he lowers his peaked hat to block his eyes. My lawyer Jackson Milan is the third one in. A tall gawky nurse with eyes like a lemur lingers by the threshold.

The hospital room is so small the men shove and push one another for position. The two officers win the standing room only positions at the foot of my bed, since they are big, buff, and have guns.

The loser, Jackson, is forced to take the chair close to me. He doesn't notice the urine bag sticking out from under the covers until he's settled. He jerks his spine so stiffly he becomes mostly a diagonal line hovering above the wooden chair with only his rigid right arm as a support.

Maybe he'll slide to the floor and the rest of us can have a good laugh at his expense.

Once they're situated, Jackson motions to the Lemur. She adjusts the bed to a ninety degree angle and helps me sit up. Not an easy task, considering my post-surgical dizziness, not to mention my bruised and cracked ribs. My pain is real; yet a few exaggerated winces help me drive my point home.

I try to catch Marciano's eye but he will not look my way. No one will, despite my best efforts to attract their attention. As is my flirty habit among handsome men, I go to sweep my right hand along my hair...only...there is no long luscious hair on that side of my head.

Oh, Gawd. I forgot. My hand hits a plastic drainage bag that is attached to my shaved skull by a rubber tube.

That reminds me, the nurses have not brought me a mirror despite my many requests. It becomes unpleasantly clear to me that I might not look my best right now.

"Ahem." He clears his throat. I focus on his tall, dark, and handsome self. I would love some Italian right now.

"Ms. Evans, I'm here with Officer Reynolds to ask some questions." He motions to Reynolds. That bastard cop has his back to me. So rude. Fine by me, he is not cute at all.

Jackson states, "My client is in a high level of pain. You have five minutes."

Marciano is all business, "Five minutes, understood." His tone softens. "Let me first say you've had a run of bad luck, haven't you." He leans forward, lightly touching the blanket tucked around my feet. "How are you feeling, Trez?"

He called me Trez. My heart swells with hope renewed. I intend to give him a sweet, genuine response to show I hold no ill will against him despite my forced confinement to a nut house and my subsequent, horrendous head injury.

I want to tell him he was only doing his job. I need to get across the fact that I will still fall in love with him if he'd only ask. But, that's not what comes out of my mouth.

"Not sooo gooood, my bbbrraaaainn uuu knowwwwwww."

Marciano cocks his head, making an effort to understand my gibberish. Not like his asshole partner who looks ready to upchuck into his oversized cop hat.

Jackson jumps up from the chair to announce, "As you can plainly see, my client is still recovering from emergency brain surgery. It's obvious she's unable to communicate."

The other cop is halfway out of the room. Marciano says, "I'm sorry, Trez, I really am."

"Trez?" Reynolds snipes, "Don't get so personal, *rookie*."

Marciano's face burns red. "Ms. Evans, I need to ask some questions. Could you nod or shake your head?"

Jackson objects but I wave them off. I'd do anything for my future lover in a monogamous relationship. Despite the dizzying side effect, I tuck my chin down and then lift it high so he can see how unwavering our connection is.

My cutie pie rookie smiles, "Thank you for cooperating. Let it be known that on Thursday, September 22, 1983 at..." He checks his watch..."At 2:47 pm, Officers Reynolds and Marciano commence questioning Trez, I mean Teresa Rose Evans in her hospital room. Her attorney Jackson Milan is present. We are investigating the disappearance of ten year old Analeese Loveland who went missing early on Wednesday morning, September 21, 1983. Let it be known that Ms. Evans is recuperating from brain surgery and currently lacks the ability to speak clearly, so we will rely on head movements and gestures to ascertain her answers."

He glances down at his notes. "Ah, the first question is do you now, or have you ever had, any knowledge of a child from Redwood City named Analeese Loveland?"

Enlarging my eyes with adamant conviction (at least the eye that's not bandaged), I twist my head from side to side.

"Okay, I'll put that down as a no. The next question is have you ever had any interaction with Analeese Loveland or any of her relatives, friends, or acquaintances?"

It's nauseating to shake my head but it's for a good cause, to express my undying loyalty to Officer Marciano.

"Did you have any contact, either direct or indirect, with any child under the age of eighteen on the day in question?"

No. Of course not. Why the hell would I hang around a kid, for crying out loud?

"Were you alone, either on your property or in your vehicle, the entire morning?"

Uh oh. A big knot is forming in my throat. Oh, God, I can barely blurt out, "Yyyyyyyyeeeeeeeeeee-sssssssssssss." I wipe my brow and try to act nonchalant.

Marciano doesn't catch my freaked out body language. I manage to smile. Wish I could tell my darling rookie how well he's doing with my interrogation. Hope that other cop is paying attention and will praise his efforts to their chief.

Marciano says, "We spoke with Sol Green, your former employer. He verified you were at his place of business on Tuesday, September 20, from 9:30 am to noon. You returned at approximately 3:00 pm, at which time he fired you. He says you spent approximately twenty minutes complaining and cleaning out your desk. Does that sound about right?"

It makes me sad to agree, but it's the truth.

"We spoke with a young woman named..." He consults his notes. "Bethany Moraga."

Now I'm the one fighting bile rising up my throat.

"Miss Moraga confirmed you attended her writing group at the Chinatown YMCA but you arrived disheveled and breathless an hour later than usual, at approximately 1:00 pm. You left shortly before 3:00 pm, which coincides with Sol Green's statement. Moraga said you and a male companion attended her book launch that evening, before leaving abruptly at approximately 9:00 pm. Do you concur?"

I nod.

"Can you tell me the name of your male companion?"

Oh, crap. Jackson Milan does not need to learn that guy's identity. I choke out long bizarre sounds that make no sense.

Marciano kindly moves on. "We'll have to come back to that. Do you know if your companion ever met Analeese Loveland? To the best of your knowledge, does he now, or did he ever know of her whereabouts?"

I shake my head twice, one for each question. Marciano pauses, frowns at his list of questions, then looks up at me.

"Trez Evans, did you have anything to do with the disappearance of Analeese Loveland?"

NO! My head is shaking so vehemently it just might come off its axis.

"Trez Evans, where were you on the morning of Wednesday, September 21, 1983 between the hours of 6:45 am and 8:30 am?"

"Ummm....?" Where was I? "Mmmm....?"

Jackson is staring at me, his facial expression impossible to read. He is playing possum, legal-style, although I detect a slight, barely discernable bulge in his right cheek where his tongue is pressed against the side of his mouth.

I'm certain my rookie is rooting for me. His big brown eyes express how much he wants me to have the perfect alibi so we can put this unpleasantness behind us.

"Ms. Evans?" Marciano motions with his index finger for me to answer.

I begin to act out my response, then stop. Jackson had warned me not to offer anything. Does that include a game of charades? I falter, which probably makes me look guilty.

Bottom line? Jackson Milan can be a five star dick, but he is a brilliant strategist so I should listen to him.

Marciano says, "I repeat. Ms. Evans, we need to

know your whereabouts two days ago, on Wednesday, September 21, 1983 between the hours of 6:45 am and 8:30 am?"

Oh, well, here goes. "IIIIIII neeeeed ta chhhheeeecc myyyyy callllllllllllannnnder."

The other officer finally talks, "I can't understand a word she's saying."

Jackson cuts this meeting short. "Gentlemen, my client has cooperated to the best of her ability but obviously, she's unable to speak at this time."

The two policemen start to file out of my hospital room. The ugly one is the first to exit, without a sideways glance to me. Hooding my one good eye, I glare daggers at him with my best Trez Evans attitude. Thanks for nothing, jerk.

In contrast, Marciano lingers by the foot of my bed. I'm yearning for him to brush his fingers along my blanketed feet again. That brief yet meaningful touch could carry me through the trials of being confined against my will.

He doesn't extend his hand, but he does something even better. He says to me, with all sincerity, he says, "I wish you the very best, Trez. You deserve it."

He probably should have whispered his sentiment since his partner bellows from the hallway, "Watch it, *rookie!*"

My conscience cannot bear the burden of my sweet rookie getting in trouble on my behalf. I make a mental note to ask Jackson to follow up, to make sure Marciano doesn't get written up for improper behavior. Improper, indeed.

I enjoy the last fleeting views of Marciano's backside as he walks out. With Jackson gone as well, what I want is relief and sleep in short order. Being interrogated is hard work.

Pressing the call button brings the droopy-boobed nurse. I hold up seven fingers to indicate my pain level.

She refers to the chart hanging at the foot of my bed. "Sorry, you have another..." She checks her wristwatch. "Another forty five minutes to go."

I wave all ten fingers frantically.

"Sorry, Ms. Evans, we follow a strict drug protocol."

I let out a mournful "Aaaaaaghhhhhhhh." How else to explain the utter devastation one feels at being denied a modicum of comfort after enduring fricking brain surgery?

I reach up to touch the gross drainage bag attached to a hose clamped somewhere inside my brain—my living, pulsing *brain* for chrissakes.

It's my attempt to *show* her my high degree of pain.

She shakes her head. Does she realize I was seriously pushing myself to get through the last half of the police interrogation? I ponder evil thoughts about her as she leaves.

What am I supposed to do with myself? There are no TVs, radios are in short quantity and high demand among patients. Since nurses brought in a radio shortly after my surgery, there's no telling when one will come around again.

I close my one eye. Might as well try to take a nap. There is nothing of interest around here.

I'M PRETTY SURE I was sound asleep, judging by the wet circle of drool on my pillow. So why does Helice yell in my ear, *Tick tock! Get ready!* Doesn't she know I'm recuperating from major surgery? That kid is so self-absorbed. She wakes me up, orders me around, and then disappears? Bloody hell.

I'm pretty sure I went back to sleep. But right now, the hairs on the back of my neck are straight up. It's not Helice this time, since a shivery feeling courses through my body whenever my hallucination shows up. My good eye pops open but I'd already smelled him, his sour milky scent.

Roman, the face licker, is standing over my bed. He's watching my reaction, following my gaze to the call button, which is out of reach. My heart is pounding so hard it's climbing up my throat. A croak escapes my clenched mouth.

He brings his right index finger up and over his lips, gesturing for me not to scream.

I obey, which is totally not my style.

He's wearing a blue two piece facility outfit that's baggy on his short, slight frame. His neck is a pencil, he has no shoulders to speak of, with hairless, spindly arms that bear no muscle mass. He probably weighs less than me.

The licker hasn't made a move to smooch me but under the bed covers, my fingers are curled into claws just in case.

His voice is surprisingly deep. "Sorry," he rasps. "I...I...major psychotic break."

He's so pitiful my fists open up. My good eye, however, doesn't break his stare. No telling what he's capable of doing.

He inhales, deeply. He does it again, his nostrils flaring. Is this a personal insult? I just had brain surgery for crying out loud. There's a drainage bag stuck in my bald head, and a urine bag by my feet. It's a hospital. Get over it, jackass.

My hands ball up again. No doubt, I would cry out in anguish from the physical action of punching him, but it sure would feel fantastic to floor this sucker.

An image of me lording over Roman like a hunting trophy comes to mind. He's hogtied by my machines' rubber tubing, with my foot planted firmly on his pencil of a neck.

Oh, Lord, now he's got his left hand extended, with fingers splayed. The way this freak is moving that hand around, he must think it's a Geiger counter. He looks to be searching for something. Oh, crap, he's closer now.

His hand is just an inch or two away from me and it's traveling down from my head, my face, to my chest. His hand lingers midway, centering around my heart area.

Roman inhales again. He smiles.

"Good," he tells me. "Good, good."

He turns around and leaves my room.

A nurse walks in. Did they cross paths? This is supposed to be a high security area. Perhaps Ross is wooing Cheryl the facility guard when she's supposed to be on duty protecting patients like me? I try to rat on Roman, to get him in trouble with the nurse but with my aphasia and my agitated state of mind, all my words come out pure balderdash.

The nurse is fiddling with my oxygen tubes. Oh, great. The anxiety of my steadily increasing pain, not to mention the bizarre visit from Roman and whatever the nurse is doing, is causing me to hyperventilate.

Suddenly, I let out a cry that is so raw, so primal, it makes both of us jump. It also dredges up a vile green bile that spews out of me so fast there is no time to redirect the projectile away from said nurse.

She goes running. A second nurse replaces her. This one does a quick evaluation as I'm holding out my hands like a crying baby. They are covered with stinky goop because I tried (stupidly) to stop the purge.

The nurse bustles around preparing a small tub of warm sudsy water into which she directs me to plunge my hands. The water turns within seconds to a murky gray so she has to pour it out and start over.

I accidently knock over the second batch when I squirm. It floods me and my bed. I put up nine wet soapy fingers to let her know my pain level.

Clucking like a mother hen, she washes and dries my legs, body, and hands. Although my busted ribs are trussed up like a Christmas goose, it still hurts like sin when she guides my arms into a new hospital gown.

She deftly changes my soiled sheets and tucks me into a freshly made bed like a swaddled babe. She then lowers the mattress to a comfy nap position and plumps up pillows to ease my piercing headache.

Finally, she loads a syringe and shoots a dose of Demerol into my left buttock. There *is* a God!

CHAPTER 8

Pee Green and Purple

Day 3 —

A NURSE WAKES ME. Once she figures out my question, she tells me it's morning. Good to know. I'm still heavy-eyed from the horror of Pria bursting through my dream last night. Ew, I still taste blood in my mouth.

The nurse feeds me bland white mush with a weak tea. I barely finish breakfast before she forces me out of bed. Once the dizziness clears, she makes me walk up and down the damn hall. Jeez, doesn't she know my scull was cracked open like a coconut?

Someone else comes in and announces a staff member is requesting a short visit. Behind her is a young attractive woman lugging an oversized black tote stuffed to the brim.

She offers me a warm smile. She's wearing a knockout dress with the latest style puffy sleeves I'd love to own. She gives off the vibe that she gets what she wants.

What she wants is for me to pay attention.

She starts right in. "Hi, Ms. Evans. My name is Hannah Harrison. I'll be your therapist while you're staying with us."

She extends her hand, and after my initial disinclination, we do the obligatory shake. Being a germaphobe, now all I can think of is the urgency to wash my right hand. Hospitals are full of germs and bugs and viruses. Eck.

I try to explain but with my aphasia, plus my torn up tongue, it's too hard to talk. Damn that Pria.

"Ms. Evans? Trez? Hello?"

Huh, what? Oh. I offer her a polite smile and point to my bruised mouth. I tap my shaved head, indicating my brain was recently probed and prodded. Not to mention a gross drainage bag. Do I really have to deal with this now?

Not getting the hint, she states, "I'm a doctoral candidate in developmental psychology at Stanford University."

If she's expecting an enthusiastic test subject for a term paper, she is sorely mistaken.

She says, "The 'father' of this field is Sigmund Freud."

Gawd, kill me now. Despite pain from the IV, I put my left (germ free) hand to my mouth. A yawn is added attitude.

She gets the hint. "I just want to touch bases with you and see how you're processing your 5150 status and, naturally, your emergency surgery."

How do you think, lady?

She sits down on the chair by my bed. She leans forward. "Trez, my intention is for you and I to forge a trusting therapeutic relationship because I truly do want to help you."

Blah, blah, blah.

She looks at me with expectation.

She's waiting for me to actually answer her? She wants to bond? Time to nip this in the bud. I point to my mouth, and shrug my shoulders with my head tilted as if to say oh well.

"Of course, I understand your current situation." She digs into her black tote and pulls out a portfolio of art paper along with a clear zippered case of colored pencils, crayons, and magic markers, along with stickers, glitter, and other crafty crap.

She's bright and cheery when she says, "Art therapy is a perfect modality for someone who can't speak."

Oh, goodie.

"We'll just do a few moments, shall we?"

She tries to place a lightweight drawing board on my lap. Holding up a hand for her to wait, I press the nurse's call button. I'm hoping a nurse will stop this nonsense, but when one comes in, she adjusts my bed to the upright position and helps me to sit up per the therapist's request. Ow!

When the nurse leaves, Harrison passes me the portfolio of art paper. I feel the top page with my thumb and forefinger. It's got good weight and texture.

"Express how you feel with color, shape, line, whatever feels right." She places a gentle hand on my arm. "Don't worry if you're not an artist, if you can't draw a straight line. This isn't about perfection. This is about tapping into your inner self and asking how you feel, what you feel, and why."

Speaking of feeling, my head is pounding so hard there must be a jackhammer breaking apart my skull into little chunks. I reach for my call button.

When a different nurse shows up, I point to my head and put up seven fingers to express my insufferable level of pain.

The nurse checks my chart and explains, "We have an hour to wait before our next dosage."

Oh, *we* do, do we?

Hannah Harrison opens the zippered case, pulls out a jumbo-sized blue crayon, and sticks it in my hand. "I know the police questioned you earlier today. How do you feel about that? Show me."

As my face crumples with confusion she says, "I'm trained to read art work. I can translate different levels of emotion that come out through one's use of color and form."

Still holding the crayon, I stare at the blank page.

"Come on, Trez, you can do it. You must have a lot

on your mind, what with being committed and your unfortunate accident. Show me how you feel at this moment."

Fine, lady. You asked for it. I throw down the pastel blue crayon and take up a chunk of black charcoal. I look over at her daffodil yellow silk dress. This could get messy.

Gripping the charcoal, I press down on the paper and make a solid black line from top to bottom. It's fun to extend the charcoal past the page onto the drawing board, which would have raised objections among my grade school nuns.

Strangely satisfying, I do it again. Before long, I've got four, five pages of lines running a close parallel to one another. They remind me of winding yarn or...strands of thick black hair. Oh, what was Helice trying to tell me in the Red Eden? Something about mites? No, that was my take.

The black on white takes me back to endlessly typing my story on a word processor: line after line of black letters in Times New Roman font, twelve point type, on eight-and-a-half by eleven inch paper contained within neatly set, one inch margins all around.

Line after fricking line. Ream after fricking ream. Ten years and counting.

I grab a fresh sheet of paper and a set of colored chalks to draw a red fire I feel rising up from within me, with dashes of murky smoke. I use my fingertips to blend a foggy blue horizon all blurred together, topped with dashes of pink, yellow, and a mauvey purple. Fricking Pria!

Will the therapist discern that these shapes and colors represent my ambition, angst, optimism, disappointment, resentment, futility, blind faith, drive, failures, tiny wins once in a great while, insecurity, lack of self-esteem, exaggerated highs, depressing lows, and everything in between?

My letting out a loud, "Aaaagggghhhh!" releases a

flood of pent up tension but something tells me to control myself and shut up. She is watching my every move.

I don't intend to slide halfway over in my bed, it just happens. Harrison calls for a nurse to push me upright.

For some reason, I feel compelled to draw thick black lines and make about six more drawings.

The therapist tries to pry the charcoal out of my sooty hand. "Okay, now. Hey, Trez, let go! Thanks. Ah, let's tap into another emotion. What about your manuscript?"

I give her a scorching look. I burned it. Case closed.

If there were matches in her art case, I would burn all the pages into sooty ashes. Instead, I shred a sheet into thin horizontal lines. It feels so good I do it again, and again.

Truth be told, something about my story doesn't make sense. I'm the writer for crying out loud. If I can't explain it, it's best to stuff it down, otherwise someone, either in this world or my made up one, will call me on it.

Next, I grab a red jumbo crayon and scribble over a fresh sheet of white paper. Now I'm using the black charcoal to outline these wild squiggles. It looks too tame, so here come globs of finger paint in dark blues and purples. As they dry I add layers of red paint to signify Helice's cardigan sweater.

For Bethany's book launch, she wore a pretty shade of green that went perfectly with her brunette coloring. To represent her, my plagiarizing archrival, I choose a sickening chartreuse color and smear it over most of the page.

For Phin, who is on my shit list for annoying the hell out of me, I make a hell of a lot of orangey red streaks.

Pria gets bloody purple.

Hannah says, "Trez, I'd like you to draw what you think about the girl who's missing from Redwood City.

Her name is Analeese Loveland. She's only ten."

She hands me a stack of fresh paper. "Can you imagine how frightened she is? Is she hungry, or cold? Show me how her parents might feel."

Whoa, that's coming out of left field. Why the hell is she asking me about a kid I've never met? Oh, yeah. I'm a chief suspect. She's clever, this one, having me play with color for so long. She got me all relaxed just so she could slam me.

I'll do this one real straight. I pick out lovely pastels for a sunset over the Pacific ocean. Serene. Calm. Innocent! I do a few more, some with trees, another with wild flowers.

The therapist gets the hint I'm not buying her sudden shift of suggestions. She asks me again about my novel. My thoughts turn to Bethany Moraga stealing my story.

My ribs are killing me from sitting upright for so long. Thinking of Bethany, I grit my teeth so hard my jaws ache, but my "process" doesn't feel done.

Digging through the supply case, I pull out a pair of blunt edged scissors, the kind kids use so they won't cut themselves. Driving the blades into the "Bethany paper" proves satisfying so I stab the pages with dozens of slashes, mostly over the ghastly green streaks.

One could say I am symbolically killing my teacher.

I do the same with red smudges that signify Helice but I stop. Helice must know something she can't, or won't, tell me. Yet the thing is, I should already know it.

I scrunch up the paper, as if I'm crushing the life out of my own self. Whatever is making me do this, I should know the answer already.

The second I slow down, the therapist motions for me to continue. Gawd, what a slave driver.

So anyway. I smooth out my crunched up paper and push more color around. Red. Helice. Even though my character has been driving me crazy for over a decade, she's grown on me. I honestly did want to kill that damn kid the other day and would have gone through with it, at least metaphorically, had the cops not stopped me. That was then.

This is now. Helice is just a child. The more I think about it, hurting the reds doesn't feel right. I can't kill her.

However...stabbing Bethany's chartreuse and Phin's orange fills me with glee!

"Okay," says Hannah Harrison. "You're definitely feeling the intensity of your experiences. Ah, thank you, you can stop now. We're out of time, Trez. Um, you don't need to continue. Oh. Just a few more then. All right, now, all done."

She slides my paper out from under me, even though it's not finished. She looks over the twenty or so pages of artwork. "You've certainly expressed yourself, haven't you?"

It gives me a smug satisfaction to watch her prissy expression build as she clears the mess her art therapy project has caused. She's putting crayons back in the box, organizing them by color. The scissors are slipped into a protective sleeve.

Eying oozing paints, she pulls a pair of plastic gloves out of her tote and puts them on. She opens a box of alcohol wipes to clean each tube before she recaps them. The chunk of charcoal, well worn down, is wrapped in a tissue and dumped into the trash.

Although she's trying not to show it, she is clearly a control freak. Takes one to know one. She lifts the drawing board and almost loses it. Underneath, the white bed sheets are blotched with charcoal powder while paint blobs of various colors have dried on the cotton blankets. My hands look like they were dipped into paint buckets. She tries rubbing me down with alcohol wipes but plainly it is not enough.

Sighing, she presses the nurse's call button for backup.

The nurse is muttering in Tagalog and she does not sound amused. The therapist tries to help. The nurse decides it's best if the therapist leaves.

The nurse is pulling off my soiled gown, telling me I need a bath. I'm pretty modest but have no choice. Yikes, the bruises on my torso resemble the blues and purples of my therapy pieces.

Perhaps Hannah Harrison would like to look over my scarred tongue.

I'll gladly stick it out at her.

Ah, the art therapist is leaving. Finally. Good thing, too, otherwise she'd want to "read my ribs."

CHAPTER 9

Teresa Evans,
The Last Rose of Summer

WHO KNEW there is no rest to be had in a hospital? Two nurses get me all dolled up...well, as best they can what with a shaved head, bum eye, and messed up ribs. They unwrap the bandages and give me the closest thing to a real bath since I got here. Then they mummy me up again.

They can't "find" a mirror; perhaps it's for the best. A little denial isn't a bad thing. They put me in a wheelchair and park it.

The reason is soon made apparent when Ross, Jackson, and Phin show up with a pink bakery box. The guys put on a show opening the box to reveal a cake decorated with Happy 33. There's a chunk cut out where some security guard looked for hidden weapons. This really is a locked facility.

They sing "Happy Birthday" off key. Ross forces me to blow out its one candle. I stick my thumb up. They cheer.

No wonder the nurses gussied me up. My surprise birthday party in the mental slammer. Ross hands me a card from brother Danny, who's out of town.

Ross helps me open a gift our older sister Janine had shipped from a boutique where she lives in Seattle. He drapes the celadon silk robe around my shoulders. The guys swear it looks lovely with my hospital issued cotton gown, but Phin whips it away saying, "Whoa! If one drop of blood gets on that it will be ruined!"

My chin starts to tremble. I don't even get my birthday present? Who are they kidding? It's my party. I'll cry if I want to.

Thirty-fricking-three. Now I only have two years to make it big. No woman wants to admit being over thirty five in this society. Some bleached blonde named Madonna says she's gonna rock 'n roll 'til she's an old broad (like fifty!) Who would pay to see such masochism on stage?

Mick Jagger supposedly swore he wouldn't be caught dead singing "Satisfaction" when he was thirty but the quote, and the cutoff, keeps changing as he ages. But he's a bad boy Rolling Stone, so it doesn't count for him.

And don't get me started about that George Orwell, Big Brother stuff. The world is three years away from 1986.

I don't want to think about that. I, Trez Nobody Evans, have only two years to figure out my novel, get it published, and debut my grand world book tour on The Phil Donahue Show, not to mention win the Pulitzer and be on the cover of Look Magazine.

Ross interrupts my musings. "Hey Trez, Jackson said, ah, he said..." He turns to him. "How'd you put it? Jackson?"

Milan mumbles, "Um, yeah, I said you look...cute." This is coming from a guy who still can't look at me.

Ross hands me my gift: a mason jar filled with ashes. "Heh, heh, the look on your face. Don't worry. It's no one you know. You seem confused, must be the brain damage."

He probably thinks he's helping me by speaking louder and enunciating, "It's your manuscript, or as much as I could sneak off with from your barbeque area."

Jackson goes into his shark mode, "Wait. When? How did you...?" He sighs. "Never mind, I don't want to know."

I'm holding the jar, staring at the inconsequential remains of ten years of work. It may as well be a funeral urn.

Ross is giving me one hundred percent of himself, at least for now. I welcome this easy going attention, which he usually reserves for his lady clients and girlfriends.

Phin is acting beyond his usual odd self on what he keeps referring to as "your special day." It must be why he's wearing a cream colored suit aka John Travolta's fever on a Saturday night costume. It's a suit made of polyester, a fabric that doesn't breathe. He looks like a trussed peacock. A non-breathing one. And it's San Francisco's Indian Summer.

At least Jackson is remaining true to character. I can respect him for that.

We have our cake with coffee from the vending machine. We've run out of things to say. Phin breaks out his boombox, which is the size and heft of a small suitcase. He sets up its detachable sound speakers on the floor on either side of roomy bed. With his cult level devotion to The Grateful Dead, he pops in his all-time favorite cassette *Scarlet Begonias*.

Phin spins my wheelchair around for a dance, which isn't much considering the size of the room. I beg him to stop as he tips over my IV stand; its tubing gets stretched and the perpetual needle stuck in the vein on my sore hand is yanked halfway out.

Ross and Jackson are arguing politics, the perfect time to discuss a delicate matter with Phin. The problem is, he is annoyingly truthful whether anyone wants him to be or not.

I'd dodged a bullet when Marciano and his partner came to the hospital and questioned me. Thank God for my brain damaged speech. Let's hope there's no need for round two.

It could go very badly very quickly if the police ever question Phin, if or when they figure out he was with me the morning that little girl from Redwood City went missing.

He and I had left my place on Kings Mountain around 7:30 am, give or take. That fits into the time period during which ten year old Analeese Loveland disappeared.

Phin's pale face goes icy white while I struggle with the words to spell out a new, corrected timeline. His voice cracks when he asks, "You mean you want me to lie?"

Shaking my head, I put a finger to my lips to keep him to a whisper. My point is he wouldn't be lying; he'd simply give out a red herring, so to speak.

Beads of sweat are breaking out along his brow. "No, Trez." Then he remembers to whisper, "This doesn't feel right." I remind him we had nothing to do with that kid's disappearance.

He's sweating so much his orangey red hair is sticking to his forehead. He brushes it away before whispering, "Okay."

Ross strolls over. "What'ya you guys talking about?"

Jackson unknowingly saves me. "Trez, you need to hear the kidnapped girl has been missing three days. What's weird is there haven't been any phone calls or ransom notes. No contact whatsoever. They're dragging Emerald Lake. Upper and Lower. Again."

Ross runs a hand through his thick hair. "She could be dea...ah, anyway, the cops are pounding her parents pretty hard, they're the main suspects."

He waves aside my sigh of relief. "Don't get smug. The cops didn't drop their suspicions against you. In fact, they'll probably ramp 'em up if nothing else breaks."

I express my outrage about the case along with a torrent of expressive cussing. Ross crunches his nose.

Phin jumps in. "I'll translate for you, Ross. I'm working on her communications. You know I'm a big Star Trek fan." He ignores Ross' groan to stress, "I've mastered a fair amount of the Klingon language, the subtle nuances and—"

"Jesus Christ," Ross bursts out. "I don't want to know this about you."

"I'm serious, Ross. I recorded her speech and after listening to the tapes over and over, I'm sensing a pattern in how she's trying to talk. I think I can—"

"What the fuc—?" Ross glares at him.

"Hey, hey. Watch your language." Phin's interject is a rare action against the alpha dog.

Ross' eyebrows shoot straight up. "Since when?"

Phin lifts both palms. "Don't' forget, the doctor told us to hang out with her. He wants us to interact calmly so her brain can reconnect, you know, to stretch her brain back to normal. Why remind Trez of her bad habits like swearing?"

Ross leans his head into his raised right shoulder, the closest he'll come to an apology.

I stare at them until Phin confesses my doctor waived the customary no visitors rule. All this time, I'd played into their conspiratorial hands by thinking we were pulling a fast one on "the man." So much for feeling special in a loony bin.

Ross changes the subject. "This has been a fun party. Right? Anyway, Cheryl introduced me to one of your nurses; she said there was an episode. You were mad as a hatter."

Who wouldn't be pissed after a whupping from the soul gutting Pria? Plus, it's my damn birthday. I explain it away as a bad dream. He stares at me as if I'd spoken Latin.

Jackson asks, "What'd she say?" Phin clues him in.

Ross turns to me. "A dream? The nurses would disagree. Here's the thing." He's making himself sound extra patient. "You had a seizure. Now it seems your brain's affected even more. They were afraid of that, so they added different medications the past two days. But, you still bit your tongue."

An adverse drug reaction has to be how Pria was able to beat the tar out of me, and why the therapist showed up to see if my brain had been scrambled even more by the seizure.

I love you, Trez," Phin coos, "but you're off your game. So, I forgive you for getting so mad at me for no reason."

Forgive *me?* My glower leaves nothing to his imagination.

He tries again. "C'mon, Trezzie, don't be like that. Just because I said you should meditate? You can lighten up now, your surgery's behind you. We all want you to heal."

He lowers his voice for my ears only. "I know what you're doing. I've studied the speech recordings. Unlike you, they don't lie. You're faking your aphasia."

Damn his fascination of otherworldly languages. Why did I ever let this Star Trek geek record me?

He whispers, "You're not good enough at linguistics to keep this up, Trez. I'm telling you right now you better start talking normal English or the staff will call you on it."

Call me on it! Oh crap, am I that bad an actor? All my plotting for nothing? A tear is rolling down my cheek. Doesn't he know that being brain damaged is the only way I'll get a private room?

He lifts the bed sheet to grab my hand. His gesture is surprisingly comforting.

I pull my hand away to give him the bird.

Phin's voice goes loud. "Hey, hey, no need for that."

Ross is going on in his annoying, Ross-like way. "About the seizure. They're hoping you won't have any more. It's why you're making less sense than usual today, heh, heh."

My lower lip juts out. Hah, hah, very funny, Ross.

Brothers can be so bratty.

I snap my head round to see Helice. She's suddenly appeared at the foot of my bed, grinning like the Cheshire cat. I tell Phin the good news.

We're both distracted when Ross and Jackson stand and head to the door. "Gotta go," grins Ross. "Cheryl's waiting. Duty calls, heh, heh. Oh, and Happy Birthday again, Trez."

Yeah, thanks, bro. But enough of you. Helice is back.

There's no telling how long she'll stick around so I start mentally blathering. *Helice, how come you disappeared? I need to know what's the real reason you were plucked out of the Red Eden to find me? Please, tell me why you're here.*

She isn't cooperating, so I burst out loud with my questions. I'm carrying on about why isn't she in the other world doing her cartwheel thing.

Jackson's turning the doorknob, he wants to take off but Ross grabs his arm.

Gotta hand it to Helice, the kid is trying. With her brows knitted and her nose crunched, she's thinking through my questions as if she's puzzling over an arithmetic test.

Problem is, she's never learned to think.

She finally answers. *To be here for her.*

"Her" again. I demand Helice tell me who sent her. Stoically, I prepare to hear Moraga's name.

Maggalena.

With Jackson and Ross gawking at me, I revert to mental communication. *I already know that, Helice. What's the plan?*

Helice lifts up her shoulders, then relaxes them. *Maybe you should talk to Maggalena.*

Ross is asking Phin what's going on, but I ignore them.

Helice says to ask the Mud Eater? That's a low blow, considering I can't figure out how to contact the damn woman. I practically spit in Helice's face. I swear to God this kid is driving me batty.

She's so dense I want to shake her. Hmm, that's a good idea. I grab hold of her shoulders and shake her like a mariachi. It's fun to shake her like a sack of beans but she's gone cross-eyed, so I stop.

I hear Ross yelling about what the hell am I doing. His voice is tight as he says, "Trez?" I peer at him. Ross' face is as white as his shirt. "Who are you talking to?" He crosses the room to loom over my bed. "Trez? Talk to me."

My good eye shuts to get a break from dealing with him.

"Teresa!" I feel my right hand being warmed by two larger ones engulfing it. There is a palpable feeling of connection, of familial familiarity pulsating through our conjoined hands.

"Trez? I need you to stop all this. C'mon, Three!"

Aw, that's so cute, haven't heard him call me Three in ages, not since he was a little boy. My eyelid flutters open to see Ross' face. My good eye crosses. We are practically nose-to-nose, not a typical interaction with my reserved brother.

That makes me laugh.

I'm so loud the nurse comes in to explain that uncontrollable laugher is a side effect of brain trauma.

I'm cackling, snorting, howling, spitting, tittering. My ribs feel like they're splintering into tiny pieces I'm hooting so loud and long.

Ross lets go of me to tell Jackson, "Look at her." Ross works out kinks in his neck. "Transfer her to Stanford hospital before it's too late."

"No."

"Come on." When Jackson shakes his head, Ross softens his tone. "She's my sister, man."

Jackson counters, "She's *my* client."

Ross tries again. "I don't think these guys know how to treat a serious brain trauma."

Brain trauma. How hysterical is that?

"Her doctor did his neurosurgery residency at Stanford," sniffs Jackson. "He brought two of his surgical nurses with him. He's assured me he would be the first to transfer her if this facility couldn't provide what she needs." Jackson adds under his breath, "Besides, the police consider her a flight risk. She stays here, end of story."

Story? I'm choking it's so funny. Get it? I'm in the

middle of my own story!

Phin keeps rubbing his hands. Ross is close enough for me to watch his greenish blue eyes turn steely gray. He does not like to be bested, especially by *Johnny Miller*.

So, Ross does what he does best. He checks his Rolex and says, "Look at the time."

Jackson knows him well. He says, "No, I'll leave, Ross. You stay with your sister." He grabs the jar of ashes. "I'll keep this, it could be construed as evidence. Ah, bye, Trez."

Laughing makes it hard to talk so I grin at him.

Turning aside to get past Ross, my lawyer is forced to face me directly. Making a loud gagging noise, he covers his color drained lips with a shaky hand.

Ross is all over him. "Heh, heh, did you just barf in your mouth?"

Jackson "Shark" Milan runs off down the hall.

As if Phin wasn't right next to us, Ross says, "By the way. Phin's had a lot to say about you. What's this bullshit about a kid in your novel showing up? She's talking to you?"

He pauses, apparently waiting for me to confirm or deny the allegation. All I do is laugh.

Phin cuts in, "That's why I asked you not to swear, Ross. The girl's only ten and since she's from the 1950s, she's way too innocent to hear such things."

Ross growls, "Was I talking to you?" He turns back to me. "So Trez, is this true?"

The jig is up. I nod my head between spasms of giggles.

Phin tries again. "Isn't this cool, Ross? Betcha you never thought this would happen, a character becoming a real girl."

I suggest they remember Pinocchio. They don't catch it. That line was right-on funny. I'm a hoot.

Phin is on a roll. "Trez will be famous for sure. She can...Oh, Trez, I just thought of something. I think...hey, maybe Helice is here to help us find that missing girl."

My head whips around so fast it must look like that chick in *The Exorcist*. Phin is an idiot. There's no way in hell the lost kid's the reason Helice is here. I don't know that kidnapped girl or her family.

Why I ever hooked up with him is beyond me. I love him like a brother, or a loyal pet, but I must have been on a binge to end all binges that first time. After that...well, familiarity breeds contempt. I can barely look at him now. That tryst, the night Helice came to haunt me, was our last time. Finis!

It's really hot in here. They should turn down the heat. I reach for the call button but my hand spazzes out on me. Sweat dripping down my forehead stings my good eye but neither hand will cooperate to wipe it away.

It's all Phin's fault. I want to strangle him. It would give me pleasure to watch his dog-doo-colored eyes bug, his stupid pink tongue lolling as drool drips down his chinless chops while I wring the life out of him. Imagining this act feels so good, I go to choke my pillow but my hands won't obey me. They're like claws. My jaws are clenched in a self-satisfied grimace while I visualize the final moments of death by constriction of one Phineas Warren McCool.

My body is shaking I'm so pissed. My bed sheets are soaked and...oh, so am I. The headboard is banging against the wall, a cacophony of rage. My teeth are clattering. I hear an oddly lyrical keening. Who is doing that?

My brother orders Phin, "Run and get help!"

Oh, Lord, I am really shaking it up. My legs are going bananas and my toes...my toes are curling...the wrong way? Shit. It hurts for them to do that. My head is moving in a weird way, it feels like it's been wedged into a vice and that vice is turning tighter and tighter in the wrong direction, like my head is being spun around backwards.

The monitors I'm hooked up to are going bananas. They sound shrill and jangly, like maybe I'm stuck inside a pinball machine, all of them braying and spewing at the same time.

Phin's back. There's bedlam with staff running this way and that. Ross and Phin are shoved out of the way. I'm not worried about them. What's important right this second is that Helice is here. There's so much we need to talk about.

Someone shouts, "She's seizing. Call Dr. Watson. Now!"

It's probably good that I'm about to pass out. That will make it easier for Helice and me to get together while I sleep.

"Let's get her lying flat," a nurse orders.

Dr. Watson rushes in, demanding, "Stats?" My doctor's orders are terse. Everyone is on full alert.

Helice holds out her hand. I hesitate. I can see myself stretched out on my bed with the medical team bustling about. I'm also pretty certain that I am standing next to the bed watching this activity centering around me.

It's weird to have two Trez Evans.

She asks for my hand again. But which "me" is the real Trez? She notices that my "self" is standing and looking down at my bare feet. She says to pay attention to that "self." She suggests I wiggle my toes as a test. It works. I delight in making them move at my command.

Apparently, in the special world we share, anything can happen. She assures me there's no reason to be afraid since I'm the creator of this story.

I clasp her extended hand. Ross and Phin are leaning against the far wall. I'm touched by how stricken my brother looks. He really cares about me; it's just our way to bat one another around like a cat with a rat.

Aw, Phin is weeping into his huge hands. I need to remember to lighten up on him.

Helice hurries me along. She says it will start soon. I ask if we're going back to the Red Eden. Can she introduce me to Magdalena? There's so much I need to ask that woman.

There's no time for an answer. It suddenly feels as if we're being lifted up by an unseen elevator.

My stomach lunges as we ascend.

CHAPTER 10

Is Paradise Lost?

HELICE AND I have a new vantage point from up high in the hospital, as if we are dangling from a chandelier in a grand ballroom. Everything below appears to be arranged with infinitesimal detail: the room's checkerboard floor, my narrow bed, its side table with supplies stacked upon it, and the lone chair for visitors. Blinking lights from numerous beeping monitors are hooked up to my body; they remind me of a miniature cityscape.

The nurses are choreographed under the doctor's direction. Everyone is playing an integral role in this live performance. Swirls of figures in white move to and fro against an unlit stage drop of a hospital. It's a collaborative dance, the goings on to remedy my medical emergency.

Funny, it doesn't feel important from up here.

Hmm, Dr. Watson has a little bald spot just south of his crown. Hadn't noticed that before.

Oh, I feel a sensation, as if something is carrying me—or whichever part of *me* this is. Helice and I are both moving up and away from the medical theatre. Wait, my body is being left behind, how can that be? I yearn to twist around and hover over the person I know to be Trez Evans, yet there doesn't seem to be a choice in the matter.

My stomach pitches. Next comes a whooshing sound. Are my ears hearing this? Does it matter?

Rapid motion cinematography in movies is annoying. I resent being subjected to mechanical motion sickness as a movie director's cheap trick to propel the story. That's what this force forward action feels like, as if someone has shoved me into a ten story high rollercoaster against my will.

Oh, no, it's gaining momentum, propelling me through God knows where. Helice comforts me as best she can.

My stomach lurches forward again. My head feels as if it's snapping backwards, a whiplash effect.

At last, the rollercoaster slows to a stop in a new area. It's a world apart from my made up heaven. Our destination looks more like a colorless void I'd put the girl in while she was in a coma, before she made it to Magdalena's pond. Everything is snowy white and while there are no specific planes, I sense a shift when we "sit down" on what feels to be a solid surface. Helice hasn't spoken since we arrived, so I take the lead.

I can talk here just fine. "Am I going to see Magdalena?"

Helice gives me a shy smile. "Maggalena says you can't go to the Red Eden anymore. She says you think about it too much. We're running out of time, you hav'ta stop."

I'm flailing my hands, talking too fast. "What the hell are you talking about? Does Bethany Moraga have a hand in this?"

Helice stands up and faces me. "No. And I'm not here for you either. You gotta help me with the missing girl."

"Why? I don't know her, what's your angle?"

"Angle?" Helice cocks her head. "Um, Maggalena doesn't think you're ready to hear stuff. She says you'll get there...eventually. But you can get started. This dream will help you figure things out. I gotta go. Bye, Trez."

"What? Wait, this doesn't make sense."

The kid disappears in a poof. Damn it. Justifying a

character's life is exhausting. My head hurts. If I were awake and present in the hospital, would it be time for a painkiller? Or, have the nurses already given it to me only they don't realize I'm stuck in an empty space not of this world?

Note to self: Title of my next book should be *The White Void*. Let Bethany Moraga shove that one up her bony ass.

Oh, crap. My "body" is lifting up again; it's making me so dizzy I might toss my cookies. The white void gives way to a sickening green color. Walls are closing in. It looks to be the lobby of this mental facility. The same green walls and bland institutional furniture. There's no way of knowing if Magdalena is behind this because Helice has disappeared.

I appeal to whoever is listening: please don't dump me here. Ah ha, my plea works instantly. I'm taken to a flower shop. The comingled aroma of roses and lavender is delicious. A woman is working on a bird of paradise arrangement. Hmm, it doesn't look that great. The question as to why I've been brought here is not addressed, nor do I linger. It's not clear what is happening, or why.

My next "stop" looks to be a typical living room setting. A man in his early forties with dark brown hair is reclining in a velour Barcalounger. His face is in shadow. Yuck, his hand is down his pants. He's reading a newspaper, chuckling over something. I "ask" to see a close-up of the article but once I get too curious, the setting vanishes.

Where to now? All this flying around has given me a major migraine.

If I were sent back to my hospital bed this instant, would the nurses believe me enough to give me a shot regardless of the time? I'd tell them there is no time in the spirit world.

As soon as I think about being in the hospital, I am swooped back into that reality. Some part of *me* lands back in the medical theatre, planting me smack dab into my body.

Oh, I'm definitely back in bed, attached to blinking and hissing machines via rubber tubes. Now that I'm here, might as well get relief from my incessant headache.

There are a few nurses hovering around, which is convenient. I won't have to fumble for the call button. I flash them the sign for pain relief. Ten out of ten fingers indicates my zero tolerance for pain.

Helice is nowhere to be seen. Hmm, wonder if she's been listening even if I can't see her? It's too much to ponder. My mind shuts down to everything around me.

I OPEN MY GOOD EYE. Oh, Ross is here. He wags a naggy finger. "You scared the shit out of me, Trez."

Ah, brotherly love. He explains my medical update. I was unconscious for a time. They've added new medications and hooked me up to even more machines, all of which beep incessantly. No rest for the weary.

He also says with all the meds they're pumping into my system, I've been chatting up a storm. He twists his body around in the chair. "Phineas, did you get my coffee?"

It does not please me to see Phin carrying two Styrofoam cups. He upset me so much about meditation, maybe he caused my seizure.

Ross tells me, "I phoned Jackson to get you the hell outta here. But..." He takes a slurp of coffee. "Ow, hot. He still insists you stay put. Says it's the best place for you. Why a nuthouse is the best medical facility for brain trauma is beyond me, but Jackson knows his stuff."

Phin takes advantage of Ross sipping his coffee to ask me, "Did you see her?"

Seeing me nod, Ross' tone hardens. "Ah yes, he told me about your character. What am I supposed to do with this?"

Phin says, "You can learn all about Helice

Polansky."

I glare at his majesty McCool. It's infuriating that Phin revealed my deepest secret without a thought to my feelings. Ross will use this juicy tidbit to best me for decades to come.

"This character coming to life bit is ridiculous," Ross is saying, "but I've decided it's due to your messed up brain. And Phin here is playing right into it."

I sputter, "Damnn straight, brooo!"

Ross lights up. "Hey, I understood that. Good job."

He has a sip of his coffee. "The cops are following a strong lead about a guy who was seen just far enough away from the girl's grammar school to avoid obvious suspicions. They think he was alone that day but it doesn't rule you out. It just puts you back a few squares on the blame game. That's why you have to stay here and keep playing the lunatic card."

Phin asks, "Do they have a physical description?" He is chewing on the ends of his scraggly russet hair.

"Not much," says Ross. "No car model or license plate. He may have been on foot. It's not uncommon for parents to walk their kids to and from class. The cops think he's approximately forty years old. His face was turned away but he's tall, with dark brown hair."

I bolt up in bed despite my broken ribs. "Ooowwww." Phin rushes to help me resettle myself among all the pillows propping me up. It's difficult to string my words together I'm so revved up, but they understand most of what I say.

I describe my weird experience during the seizure. How it felt like I wasn't part of myself while watching everyone working on me from a high up perch, then flying around.

Phineas butts in with an emphatic "Far out! Sounds like you had an OBE." He answers my *what's that* question. "A classic Out of Body Experience. You should know what that means, you did years of research on esoteric...um, stuff."

My stink-eye scowl is enough for him to shut up

around my left-brain brother. But like a dog that can't give up a bone, Phin continues, "Ah, like I was saying. It's totally spontaneous, you can go visit friends or places on your mind." A faraway look crosses his face. "You basically trip through space without a care in the world."

Ross rolls his eyes. "That's a great description for the police to follow up."

I snicker at my brother, "Youu know what, Ross? Youu don't know jaackk."

Ross holds up a hand. "Jackson's source gave him gold. There's one thing about the guy's description that hasn't been released. Let's test your vivid imagination against reality. Wanna take a shot, Trez?"

Ross is baiting me, yet I don't want to fool myself and everyone else. I am a creative writer after all. Relying on Phin? He's so certifiable, he uses this facility as his personal "tune-up" center.

He's also quite convincing. Has he been leading me down the yellow brick road of craziness?

Taking in a breath to clear my thoughts, I tell myself to think back to that man in his chair. What was he doing? He had his hand down his pants, disgusting pig, but that's not it. What was different about this guy?

As if viewing a movie screen, I go through every "square inch" of my memory picture of him sitting in his living room. My good eye squints with effort, as if that will give me a better perspective. He seems vaguely familiar but now is not the time for a visual check list of all my love conquests. Oh, too late, it is delightful to run my mind's eye across the bare rumps of my many man friends.

Focus Trez, focus! There has to be something striking on his person for an eyewitness to recall this bastard kidnapper. Most likely, their encounter was only a matter of seconds.

I take another deep breath, holding it in before expelling. There's something about the guy's lower jaw or neckline.

Oh. I shout out, "A b-big ugly mole."

Ross' jaw drops. Normally I'd relish a win like this over him since besting one another has been our game for more than twenty years, but this ante is too high.

Ross mutters, "Jesus, this is freaky." His shoulders tighten.

Phin says, "It'd be immoral not to *try* to figure this out. And man oh man we have to hurry. You know how these things can turn out real bad real quick."

Ross' forehead crinkles in thought. "I feel for the kid's parents, they must be going through hell." He steeples his fingers together. When he speaks, his voice is terse, "Okay, I'll buy into this, for now, however bizarre it seems. There's no real proof, though. We can't tell Jackson any of this, not yet. Trez, you claim you saw the guy. Give us the details."

This worsens my headache. Despite that Phin said about me exaggerating my speech problem, my tongue is the size of an eel. With Phin helping to decipher, my description of the man and his living room emerges.

Phin says, "According to Trez he was wearing a red and black plaid wool shirt, the lumberjack type. Third button missing. Jeans, acid washed, frayed at the edges of both his pant legs where they've dragged on the floor because they're too long. Big hole in his sock, toenail sticking out, way too long and ragged. Trez thinks that must mean he doesn't have a woman in his life."

After he delivers that information, Ross cuts in, "How would you know he doesn't have a woman if you saw him alone in his house?" He waits a second or two. "Trez?"

"G-gut feeling. Women in bed don't like scratches from a guy's toenails. They, um, n-nag." I blow out an exhausted breath.

Ross urges me on, "You speak fine now, just tell us!"

I am spent. Phin goes back to interpreting and is able to get the gist of my account.

He announces, "Here it is. Trez says there was

nothing in that house other than what a man would buy: a bulky recliner, a lamp with a funky shade twisted so he could read. Piles of newspapers stacked knee high along one wall. Dirty dishes, no paintings or photos. "

Ross spreads out his hands, palms up. "Where is this house? Think."

A moan escapes me. There was no aerial map to follow, I just got there.

Ross presses, "How did it end?"

"He was reading a newspaper, g-gloating." It's an effort to explain that when I wanted to see the article close up, the experience ended in a blip. I woke up in my hospital bed.

Phin's cheeks flush a rich red, the same shade as his hair. "Your logical mind shut everything down, Trez. Too bad. He was probably reading an account of the kidnapping."

Ross tells us, "The latest articles report no new clues, no leads. Police are stymied." He grows pensive. "I saw Tobey Vallencourt interview her parents on TV. They begged the kidnapper to let her go, no questions asked. It was heartbreaking." His voice cracks. "Goddamn bastard."

I ask for her photo and other information.

Ross shakes his head. "No way. Jackson would pitch a fit if he knew I'd told you this much, and he'd be right."

He clicks his tongue against his front teeth, tsk-tsking like an old lady. "You can't be linked to her, or any of this."

I happen to look up as an orderly walks by my door. He's carrying a bird of paradise floral arrangement. Exactly like the one I saw the woman making! I whistle to get Phin's attention. Like a loyal dog on a mission, he races out into the hallway to follow the man and find out who gets the flowers.

Phin returns with intel. The flowers went to an elderly widower who'd tried to cut his wrists. Not from around here, he's only been in the area for a few months. He was brought in from a nearby nursing home. No children. No visitors.

"Nothing there," says Ross. "Who ordered the flowers?"

Phineas sighs, "It's the nursing home's policy to send a floral arrangement to each of their hospitalized patients."

Ross argues, "But still, Trez was right. She described those flowers perfectly. It proves she saw the kidnapper." His eyes glint. "What do we do now, how do we follow through?"

Phin draws himself up to his full height. "Man oh man, I gotta tell you, I really, really don't think Helice is here for Trez." He gives me a look before saying, "Or Bethany."

Ross surprises me. "Go ahead," he says calmly. "Tell us."

Phin hesitates, but Ross gestures for him to continue. Phin explains, "I'm thinking she's here to find Analeese. Trez will be her rescuer. Think about it. Helice is ten. She shows up right before Trez is suspected of kidnapping another ten year old. You know how kids stick together."

Ross nods. "We have nothing else, why not run with it?"

With that encouragement, Phin adds, "We just have to ask Helice where Analeese is. Problem solved."

Ross agrees, which is akin to a golden seal of approval.

Maybe Phin's right. Helice could be helping me fulfill my destiny. This could be what I've always secretly yearned for. Purpose.

CHAPTER 11

Never Never Land

Day 4 —

NOW THAT IT'S CLEAR I am destined to save Analeese Loveland's life, my adrenalin is pumping. After years of not knowing what to do with myself, of drifting from one meaningless job to another, my path is clear and bright.

I, Teresa Rose Evans, humbly accept the mission of rescuing an innocent child from the clutches of a monster. We just need a plan to catch the kidnapper and return sweet Analeese to her parents.

Phin and I are drunk with joy over this development. Even Ross is enthused. Or, as involved as he can be for the next two minutes. Then he checks his Rolex. "Gotta go, heh, heh. Promised to meet her at Sam's Grease Shack. He winks. I plan on eating more than fries, if you know what I mean."

Ross' mind is clearly on other things, so he leaves us to go rendezvous with his gun toting security guard. Whatever.

I assure Phin all we have to do is figure out where the girl is being held and then, of course, we'll rescue her and bring her home to a hero's welcome. I can picture the parade down the Peninsula's El Camino Real, of me sitting on the back of a sleek convertible and waving to the adoring crowds.

He grins. "This is perfect for you, Trez. You've always wanted a reason to wear a red cape. Here's your chance to put someone else's life ahead of your own."

He springs from the chair. Throwing back his shoulders and puffing his chest with melodramatic flair, he throws on my green silk birthday robe and breaks into an operatic anthem from our childhood. "Here I come to save the day..."

I sing, "That means that Mighty Mouse is on the way!"

He takes over, "Yes, sir, when there is a wrong to right, Trez Evans will join the fight."

I swoon with theatric gusto. Mighty Mouse may have been a flying cartoon savior from the 1950s but that tiny buff guy was hot with his dashing cape. He was my first crush.

I leap into the daydream. "I'm more of a modern day Wonder Woman. I like her costume, the gold crown. Oh, and her power bracelets. The boots are cool. So is that cape of hers, all red, white, and blue drama."

He says, "You're talking great now that you're happy."

I grin, "M-maybe you're r-right." Pretending to swirl a cape feels surprisingly rewarding. I've always harbored a secret yearning to rid this world of bad guys. The opportunity to do so while wielding superhero abilities would be the ultimate career for me.

I warn Phin, "Don't tell. Ever. P-people will think I'm off my...um, my...rocker."

"Yeah," he jokes, "especially the people in here." His green cape flags and one hem drags the floor.

I've been laughing so hard my ribs hurt. Enough fun, down to business. We brainstorm on what steps we'd need to identify the kidnapper and then, how to find him.

It's harder than it seems to track an elusive bad guy. I blame my lack of a plan on brain trauma, headaches, and incarceration. Phin has no excuse. We think some more.

He buys sugary snacks from a vending machine. He goes back for coffees. He makes a run for a nearby dim sum place. After all, starving rescuers can't think effectively without takeout.

Helice hasn't been around since my visit to the kidnapper's house. You'd think she'd be chomping at the bit to resolve the dilemma and get back to the Red Eden. The way it's going, we have no clue why Helice hasn't appeared.

Dr. Watson comes into my room. "Sorry my rounds are late, I've had to admit several new patients."

Phin steps into the hall to allow us privacy. Without thinking, I burst out, "What's up, Doc?"

Watson smiles. "How are you feeling today, Trez?"

Uh oh, I'm supposed to be sick. "Um, not soooo gooood."

"Is that so? I could have sworn I heard you singing."

Oh, crap. I need to play up my aphasia.

"W-who, mmmmeeeeeeee?"

He reads my file. "You went through a bout of hysterics earlier. No worry, it's a side effect of the brain trauma."

He goes on, "Don't fret about the seizures, they're common after a surgery like yours. Don't be alarmed if they continue for a few weeks, or even months."

He checks the stitches on my head. Staples actually, forty of them. He assures me they are healing nicely. My blurry vision is clearing on schedule, he notes. While switching out the eye bandage he leans into my chest, which hurts exactly like one would expect.

He says, "It's time to eliminate the Demerol shots. I'll switch you to an over the counter painkiller. Certain drug classes can cause dependency issues if they're used too long."

No more drugs? "Pleeeassse, mmyyy head. It hurtsss."

He pats my hand. "You're doing great. With the influx of admissions we might need your bed so we'll get on with your psych eval. There's no reason you can't meet with the team in here. The art therapist already filed your session report."

Uh oh. That was for real?

He flips to a new page in the file. He studies it. "Huh, is that so?" He frowns. "I hadn't seen this. "The staff has been tracking your speech patterns. They say you're prolonging the aphasia to avoid transferring to the involuntary section."

He takes a long look at me. "You were clever enough to devise this scheme. It took mental acuity to pull it off. That's it, we're moving you. This afternoon."

The minute Dr. Watson leaves, Phin comes in and plops into the chair next to my bed. There goes his redhead topknot, wobbling as he talks with increased excitement.

"They busted you? Man oh man, I don't blame you for not wanting to leave the hospital. Seizures are freaky. It's hard to believe the doctor thinks you're ready for your evaluation this fast. And you knew you couldn't have a private room forever."

A shiver runs through me.

"Betcha you're scared stiff to be moved to lockdown."

No shit, Sherlock.

He continues, "It was pretty brilliant of you to fake-talk. You had me going there, but I gotta tell you, charades don't work there. Trust me," he says with a level of seriousness I have to take seriously. "I've tried stuff like this. One time I pretended to be catatonic for so long, I went off the deep end. I'm talking stark raving mad. They kept me in lockup for over a month."

Oh, crap, I hadn't thought about that.

"You shouldn't be here. Yeah, you got drunk and burned your manuscript. But you're not mentally unstable." He titters. "I oughta know."

I make circular motions with my index finger to wrap him up. He says, "You gotta go through the psychological evaluation whether you want to or not. It'll last seventy two hours. I won't be allowed to see you, Ross won't either. You'll be on your own. So here are some sure-fire survival rules."

His voice changes. Phin sounds like my father when he told us ghost stories, all hallowed and creepy. "Go along with whatever doctors and nurses tell you no matter how stupid it sounds, since believe you me, they have a reason for everything. If they say the sky is green instead of blue, don't argue. Don't totally agree since that could be a test too. You gotta let 'em know you're participating in the conversation, that your mind is ready and able. Don't play brain dead or you'll end up in long-term care for sure."

I snap, "For chrissakes, you make it sound like a prison."

He throws up his hands, a frustrated gesture that concerns me. I fake a laugh and say, "I'll make friends with everyone, the staff and the 'inmates.' Everything will be fine."

He wags a finger at me. "At this point, just be agreeable, okay? Answer the evaluators' questions, or at least show you're trying to give an appropriate response. It's all about letting 'em know you're 'in there,' that your mind is intact and firing on all...or um, at least most of your ah, cylinders, and...ah..."

Squinting my good eye, I fix my gaze on him. Although my vision is blurred, there is a haunted look in his eyes, like he's the fox all the dogs are chasing. I reach for his hand and he grabs me so immediately, so thoroughly, it makes me want to cry for him instead of for myself.

We sit in silence before he eventually says, "Want to talk about the kidnapper?"

I let out a sigh. "What difference does it make?"

"Man oh man, it's not your fault you can't figure out where that guy lives. You said Helice doesn't know. The cops haven't found him either. And, you don't even know—" He stops to draw in air. "You don't know if what you saw in your dream means he *is* the kidnapper so lighten up on yourself."

I tell him to go away.

"You know, Trez, maybe it's too hard for you to deal with this *and* a psych eval. How's about we hire a private investigator?"

"N-no. Jackson would have a conniption. H-he'd say it's tampering with the evidence, or the p-police, whatever. Besides, he'd never authorize payment while I'm in here."

Phin says, "I could pay for it, anything you need. I want to help, Trez. Let me do this for you."

Bless his heart for offering. Sadly, I shake my head. "I-I just told you Jackson would blow his top. He'd be right. We'd s-screw it up. I can see Mighty M-mouse taking a nose dive and crashing. Wonder Woman might shriek at a mouse, even if she does wear a cape." I sigh and sniff back a tear. "I think we're done being superheroes, Phin." In my mind, my red cape shrinks like a punctured birthday balloon. And Phin's cape, my birthday beautiful celadon green real silk robe, is a crumpled heap on the floor.

LORD HELP ME, I'm being transferred from my private hospital room to the "involuntary" population. They have me change out of the standard issue gown with no back, and into a scratchy pair of green elastic waist pants and matching pull-on top. They're huge but the nurse says they don't have smaller sizes. Ugly white canvas slip-on shoes with orange rubber soles complete the ensemble. Used shoes, by the way, scarred by years of laundering.

As fate would have it, Virgil, the head orderly, shows up to escort me to the next chapter of my life in Crazy Town. I cringe, what with our past history, but he's acting as if we've never set eyes on one another. Fine by me. Reminding a gigantic guy who wields all the power that I'm the one who broke his nose is not in my best interest.

He flirts with nurses of all ages when he's given my chart, he asks them for dates as he scoops up my meager belongings, and he vows to return wearing his dancing shoes.

Virgil is a' grinning and a' smiling until we're out of view. Then, his eyes glint. "Listen up, bitch. You're in my turf now. I own it, you got me?"

A whistling Virgil escorts me to a nurse's station. He's acting smiley to a new set of nurses, all of whom go giggly.

My quick glance around the general area reveals more ubiquitous puke green walls, cracked vinyl clad institutional furniture, and a linoleum floor in need of a shine. My nose scrunches at lingering aromas of the cafeteria's lunch special, some concoction made from broccoli. It's still wafting through air made stale from barred windows shut tight.

It reminds me of the scene when Helice was rushed to a hospital in Detroit. I'd used the same boiled broccoli stench from a nearby cafeteria to set up the climatic moment. Her mother Basha broke down over a homey smell infused with Clorox when she tucked a freshly laundered sheet around her paralyzed daughter. A sensory déjà vu. Does it matter if this sensate memory is only for me, that Helice and her mother aren't real enough to inhale anything?

Back to my new world. The show playing on TV must be boring since the viewers choose to watch me. The nurse goes over the chart Virgil hands her. She's looking down and doesn't notice the evil eye he's flashing at me. He bids her adieu and takes off, but not before flipping me a universally understood gesture.

The name on her I.D. badge says Jennifer Harbine. She doesn't introduce herself. She makes an "uff" sound lifting herself from a groaning office chair. It isn't until she comes round from the other side that I can take in the vast expanse of her "south forty" nether regions. I fail to stifle my own "augh" sound. She hears it. Strike one against me.

She has a way-too-high-to-be-real-voice that's right up there with grating one's nails on a chalkboard. She wants me to follow her, seemingly oblivious of the lamentable task she's given me of watching her polyester-clad buns and thighs undulate from behind.

Harbine's going over the ward rules as we walk. It's hard to concentrate what with the friction of her pants. The shiny artificial fibers being rubbed together are making a whish, whush, whish song. But it's the crowd I seem to have attracted that's giving me pause.

I realize that a new inpatient would be of interest, but these people are gawking at me with open mouths.

Nurse Harbine opens the door to a cramped dorm with a set of bunk beds. Oh, thank God she's pointing to a bottom bunk. I couldn't climb up anywhere. I ogle at an unmade twin mattress and pint-sized personal foot locker that will be mine. Sheets are stacked on the mattress for me to make the bed. The room is crowded with furniture yet a couple of patients manage to cram in. A single transom is so narrow and high up, it doesn't let in much light and as mentioned, there's scant fresh air what with every door and window being locked down tight.

Harbine intones, "As you can see, women bunk four to a room and share a toilet area. Showers are down the hall."

Of course they are.

"Mirrors are not allowed," she says, "since they can be broken and made into weapons to harm others."

Oh my God.

Harbine continues her tour as if handmade shanks are a normal topic of conversation. She gestures toward the "bathroom," which is set in a corner of the room without a privacy door. It offers a toilet, no stall, and an undeniable tinge of old urine. Above a trough sink is a reflective aluminum panel mounted on a white tiled wall. It provides enough of a reflection to take in the first view of myself.

There was a reason the hospital nurses could never find a mirror. Horror of horrors, I gawk at the drainage tube sticking out of my partially shaved skull. I knew it was there, but to see it? It reminds me of a sewer pipe since it runs brain ooze into a pouch taped to the side of my head. It's transparent so the staff can make sure the slime is not infected. Does that make me sound like a typical woman? Fitting in with my "peers" does not factor into this equation.

No wonder my lawyer still can't look at me without gagging. Who can blame him? My blurred vision has cleared up enough so I can catch the other residents' aghast looks and believe me, there are plenty.

One of the last things Phin had said to me was, "The other patients could be a problem for you. Use whatever you've got to get by."

He'd stopped short of calling it survival of the fittest but I'm pretty sure I'm surrounded by predators.

I'm thinking my best strategy is to use the pity card, for obvious reasons. If that doesn't work, I might have to switch to the "monster" card. Go all Frankenstein on them.

CHAPTER 12

Crazy Town

I'M BUSY SETTLING IN. Thank goodness my hospital issued comb and toothbrush are wrapped in plastic. I'm arranging them and the underwear—God only knows how many other people have used them—into the metal locker at the foot of my bed. The locker is so low to the floor I'm on my knees with my head down, which is making me dizzy.

My entire body seems to be in a hyper-reactive mode, come to think of it, what with the sensation of hot air blowing on my neck. Is there a fan nearby? There's also an odd click-clack sound, akin to tapping a porcelain cup with a spoon. And, two distinct odors. Cloying. Lilly of the valley. And...garlic...?

"Augghh." Recoiling, struggling to get my bearings I screech, "What the hell?"

"You're it!"

Looking up at a wrinkled woman with frazzled pink tinged hair, I pucker my nose. Aggh. She reeks of old lady stinky sweet perfume. I demand, "What are you doing?"

"You're it!"

Nurse Harbine comes into the room. My voice pitches high as I exclaim, "Thank God you're here, there's no telling what she would have done to me."

The woman removes her dentures and flashes me a toothless smile. Phew, her garlic breath is overpowering.

Harbine addresses the intruder, "Gladys, we've told you a million times not to come into other people's rooms. You have to respect their privacy."

The nurse turns to me. "Don't worry, she's harmless. Like a child, actually. She's always looking for someone to play hide and seek."

My cheeks must be flame red they're burning so bright. "Yeah, well, I didn't know that." I point to the bandage covering my right eye. "I don't have the best peripheral vision right now. I was scared she, um, she could have snuck up on me and... and, hurt me."

The nurse arches an eyebrow. I follow her gaze to the little old lady with bones jutting out of tissue paper thin skin that has blue veins running like rivers up her stick arms.

"Uh huh," says Nurse Harbine, as she escorts Gladys out of my room.

Strike two.

THERE IS NO PITY for anyone passing through Crazy Town. All variations of freaks and monsters are running amuck, including several interpretations of Frankenstein. So much for my survival strategy. My new Plan C is to shut up and keep my head down. And watch my back. Literally. Not only does Gladys like to play tag, one of my roommates has made me the newest unsuspecting participant in her game. She sneaks up from behind and screams bloody murder. I learned through an awkward experience that this chick gets her sexual kicks by scaring the bejeezus out of folks. Literally.

Why bother to seek out a make believe child when there are real life characters acting out around me? I can't worry about where Helice Polansky may or may not be hiding when a demented nymphomaniac is bunking next to me. I'm also wondering where the ferret-faced Roman, the licker who lingers in the shadows, might be.

Those people in the know tell me the involuntary population is mostly made up of peaceable people (like us) who have found ourselves on the wrong side of a situation without the means, or a clever excuse, to get out of it. Simply put, a 5150 is when "the man" holds innocent folks like us against our will by a court-ordered, seventy-two hour enforced mental health observation for "probable cause."

They're outraged my three day hold has been postponed due to my brain surgery, since it means more time in here. A man gives me a high five. Hmm, this has earned me a status.

A good number of patients have landed here due to heavy and/or ill-advised intoxication aggravated by innumerable tales of woe. Keith regales me with a spirited account of a two hour bar standoff he waged before five cops could lay him down. It makes me laugh but my story takes the prize for most original "plot."

I must admit to sneaking a second look at Keith. Well, actually about five or six peeks. It's been too long. A girl can't let opportunities pass, even if it means digging "among the ruins" of a locked facility.

My eyes wander away from Keith to spot Jackson coming my way. It's time for my daily patient/lawyer consultation. It's allowed under the timeframe of a three day 5150 hold, which began when they released me from the medical wing.

I burst out, "I shouldn't be here, get me out. N-now!"

"Your speech is getting much clearer, that's good." He still can't look at me.

Next, he explains the legalities of my situation to prepare me for the important decision I must make at the end of my evaluation. Although I am still considered a "person of interest" in the Redwood City kidnapping case, police haven't found enough evidence to formally charge me and tensions are high. The community wants justice to be served, even if that means taking a detour and running over my constitutional rights before declaring me innocent of all suspicions after the fact.

No matter how real my out-of-body experience may have been to me, Phin and Ross weren't able to substantiate any of the clues from my astral "visit." Even before Ross grew bored of playing detective, he was pretty sure there was no legal ground to stand on. In other words, he told me to keep my mouth shut and never, ever mention it to my proper, analytical lawyer.

It's no big surprise when Jackson tells me, "I've told you all along that it's in your best interest to play nice and stay put, which means voluntary inpatient treatment."

"Yeah, but," I fret, "d-doesn't that mean I'll be classified as mentally ill?"

"You? His hand flies to his heart. "A mental case?" He's quickly losing his veneered professional persona.

He's trying, but he can't help breaking out into raucous laughter. "Didn't you realize you've been *committed?*" He looks at me, really studies me, for the first time since my surgery. "

"I'm not paying you $400.00 fricking dollars an hour to insult me, you cold blooded shark."

He says, "Well, those words couldn't have been clearer."

That's true. As long as I'm not too stressed out, the more I talk, the easier it gets. He doesn't need to know that. I may need to use the aphasia card again.

Jackson puts his poker-slash-lawyer face back on to advise, "You'll win points with the court. The shrinks will give you at least one bullshit psycho label like brief reactive psychosis. I'll make sure it remains in a closed record. Your medical insurance won't be affected."

"Yeah, but, can't you transfer me to a private clinic?"

"No, it'll look better to stay here."

My voice turns shrill. "You have no idea how bad it is in here. One of my roommates speaks in tongues, Jackson. Tongues! It's not even nighttime yet. What'll she be like when they turn off the lights? It's freaking me out."

He's checking his calendar.

"And, I saw that weirdo who licked me. He *licked* me."

Jackson does not seem at all concerned.

"Then get me a private room. Please," I snivel. "Or I really will go insane."

He stifles a chuckle. "5150s don't warrant any luxuries." He brightens, "I might be able to pull it off when you extend your stay." He checks his watch. "Our time is up. The bottom line is you have to stay here no matter how much you cry."

So much for my crocodile tears. Time to amp it up.

"C'mon, Jackson, I am totally afraid of these people. Once you leave there's no telling what they'll do. Seriously."

My lawyer closes his outrageously expensive Italian leather briefcase. The one I gave him last Christmas, for crying out loud. He informs me, "Your brother figured you'd balk at staying here indefinitely."

"No shit, Sherlock."

His finger traces the fancy *JM* monogram. As if the price of the briefcase weren't enough of a sticker shock, I paid extra to have his initials engraved.

He says, "Ross is holding certain items of yours." He pauses, "Items you wouldn't want revealed."

Oh brother, he sure does! Ross wouldn't think twice about releasing photos of me on holiday with a well known married public official. Maybe he wouldn't actually go through with it but then again? It'd mean he won our besting game and he would surely celebrate.

I snort, "Well...fine, I'll stay. Speaking of Ross, where is that asshole? He should be back by now." It is well known his paramours have a short shelf life. The best way for Ross to kill a budding relationship is to take the lady out of town.

"Ross extended his vacation," says Jackson with an attorney's nonchalance.

My jaw drops. "You mean, he's *still* with the

security chick? She must've brought her gun."

"He booked the best suite in the best resort in Sonoma."

"Damn. She must've brought her entire arsenal."

Jackson's eyes explode with a gleefulness he rarely allows to escape. He's showing his teeth he is so amused. Even though he hasn't made a sound, I know from knowing him most of his life, when he was still Johnny Miller, that he's cracking up on the inside where he hides such things.

He starts to leave and then flashes me a real smile, a genuine gift he does not often give. "Don't worry, Teresa Rose, you're tough enough for this place." He comes over, bends down and to my surprise, kisses my cheek before heading out.

IT WAS INEVITABLE. Cooped up for so long. Recovering from a traumatic brain injury. Alone in a hostile environment. Can you blame me for seeking a little comfort?

Keith is being released tomorrow morning. Tonight we must seize the moment. Hmm, let's hope it lasts longer, a lot longer than just a moment. I figure we'll need several if you know what I mean. We've been engaged in a nonphysical foreplay with our eyes all afternoon and finally, we've slipped away during the ward's evening recreation time.

Keith leads me to a secret rendezvous. He says he knows this place inside out. He answers my "Why, how?" with, "I've been here three or four times, what does it matter?"

It doesn't.

His hand feels hot in mine and I can only imagine... Hey, wait a minute, where are we going? A broom closet?

"Are you kidding me?" I pipe up. "What are we, in seventh grade?"

His response is a big wet kiss as he presses me

against a...oh, yuck, it's a broom. A wet broom.

He's going at it so fast and furious the back of me is being banged against the wall. I warn, "Hey, watch it. My ribs are messed up." He doesn't say a word. He's too busy getting all over me. Gawd. He's acting like a pubescent octopus.

I forgive him when he peels off his facility issued shirt. Yum. Even with only one available eye, blurry as it is, I like what I see. Biceps and abs like a romance novel cover boy. I've been especially enthralled with his pouty fish lips, the pair of which I've spent several delightful hours imagining how they'll glide all over me.

Oh man, hold on. He really is a fish, what with his breath. Phew. I need to turn away, grab gulps of fresh air.

We go back to kissing but it's weird, the lower half of his face feels as if it is collapsing whenever our lips press. I turn my tongue into a whirlybird to investigate inside his mouth. Oh, dear. It turns out lover boy ain't got many teeth left in his pretty head so when he puckers up, he really does pucker.

In the dim light of the broom closet, I happen to see a large tattoo of a snarling tiger across Keith's chest. It looks vaguely familiar. All of a sudden, it hits me: he's a biker in a notorious Bay Area motorcycle gang. A gang that's earned a permanent placement on the DEA's *let's nab these guys* list for drug trafficking cocaine and methamphetamines. Hence the rotten, missing teeth.

The mood abruptly shifts in our love shack. Soon as I fling open the door, he starts carping that I should finish him off. He's crying about me leaving him with blue balls.

Exiting the closet, I am smug with righteousness. There are boundaries, for crying out loud and... Oh, damn it. With impeccable timing, here comes Nurse Jennifer Harbine. Her arms are folded tightly, her frown is so low on her face it has merged with her twin chins.

This is my undeniable strike three, and it's not even the end of my first day here.

We hang our heads like the two school age kids we've reverted to as soon as she caught us. We march ourselves to the principal's office, i.e. the nurse's station, where the staff had coordinated a systematic search for us.

We also must walk the gauntlet of shame: the other patients split down the middle for us to pass through. Keith's circle of friends let it be known that he has impulse control issues. They insist it's not his fault the poor innocent guppy got sucked up into the inky inlet of my turgid bay.

Great, even Roman the face licker is passing judgment. Hey, he's the only one among us not dressed in green. I think that means he's a voluntary patient. Why is he in the locked ward? Virgil, the head orderly, probably let him in.

Ack, no time to worry about Roman. Most patients are siding with the staff on this one since it's a big thing, sneaking off. The staff probably assumed we'd gone off somewhere to get laid and went on full alert.

Patients are abuzz with what this means.

The alpha female speculates, "Keith's evaluation team will have to meet again to discuss all this —"

"It's a serious infraction," interrupts her cohort.

Alpha continues, "I'm worried for Keith. I don't see how he could be released tomorrow, not after this."

Darn it, I was hoping to never see the guy again.

"Eww!" The town crier cries out, "What's going on with her head? That thing. It's leaking." There rises up a cacophony sounded by my disgusted peers.

Harbine takes a look at the pouch that's hooked up to a tube running from inside my skull. The pouch is supposed to be discretely taped to the side of my head. She sets her mouth and goes into triage mode. I reach up to investigate. The pouch has dropped down to where it is now grazing my shoulder. My gooey probing fingers tell me the thing has popped. It's gushing blood and God knows what else.

She shoves me into a wheelchair and hustles me

over to the medical wing. I can't help but smile at this development.

The nurse bursts my bubble. "Don't assume you're staying in the hospital. We're just going to patch you up and then back you go. You'd better settle in and play the right game, Teresa, or things will get a whole lot worse for you."

CHAPTER 13

Here It Comes

Day 5 —

THE PSYCHIATRIST INTERRUPTS my revelry with a cheery, "How's it going, Ms. Evans?"

Mindful of playing the game, I give him a thumbs up. I'm set up at a table so he, the third health care professional to assess me this day, can give me yet another test. This court ordered evaluation process is no joke. Since eight this morning, I've been volleyed back and forth among the staff so they could assess my personality, my logic, my perception, my puzzle solving ability, my intelligence, my sanity. Shoving a square block into a round hole, that kind of thing.

I'm currently suffering through a multiphasic personality test. Answering over five hundred true/false questions could make any normal person go absolutely bonkers. It makes me want to sabotage the test it's so lame, but that would be a dumb move. The shrinks are in control of the asylum.

He interrupts again to remind me, "It's almost time. You'd better finish up."

Yeah, yeah, yeah. The clock on his desk is across the room from me, but it's ticking so loudly it feels like I'm inside Salvador Dali's crazy painting. On acid. That thought gives me a giggle. Or, or...I think of a better one.

It's like Hollywood's classic *Hunchback of Notre*

Dame. Quasimodo tries to quell the thunderous reverberations of the gigantic bell in the tower. He clutches his hands so tightly against his ears his skull might crack like a walnut. He is a sympathetic character everyone roots for, yet the universe couldn't allow Quasimodo to get the girl. Esmeralda.

Hey, that's the same name as my housekeeper. What are the odds? Wonder if she's cleaning my house now that her "mistress" is AWOL. While the cat's away...

Mary. How confused my poor dog must be, wondering where I am. All I did was burn my manuscript on my private property. As if I don't have a right to kill off a character, a girl of my own making. Mystery novelists have the luxury of committing pretend murders and they get paid big bucks.

Still think those cops did an illegal search and seizure. Cops. Oh, goody. Here comes hunky police boy Marciano prancing into the delights of my mind like he's about to ravish me. Hmm. Italian would taste so good right now.

Can't help fantasizing about what could have been, if the other cop hadn't almost croaked on the edge of my land. Why they let an old fat guy with high cholesterol run around with a gun on a hot day—that's the real crime here.

The psychiatrist warns, "Two more minutes, Ms. Evans."

Jesus, the sound of his voice is making me crazy. Oops, I shouldn't use that word around here. I have to play the game, prove I'm not a threat to myself or others. Looking down at the rest of the true/false questions I answer with fake enthusiasm, "Okay, thanks."

Getting back to Marciano, I'm sure he would have fallen for me if it hadn't been for his aged sidekick fainting like a diva and getting all the attention. Marciano could have been the one. Well, truth be told, he's a tad younger than me, but it felt like kismet, it really did.

Wonder how Mary would react to a stepdad? She hasn't liked sharing me with men, and to be honest, I've had an endless stream of them. Mary is a one person kind of dog.

Ross told me not to worry while I'm here. He said she's "just" a dog, what does she care as long as she's fed? He assured me there's a new vet in town who's taking great care of her but what does my brother know, he's a self-absorbed bachelor without any responsibility to house and home.

Mary is the closest thing I have to a family.

Speaking of dwarves, I suppress a chuckle over memories of Spud. My little person boyfriend was an exotic dancer at one of my favorite clubs back in the day. Hmm, haven't heard from Spud in a while, wonder if he ended up moving to the Florida Keys to run that fishing boat he was always going on about. Now, Spud was a lip smacking milk chocolate nugget if there ever was one. Yummy. Always left me watering for more, the way fine chocolate does. He's a tortured writer, just like Ernest Hemingway, which is probably why Spud wanted to live in the Keys. To get the ambience, you know. Think I'll look Spud up and—

"Ms. Evans," the doctor says, "I can't give you any more time to finish this test."

"Huh? Oh." I sputter back to my present day reality in the nut house.

The doctor, a middle-aged man with rimless glasses, has not been unkind. He leans forward with an encouraging smile and says, "You look like you need a break."

I haven't been able to stop yawning. The clock on his shiny spotless desk has been assaulting time tick-by-fricking-tock. It's only half of day one of my three day evaluation.

My brain is bloody well fried.

Frankly, I don't give a damn what they think of me at this point. I am done. For emphasis, I flick the yellow #2 pencil away from my test sheet. The doctor and I watch it roll off the table and onto the floor. Neither one of us makes a move to pick it up.

He tries to placate me by lifting his hairy hands. "Well," he prompts, "it's been a long stretch, huh?" He motions for me to come sit at a chair on the other side of his desk.

He's worked hard to figure me out, let's give him a bone. Let's give him something true. So I say, "I didn't sleep last night." I punctuate my statement with a sad grimace.

He looks interested when he gives me a friendly, "Oh, why's that?"

I decide to level with him. "One of my roommates is a nymphomaniac. I was worried she'd jump me in my sleep."

The doctor raises his eyebrows. "Are you afraid of sex, Ms. Evans?"

"Are you k-kidding me?" I can't help it. I burst out laughing in spite of his serious expression. "Doctor, trust me, I have a healthy respect for sex. With men, that is."

Uh oh, I have to be careful. That gorgeous cop Marciano is lounging atop the dirty sheets of my mind with a come hither look that's to die for. But I have to concentrate on my evaluation. Focus, Trez, focus.

I tell the doctor, "What I mean is, I don't go in for gaga women, especially one in a locked facility who isn't chained to her bed." Uh oh, bad choice of sadist/masochistic imagery.

"I mean, ah, humanely restrained of course."

He's looking at me through glasses perched low on his nose. This makes me think he's annoyed, or is he being condescending? He's making me feel defensive.

I start jabbering, "I mean, sex is fantastic, right? Seriously, who doesn't like sex?"

Oh, the joy. Marciano is stripping out of his policeman uniform. Yummy, now he's buck naked.

The doctor clears his throat. "Is that why you and Keith locked yourselves in the broom closet?"

"Huh, what?" I have got to concentrate. I'll think about fish-lipped Keith. That'll cool my libido.

The doctor is peering at me with one of his thick eyebrows pointing up. It looks like a woolly question mark. Back to the question he asked about Keith. Toothless methhead Keith.

"Oh, that." I fake a cough. "That wasn't the best idea in the world but, well, I was ah...um..." Phin had advised bonding with the psychiatrists so I go for the gold here. "I was so scared and, and...feeling all alone and...vulnerable. My oversexed roommate had already felt me up before I knew what was happening. I felt totally violated, by the way. I...I...oh, it's still hard to talk, what with my aphasia and all."

The doctor nods in support of my emotional pain and suffering. He doesn't say anything, so I go on. "One of my other roommates speaks in tongues. I kid you not. She's all about 'the spirit' with the holy water, t-the whole nine yards."

His woolly eyebrow arches again.

"So," I stammer, "I've got a religious fanatic on the bunk above me , and a n-nympho on the other side of me. Is it any wonder I was afraid to go to sleep?" I sigh like a tire losing air. "I'm not sure if there is a third roommate or what she'd be about."

I stop to give him my doleful Trez look. "Do you think I could have a private room?" My eyelashes flutter, my automatic response to a male whenever I want something. It happens before I remember where I am.

His nice guy demeanor fades. "No. That's not possible."

Great. Now he thinks I'm manipulative, which might be a pathological diagnosis. Got to get back on his good side so I blather, "I'm sorry, I didn't mean to ask for special privileges or anything, I'm just so exhausted, I had brain surgery a few days ago, it's hard to keep track of time in a place like this, you know? I gotta tell you, it's a traumatic experience, dealing with brain trauma. Oh, I just said a double entendre."

I let out a frothy giggle but the good doctor appears to miss my humor. Wait. Doesn't that mean risqué? Great. Now he thinks I'm coming on to him. Not that he isn't attractive in an old man sort of way, surely some women of a certain age must dig him but ick, he is not sexy to me at all.

I have got to get myself out of this faux pas before it gets any worse. It's best to not look him in the eye otherwise he'll think I want him to kiss me. Kissing Keith is what got me in trouble. Speaking of Keith, he didn't show for breakfast.

What happened to him? He probably ratted on me, threw me right under the bus to get himself out of trouble. Hey, maybe he got sprung like he was supposed to. Good for him, he served his time. He left me for the lions but hey, it's a dog-eat-dog world after all. Dog. God, I miss Mary.

"Ms. Evans." The doctor again raises his hairy hands. "Are you still with me?"

I flash him a brilliant, tried and true Trez Evans smile. "Yes sir, I sure am."

JACKSON GETS IN MY FACE. "You screwed up big time, Trez."

We are in the tiny room assigned to us for my daily legal counsel. While I sit in stunned silence, he's pacing the small space. He's as pissy as a nag on the rag.

"What the hell were you thinking?" It is not a good sign when Jackson speaks in terse short clipped sentences. "Being sexually engaging. With the doctor?"

I laugh it off. "Oh, that. Come on, it was an innocent misstep. If I'd wanted him, there would be no question." Uh oh, the jerk of Jackson's upper lip tells me that went too far.

"A misstep?" He kicks a folding chair away from the table he's using as a desk. "You messed up the evaluation."

I must fib to fight back. "You said to play nice, but my speech is still screwed up. It's hard, it's *super* hard to think and talk at the same time."

"Really?" He clenches his fists. "You were fine earlier."

"Couldn't you tell them that anyway? Let's just blame it on my brain damage."

He snorts, "There's no way out of an extended stay now. Even if the police were to clear your name this minute. You dug your own grave, you idiot." His pacing is getting faster.

"But you said you wanted me to stay here longer."

"Voluntarily. That's a big difference from being declared mentally incompetent."

"C'mon, stop being a drama queen." That usually works when Ross says it but my blustering lawyer yells, "I swear, if you weren't Ross' sister I'd—"

"You'd what, Jackson? Give up the exorbitant fee you charge Lawton's estate? *Annually.*"

A little groan escapes my lips before I pull it together. Even after all these years, it hurts to talk about my late first ex-husband Lawton Pennalton the fourth. I'd met the sixty-seven year old playboy in 1969 at a "love-in" in San Francisco's Golden Gate Park during the Haight Asbury heyday. We eloped a month later.

A gray haired Peter Pan in paisley velvet bellbottoms, my new husband cowered under his dowager mother's threats to cut him off if he didn't annul his marriage to a nineteen year old girl who loved him with all her might. He set me up with a whopping trust fund before he died so "Mommy Dearest" and his three scheming ex-wives couldn't claim a cent. Lots of women still lined up with their hands out. Paloma Del Mar, his longtime lover, sued for palimony. Hers was the only suit to win, a legal defeat Jackson still takes personally.

On my end, Jackson was among many friends and relatives who questioned how I could marry a man who was older than my father.

So it feels good to glare at Johnny Miller, the neighbor boy I used to babysit. The guy who borrowed my money for law school so he could become Jackson Milan, Esquire.

It feels even better when I hiss, "What'ya wanna do? Give up your *annual* fee?"

That second zing should do it. Jackson should roll over and offer me his soft underbelly.

Steam is practically spewing out of his flaring nostrils. "Legitimate costs to protect your estate from Lawton's conniving ex-wives and relatives, you ungrateful bitch."

"Whoa." My hands fly up. "Stop it right now. What's really going on?"

Plopping down on the folding chair across from me, he runs his fingers through his perfectly styled hair. "Bad news. Police swept the Loveland's home again. One of the dogs found a trace of Analeese's blood."

"Oh, God." It feels as if my lungs have been punctured. "I...is she...dead?" This news makes me feel like a failure, just like all my other "projects" that went amiss. What about my destiny to save that kid? So much for being a superhero.

Jackson sighs. "No one knows." But this is bad for you. Even though they're reviewing all the suspects, your name is still at the top of their list again. Their very short list."

I confess to being relieved they haven't found a dead body, but Jackson looks so pained, there must be more.

I protest, "Why? You said they didn't have any evidence."

"*Why?*" Jackson is pinching the bridge of his nose so hard his skin is reddening. "What does it matter who they arrest?" he grumbles. "They need someone to crucify. Why not a spoiled, demented heiress?"

"That is so not true. Or fair. Just because Lawton named me his only beneficiary..."

He breaks into a snooty laugh. "Jesus, you *are*

oblivious. Ross brought up your narcissism when you were hauled off on the 5150, but of course, he was trying to save your ass."

"Hey, hold on. Ross is the narcissist, not me."

Jackson ignores my protest. "Phin said the same thing, but no one listens to what he babbles on about. The bottom line is they both insisted you couldn't have had anything to do with a kidnapping because you're one hundred percent unaware of any one other than yourself." He raises and then drops his shoulders as he mocks, "Who was I to argue?"

My eyes tear up but he will not have the satisfaction of seeing me cry. Not today.

Jackson pounds the chair he was using as a table to command my attention.

"Listen up. This is precisely what you are going to do..."

I'M SITTING AROUND a conference table with the team that evaluated me: three psychiatrists, my surgeon, and Nurse Harbine. It's hot in here, I'm nodding off, but the cafeteria serves only decaf coffee, and they haven't recessed for lunch. OK, so I don't have aphasia, but it's still tricky to answer questions when my brain locks and my mind goes off on a tangent. Jackson can't comfort me, he's by himself at the far end of the large room. He can't interfere with the process unless there is a legal issue to discuss.

The woolly-browed psychiatrist is sitting across from me. If he's upset over my inopportune sexual innuendo from this morning, he's not showing it. One down, four to go. My surgeon, Dr. Watson, seems supportive. I grew fond of him during my hospital stay. He never judged me for my stupid stunt that landed me in his operating room. It'll be interesting to see how he votes.

Nurse Harbine might have been sympathetic before she found Keith and me in the closet. But, we'd already gotten off to a bad start when she admitted me. I couldn't help it if my eyes again bugged out at the sight of her massive behind. I wonder if she's forgiven me for the little squeak that escaped me while following her big butt and ham hock legs stuffed into tight pants. I'm still having nightmares about spontaneous combustion.

There's the student shrink whose name has slipped my mind. I recall her saying she's an art therapist, whatever that is. She's doing her residency here and I'm thinking she's likely to be sympathetic to my case, if for no other reason than she's young and new to this game and I'm a girl like her.

When Dr. Watson motions for me to begin, I stand up.

My chest is heaving I'm so nervous. "I, um, thank you for meeting with me before the official evaluation is over, I know it's not the usual case." I look down at myself and try to press out the creases in my oversized hospital issued two-piece.

Dr. Watson says, "You can sit, it'd be more comfortable."

I thankfully sit back down. "Ah, please accept my apology for any im...ah, impro...priety. Excuse me, it's hard to speak what with the brain damage, my tongue gets tied. Anyway, it's been a tough few days for me here. I've been physically and emotionally exhausted."

No need to mention it feels as if my heart is stuffed into my mouth. "I, ah, this shouldn't be an excuse, but I've been recovering from emergency surgery. I've had headaches and dizziness ever since."

Which is totally true.

Dr. Watson nods. "We're taking that into consideration, along with the progress you've made. It'll take time but you will fully recover." He gives me a smile. "I promise."

"Thank you." I address the others. "I'm sensitive to drugs and as you know, I've been given a lot."

Pausing for emphasis, I go to brush my hand through my hair. As one of my practiced habits, I've always brought attention to my hair. It's usually thick and shiny but I'm suddenly conscious that my long locks are no longer there. Instead, my fingers hit the plastic pouch taped to my head, the one that's connected to the gawd awful tube sticking out of my skull. The tube that's draining muck from the giant hematoma.

Oh, my God. I can't think about the horror of that now. I have to concentrate on this evaluation. Focus, Trez, focus.

"Ah, it's hard to cope with...I, ah..." This is no ruse, my voice is cracking, and my throat is tightening up.

When my chin quivers (for real) Nurse Harbine pours me a glass of water, which I accept with a shaky hand and drain in a few gulps. With everyone's attention riveted on me, there's nothing else to do but to keep talking.

First, I let out a long slow breath. "Ever since they brought me in I've complained it's all just a big mistake, that I don't belong in a loon—ah, a locked facility."

Harbine pours more water. These people seem genuine; they're acting as if they care. They outlined how each patient's evaluation and treatment plan is customized for the best end result possible. Maybe I should stay here, work on those "issues" they told me I have.

At least they're listening to me. It's more than I can say about my writing group. The only attention they ever paid me was like that of a pod of killer whales attacking baby seals for dinner. Reminds me of Bethany Moraga, who may be an anorexic, but she's the fiercest orca there is.

"Um, so..." I stammer before taking another sip of water. I link my one good eye with Dr. Watson. He's nodding again.

I let out another breath to steady my nerves. "Guess I haven't owned up to what brought me here, and resisting everyone's efforts to help me through, um, a difficult time. This morning was a real turning point. It wasn't until the session ended, I had time to think."

I drain the glass again and set it on the table. "That's when it hit me. My life has been super stressful the past few months. I've been trying to write a novel for years. It's not going so well. When I lost my job it all came to a head."

My voice breaks again. "The best thing to do for myself, the healthiest thing, is to...um, I'd rather stop this evaluation process early and instead, if you all agree, that is, I'd like to sign in here as a voluntary inpatient to...um, I'm ready to receive proper care."

I almost add, "For however long it takes" but my crafty lawyer had coached me on exactly what to say. He didn't warn me it would be so emotional, though, or that my heart would be aching as if it's being wrenched from my chest.

Dr. Watson is the first to consider my proposal. He tells the others, "It'd be easier to manage her medical care if she stays here longer. I'd want to continue the anti-convulsion drugs for at least another two or three weeks."

Dr. Woolly Brow says, "She'd have to stay on all the psychotropic meds, at least for now. We'd monitor her very closely to watch for side effects. That is—" He turns to the young shrink in training. "As long as you agree."

She's eyeing me, on the alert for any facial tells to let her know if my words are sincere. Returning her gaze, I try not to be cocky or assertive. She nods her approval.

A negative vote is cast after a psychiatrist I've never met reads a statement on behalf of her colleague. Dr. Lively is on medical leave for a broken hip, a hip they say I am somehow responsible for breaking. It feels surprisingly hurtful when the psychiatrist uses words such as "inappropriate reaction," and "alcohol-induced delusion" to describe my "affect" that day. What about my side of the story? Nobody bothers to ask.

Jackson had told me not to bring up how my "hysterical hallucination" got the better of me. I dare not mention I charged the wall to get at Helice, who was egging me on with her freckled smiley face. Speaking of which, I'm mad that she ran out on me. She hasn't been around for over two days, the little stinker.

So now, the score looks to be two against one with two votes to go. Nurse Harbine brings up my fake aphasia stunt. Maybe I can't count on her, is she going to be a turncoat vote? A debate over various treatment plans for my malingering ensues. Jeez, that nurse is passing judgment as if I'd robbed a bank or something.

They ask me to step out of the room so they can discuss my proposal. Jackson stands with me in the hallway. We do not speak. He's in his lawyer mode, his expression impossible to read. Who would have thought I'd be praying for acceptance into an asylum? Who's the cuckoo now?

Eventually they call us back in. Nurse Harbine is smiling. I practically leap for joy when they announce they've agreed to my voluntary admittance into the facility. The student shrink will be my therapist for the rest of my stay, however long it is. Her name's Hannah Harrison. Hmm, why does that name sound familiar? Whatever. She'd mentioned our "first session together" but I just played along. I love her perky haircut. Maybe I'll do my hair that way. When it grows back, that is. Us two girls can have lots of fun together.

Jackson looks visibly relieved. He pays attention to the specifics the team is spelling out, such as meds and treatment plans. They mention code numbers for psychiatric "disorders" they say I have. Apparently, they have given me a few diagnoses, probably to justify bilking my insurance company for outrageously priced treatment. I'm too relieved to listen to specifics. It's all bullshit anyway. They eventually disperse and go back to whatever they were doing.

Even with my prodding, Jackson refuses to explain what might have happened without the team's vote. Denial can be a good thing. My triumphant lawyer turns on his Italian leather clad heel and leads me to our consultation room.

As he closes the door behind us, he says, "You're

lucky, Trez. Damn lucky."

He rubs his hands with brisk efficiency. "Okay. First things first. Ross is back in town. He's ready to do anything he can to help you. In fact, I had an interesting discussion with him and Phineas last night. Eye opening."

Jackson pauses, and gives me an odd look. He holds that stare long enough to get my full attention. Then he says, "We need to talk about the man you think kidnapped Analeese Loveland. But first, tell me everything, and I mean everything, about Helice Polansky."

CHAPTER 14

New Man, New Chance

I'M BREAKING OUT OF HERE! An irresistible urge has been welling inside of me to call out to one and all, "So long, suckers." But I can't bring myself to do it. Some of these deranged people like it here. They don't notice my departure.

Since the powers that be granted me an extended stay in Crazy Town, they're moving me out of the involuntary population. Judging from folks I've encountered, this locked ward is the apex of the asylum. Patients don't know they're certifiable, even if you tell them over and over. Being licked on the face, for instance. That's the definition of madness.

It's a relief to be transferred to the voluntary population. People here recognize they aren't right in the head and need to be redirected with therapy, positive reinforcement, and healthy coping methods. Blah, blah, blah.

The bottom line is, they know they need to be here.

Except for me. I'm in here under false pretenses. But being moved from the psycho floor is a good thing.

So now, I'm again following the broad, polyestered butt of Nurse Harbine around. "Admitting you will take a while," she says in her high pitched little girl voice. Harbine is twisting her neck around to talk while she walks. She advises me to, "Take a look around, get familiar with things."

I am so over watching her undulating pork chop

thighs rub together as she leads the way. Since they haven't caught fire from the friction, the novelty is over.

As for coming into a new environment, I can't help being pensive. To be honest, my biggest fear is if I'll ever see Helice again. I blew it, being so mean. No wonder she went away.

Harbine bustles off with my folder. "I'll be back in five."

I nod. There's nothing new here. Same floor plan with walls, ceilings, and doors painted in the puke green color that covers every square inch of this building.

On the plus side, everyone here wears a blue two-piece uniform rather than the green that designates involuntary patients, one more way they cull the herds around here. The same used white canvas slide-ons with orange rubber soles complete the ensemble.

If I have to be in a mental facility, this section is probably the best place to be.

I'M ALMOST THROUGH my first group therapy session. Being stuck with a bunch of nut jobs blathering about issues is as much fun as filing one's tax return. It's turned my bum mood around, though. Listening to emotionally charged whining (versus mental illness torment), is like being part of a live theatre performance. You wonder what's gonna happen next.

Granted, a few of them are in real pain. A young mother checked herself in to learn how to cope with a serious illness so her kids won't be affected by her fear and worry. I was close to tears listening to her story.

Then there's a World War II veteran who tried to kill himself because everyone he loved is dead. The irony is, he's the patient in the hospital ward who received the bird of paradise arrangement I saw being created during my OBE out of body experience. How trippy is that?

Those two patients have legitimate gripes but the others? Give me a break. It's up to me to set the rest of the folks straight. It's hard work, given their personality disorders, but someone has to do it. The therapist seems to be out to lunch.

Speaking of lunch, it's time to eat. The staff follows a strict timeline so we are taken to the cafeteria. Who knew sharing feelings works up an appetite? Not that I'd ever disclose anything personal.

I grab a tray and join the buffet line with others from our therapy session. They tell me different wards eat in shifts and I'm relieved the unpredictable green-clad, court-mandated patients are long gone from the cafeteria. Their absence should lend a leisurely ambiance to the meal.

We find an empty table and dig into the food. It's barely edible, but my stomach is no longer clenching from apprehension worrying what intensity of fruitcake might sit next to me. My gastric distress is now due to the greasy hot dog and bean casserole. Funny thing is, this food reminds me of the dinners my domestically-challenged mother cooked.

We're discussing baseball, notably the San Francisco Giants, when I gasp, "Who is *that*?" With radar precision, I zero in on a guy who's the incarnation of actor Paul Newman.

This hunky man is in his late twenties, circa Paul's early years in Hollywood. It's eerie; this guy has the exact heart-stopping turquoise eyes that turned Newman into a major movie star. Turquoise is a rare eye color. Not baby blue, which is a common color. These have just enough of an aqua overtone mixed with the perfect percentage of green. Believe me, I've hunted for men with eyes like these. This guy's brown hair is wavy, he sports the dimpled chin, and he's even the same height and weight as Paul Newman. Betcha anything, he has the endearing smile as well. My kind of guy!

I need a napkin to wipe the drool off my face he is so drop-dead gorgeous. He's standing with a small group of men. They're not debating like folks at my table; in fact, they're not talking at all. "Paul Newman the Second" seems to be the strong silent type.

Speaking of his name, calling him Paul makes me think of the actor nowadays. He's an old guy, almost sixty. Besides, my favorite version of Paul Newman is when he was new to the game in the '50s, fresh out of "the Method" Actors Studio in New York City. Hmm. New. Newman. Think I'll call him "New Man." He's my new chance at finding love.

My first thought is to rush over there and claim him as my own. However, the memory of toothless Keith jumping my bones in the broom closet keeps me sitting at the table. My hormones may be in overdrive, but my mind is warning caution. This is the nut house after all. First make sure this New Man is not off his rocker, a druggie, or a parolee.

I jump up, grab my tray, and head over to the cleanup area where my potential new boyfriend is standing. I begin to slide my plate and glass onto the vertical dirty dish rack. Oh, my goodness, I've accidently dropped my tray.

The plastic tray hits the linoleum floor with a satisfactory amount of noise, certainly loud enough for him to hear it.

"New Man" does not make a move.

I let out a coquettish giggle, "How clumsy of me." He doesn't react. I go to make my signature flirty move, where I take a hand and flip my hair back but instead, I hit the goop bag attached to my head. He doesn't notice that either, thank goodness. Let's try this again.

I add volume and emphasis to my situation with a lustfulness worthy of Marilyn Monroe, "Oh dear, I'm all thumbs today." When he still doesn't come to my aid, I wail with theatrical gusto, "Of all days for my back to go out. I don't think I can pick up this tray."

A bald man on dish duty gives me a sour glare as he bends down to retrieve the tray. Distracted by this server's surly attitude for a moment or two, I turn back to discover that Paul Newman the Second has left the cafeteria. Ah hah, my New Man's playing hard to get.

I'm all set to follow his tracks when the PA system buzzes and a woman announces, "Trez Evans, please report to Room 113. Trez Evans, report to Room 113. Immediately."

CHAPTER 15

Call Me Trez

BEING FIFTEEN MINUTES LATE for my first individual session is not the best way to forge a relationship with my new therapist, but the show must go on, right?

Hannah Harrison is pretty cool about it, although she is quick to establish our pecking order by stating her rules. One is for me to respect her commitment to help me achieve my therapy goals. Secondly, in order for this to work, I must agree that we will meet at 1:00 p.m. sharp Monday through Saturday. Sure, no problem.

"I'm glad you understand, Trez. We have to be on the same page if we want our sessions to be meaningful." She launches into the rest of the rules along with how entering into therapy will be beneficial to my emotional well-being.

"I want you to feel you have a voice in this relationship. For instance, some of the other therapists prefer to be called Doctor. My title won't be official for another two semesters so I'll let you decide whether you'd like to call me by my first name or Ms. Harrison. You choose. All right? Hello? Trez!"

I jump at the sound of my name. "Ah, I like the name Hannah, so yeah."

She starts in again but everything she says sounds like the grownups talking in Charlie Brown cartoon specials. I hear "Whah, whah, whah," when all I can think about is my hunky boyfriend-to-be Paul Newman the Second.

It was a miracle my turquoise eyed New Man didn't notice my goop bag but next time it could be a real deal breaker. I make a mental note to see my surgeon Dr. Watson immediately so he can remove it. Can't afford any unnecessary hindrances to nabbing my true love.

Uh oh, here comes a naggy thought about hooking up with a deranged serial killer. But first off, a serial killer would be shackled in the dungeon of a high security prison and second, one shouldn't be picky about where one finds love, one should seize the moment. Be on the lookout for unique opportunities in unique situations.

Harrison interrupts my thoughts. "Trez, how do you feel about what I've outlined? Do you agree with the plan?"

When is she gonna stop talking? The therapist may have said something I should pay attention to, but what the hell, daydreaming about my new dreamboat is way more fun.

Hey, while envisioning the future with my boyfriend-in-a-serious-relationship, I've just realized he and the others in his group weren't in "uniform." They wore orange smocks over regular clothes like shirts and khakis. That could mean he can leave this place at will. Wonder if he's part of the staff? If he's management, he's not certifiable.

That would solve everything. We probably won't be able to date openly while I'm still a patient but as soon as Jackson gives me the nod to check out of this dump, we can take our relationship public.

I really need this win, this chance at happiness. I wonder if New Man believes in love at first sight. I sure do, always have. In fact, the day I met my second ex-husband Philip "Flip" Haggerty comes to mind. That didn't work out so well but it would be so great if New Man—

"Trez, we can't get into our session if you won't even answer a basic question."

My cheeks blush hot and by the looks of her, she knows she has me by the proverbial balls. I mutter, "Oh, sorry. I was taking a moment to make sure I understand all the rules."

She's been holding a crisp new case file with my name printed on the label. Putting it down, Hannah Harrison leans forward in her chair. "I'm not buying it. Want to try again?"

Busted. It's time to put New Man down for a while. I will pick him up later.

I flash her my tried and true Trez Evans smile and say, "I love your shoes, Hannah. Did you get them around here?"

She smiles back, giving me the impression we can carry on fun girl talk. Then she speaks. "Trez, you need to understand that in order for us build a therapeutic relationship together, you and I can't get personal. No doctor and patient can. It simply doesn't work that way. You need me to maintain an objective viewpoint so I can point out behaviors or negative beliefs you might not be aware of." She smiles again. "If you'd like, we can plan an extra session when you could tell me about some of your friends."

"No thanks. But, I get it. I'm nervous, and embarrassed about being late. Don't worry, no more personal questions." I glance down. "Although, I really do like your shoes."

Hannah Harrison's laugh is soft and lilting. "In that case, I got them at Brinkley's."

"Gotcha." My body relaxes into the chair. "So, tell me what to do."

She smiles, "Let's start with what brought you here. Tell me about that day."

Oh, brother, here we go. Without admitting too much, I provide enough so she can get the nitty gritty. As Ross always tells me, *"Never show your hand, Trez. Keep a little mystery."*

There is no mention of a ten year old from 1953 Detroit.

THE ROUTINE AROUND HERE is getting old and my first day isn't even over. After my therapy session, they sent me to the kitchen to scrub pots. Hot wet work. At least I'm safer in this ward. 5150s are too volatile to mix with us regular patients. Problem is, there's no trace of New Man, or any of his orange smocked buddies I could befriend. Where could he be?

I'm elbow deep in dirty water scrubbing hot dog and bean casserole-caked pots and yet I'm grinning like a fool due to the most lascivious fantasy about my new man.

All of a sudden, the thought of Helice pops into my head.

Quick as a flash, here she is sitting on the floor next to the sink. After being away so long, she barely notices me, what with her studying a book as if her life depends on it. She eventually looks up to explain it's a Girl Scout manual about how to survive in the woods. Where did she find that?

She's not excited to see me but I shrug it off. I give her a mental hello. Our exchange over, she goes back to reading.

The kitchen supervisor tells me to dry my hands and go with the others who are heading to the arts and crafts room. It's called Creative Modalities. The others explain this play-fest will go on for the rest of the afternoon. Fine by me if people want to finger-paint, it might help their mental state.

I'll pass, thank you very much. Oh, crap, this is mandatory? I hate arts and crafts, my fingers get glued together and glitter sticks to my hair. Well, I don't have much hair these days but trust me, nothing good will come out of me creating art with these fruit loop patients.

Hannah Harrison is greeting everyone at the double-doors. Oh, that's right, she's an art therapist, whatever that is. We file into a huge sun-filled room with a bank of picture windows overlooking a lovely garden.

There are several twelve-foot long worktables near shelving units stuffed with art supplies. Freestanding easels abound, along with two pottery wheels in the corner near a kiln. There are also shallow translucent plastic boxes filled with sand that are set on card tables. Don't ask me why they have litter boxes. There are no signs of cats but just in case, I won't be digging my hands in sand.

Helice goes over to one of the easels. She's checking out the paints and brushes. Hmm, if she painted, would there be an end result? If so, her artwork would be evidence of her existence. A part of me wants proof but I take a good look at her earnest face, how her eyes are so bright and full of life. She seems real. Do I want to open that door?

People get to work but I'm not sure what to do. Helice picks up a brush. This should be interesting. I want to see if my fictional character can create in real life, but Hannah comes over and distracts me.

"Pick an art medium, Trez. Just start and see what happens." She hands me a sheet of paper and just like that, it's déjà vu. All of a sudden I remember. She'd guided me through an intense art therapy session in my hospital room. That's why her name sounded familiar. Plus, I totally loved her cute hairdo.

I have to maintain my cool. "Yeah, well, I'm not into this artsy stuff so can I leave?"

There's a roguish glint in her eye. "I'm interested in the things you create, Trez, especially with you being a writer."

I fold my arms, crinkling the paper. "You don't expect me to draw a typewriter do you?"

"Don't be so quick to judge, it might be fun to build it out of Legos." My reaction leaves nothing to the imagination.

She thinks a moment. "I have just the thing. Follow me."

I can't leave. It appears Helice is painting. Squinting, I strain my good eye to watch her apply streaks of orange and red against a lilac backdrop. She switches to hues of green in the foreground. Oh, wow. Is she painting the Red Eden?

"Come on, Trez." I give Hannah a sharp glare that clearly tells her to back off. My fictional character could very well be painting a scene from my made up world.

Hannah insists, "Stop stalling." I'm forced to follow her to a library alcove with shelves of books and magazines. There are fairly decent word processors with built-in printers. She leans down at one of them, punches a key and voilà, a new document page appears on a little screen. She states the obvious, "You're a writer, so write something for me."

I point to my bandaged eye. "It's too hard for me to see."

"Really? You seem to see just fine when you want to. In fact, you keep stretching your neck to look across the room."

Helice's painting is so lifelike I need to grab it before the therapist catches on. It'll be proof I am not bonkers.

"Are you listening to me? Trez?"

"Fine, then, I'll try it." I'm thinking I can easily retype one of my short stories from memory and then call it quits.

"You didn't offer much about yourself during our session. I'll chalk it up to your being nervous on your first day. Remember, I asked why you spent ten years writing an epic novel and then, why you abruptly burned your manuscript? You focused on police harassment instead."

I start to mouth off about the cops but she puts up her hand. "Your protest was after the fact, wouldn't you say? I want you to go back to the beginning, to the origins of what prompted you to destroy all of your hard work. Give me your history. You know: who, what, where, when, and why. I especially want to know *why* you did it."

A hiccup escapes me.

She checks the wall clock. "You have plenty of time to produce, oh, let's say a minimum of a thousand words. And please, do it properly. You wouldn't want to stay after class and miss dinner to write it all over again, would you?"

Still straining to watch Helice paint on the other side of the room, I bark, "Are you kidding me?"

It turns out that the fresh-faced doctoral candidate with the perky haircut and cute shoes is tougher than any ruler-whacking parochial school nun I've ever come up against.

With a twirl of her fashion-forward skirt, Ms. Hannah Harrison leaves me to it.

EXPELLING A LOUD BURST OF AIR, I delete my third attempt at writing my story. Not my novel, of which there are probably thirty different versions over a ten-year span. *My* story.

Ms. Harrison has turned out to be a prig. She was so nice and understanding, all the while playing me. Her shoes aren't cute at all. I was just placating her for my coming late.

Everyone has left, including the therapist. But I'm stuck in the arts and craft room like an errant schoolgirl doing time in the principal's office. One day I broke out of that parochial grammar jail and ran all the way home. My mother brought me back and Sister Mary Mean loaded me up with even more remedial work.

While Helice and I were separated, she'd painted what looked to be an entire portfolio of Red Eden artwork. Whenever I wandered over there, Helice had asked me not to peek until everything was finished. Wish I hadn't been so agreeable. It looked real but then again...? I was distracted with my story and didn't realize Hannah collected everyone's drawings. Did she notice artwork from an imaginary child?

Where is it now? I jiggle the desk drawers. Locked. Where is Helice? Wonder if she followed the therapist home.

It's too quiet in here. First time I've had a chance to be with myself since they released me from the hospital.

I can't stop thinking about Analeese, how I've failed her without ever meeting the girl. That's me, Trez Evans screw-up. How I thought I could make a difference, well, fool me once, etcetera, etcetera. I can't blame Phin for this.

This is my punishment. I read a few sentences, rewrite them, and then press delete. Over and over like a lunatic.

I've been trying to justify why I shouldn't be held in this place; it's coming across as more of an article. I am not a journalist. That's why the words aren't flowing. My therapist specifically wants to know what was going on with me, what led up to destroying my novel. She doesn't realize I've been writing this story my entire fricking life.

I close my eyes, take in a breath, hold it, and then release it nice and slow. I do that two more times to clear my head.

Okay, a concept is forming. It's best to just allow it to unfold and to trust the writing process. Hmm, what's coming through is not half-bad. An interesting title for the piece comes to mind. Here goes:

CALL ME TREZ
Musings from the Other Side of the Moon
by Teresa Rose Evans
Tuesday, September 20, 1983

Call me Trez. Some do. The others probably never took this name seriously, although I did ask them to honor what I want to be, rather than what has been. I have long been searching for my place in the field.

My family origin is Germanic, mingled with Celtic blood under the sod from the other side. Evans is not our original surname. My father's father was shuffled from a ship's steerage with throngs of fellow passengers onto Ellis Island in 1898. He clutched a promissory note of employment in the cattle stockyards on Evans Avenue, San Francisco, California. Since harried immigration officers couldn't pronounce his last name, they figured no one else in the U.S. of A. would either. Josef Razgorshek was reborn as Joe Evans, brand new member of Uncle Sam's club.

The Slovenian-born wife he met here in the City bore two sons. One lived. My father Joe. Then, when Joe married, I was his third and final girl. He and my mother saw the leaves change to red in the fall and they named me Teresa Rose Evans. 'Last rose of summer' is what my father called me.

I go on here about what I liked as a child, more stuff about my name, my siblings, and all that. Then in a burst of energy the next line popped out.

I can't seem to find a place for myself in this world. Nothing I try works out. Perhaps it is my family's legacy.

In my generation, the fourth in San Francisco, our family was planted atop sand dunes in the Sunset district, where sun was a rarity. Perhaps salt and fog desiccated our roots. Like branches breaking off a tree in a windstorm, two parents and two siblings have tumbled to the ground, marking those of us left behind as petrified as its wood. We tucked our fallen ones into earth nests, blanketing them with layers of leaves.

Since my parents' deaths left me alone to my own vices at an early age, I can be labeled as passive or aggressive, depending upon who asks, and when.

Family. These days, I don't seem to belong anywhere.

I stop writing and read my story aloud, tracking the words on the word processor's screen. Being a consummate editor, I print out the newest revised copy.

Do I want my therapist to know this much about me? Grabbing a red pencil, I circle a few errors and ponder deleting lines here and there. Too personal, revealing a bit much.

Then again, my gut's telling me this story feels finished. Granted, it's but one of many in my head and yet, it stands alone. Perhaps it is time to take a chance. What the hell.

Without adding any more corrections, I print out a new copy, sign it, and stack the pages into a neat pile on Hannah Harrison's desk. It's not often that I allow my words to take me so far underground.

It's much easier to skim along the surface of life.

CHAPTER 16

A Remote Point of View

I MAKE MY WAY over to the double door entrance, and push down on all of the room's light switches at the master outlet. The entire space turns a moody midnight color softened by one yellowish beam of light, what with the moon casting its presence through the windows.

That's when I spot something out of the corner of my right eye. A shadowy shape most people wouldn't even notice. It moves toward me.

I burst out, "Helice!"

I flip the lights back on. Hmm, she doesn't look the same. Her cheeks are smudged, her clothes are dirty, her saddle shoes are caked with mud.

It's good that we're alone, we have a lot to discuss. And I need my mouth to say what's on my mind.

"Where have you been?" I sound like a typical mother. "What have you been doing?"

With a tantalizing smile, she lifts up her shoulders, letting them linger. Cocking her head, she drops her shoulders back down. Almost as an after-thought, she adds a taunt.

That's for me to know and you to find out.

I feign indifference.

She is quick to appease me. *I was just funning with you. I'm sorry. Maggalena said to make things fun. She said you're too serious. I thought if I made it a game you'd laugh.*

Helice slips her hand into mine. I look down and

169

am filled with a sensation of...what?

I point to a sofa. "C'mon." Once we plop down I ask, "Why are you so dirty all of a sudden?"

Maggalena says we're running out of time. We have to work fast. She says you're kinda...well... Helice's cheeks are reddening. *Um, so anyway, Maggalena told me to hurry you up so we can—*

"Magdalena says I'm kinda *what*?"

Um...you see... The girl tucks her chin down, as if hoping I won't be able to see her all of a sudden.

"Tell me already."

Maggalena says you're kinda dumb.

Despite my sore ribs, I am up and out of that sofa so fast it makes my head spin.

Helice is a pretty good peacemaker for a ten year old. She is quick to admit she might not have understood Magdalena.

I tell her that's a reasonable mistake, so I sit back down.

Helice has more to say. *She's been missing too long.*

"You mean the kidnapped girl? Analeese Loveland?"

Analeese? That's a pretty name. I never heard that name before. Analeese.

"Is she the one you're here to help?"

Helice lifts her chin so she can nod her head.

"So, this has been about Analeese all along?"

Helice puts her head down. *I didn't know her name.*

My voice is rising rapidly. "Why didn't you mention you were talking about a *kidnapped* girl?"

Helice gives me a sweet smile. *She wasn't kidnapped, Trez. She walked away.*

"Walked away? She just left her family and never came back? How would you know that? Helice?"

Maggalena told me.

"When?"

Before it ever happened.

"Before she ever left? How could Magdalena know

that?"

She lifts her shoulders. *I dunno.*

"You came here specifically to help Analeese. She's been missing for five days. Why the hell didn't you let me know?"

In her innocence, Helice's eyes go wide at my evidently stupid question. She nonetheless explains. *You didn't ask.*

I'm clutching every strand of my remaining hair. I'm pulling so tight it makes my eyes pop.

"It's true." Someone from behind me says, "No one kidnapped that little girl. Analeese. She took off on her own."

Springing up from the sofa, I whip around to see where the male voice is coming from. There he is. The ferret-faced Lothario with a penchant for licking unsuspecting women.

"Roman!"

"Hello, Trez. It's nice to see you again."

I bellow, "Nice? Are you kidding me?" My heart is climbing halfway up my throat as I'm wagging a finger at him. "You've been stalking me."

He hangs his head.

With his narrow angular face, long torso and short legs, he really does look like a weasel. All he needs is a furry tail.

Roman is staring at me, waiting for my response.

What I really want to do is charge Roman and wring his scrawny neck. If my stay in Crazy Town has taught me anything, it is to think before I pounce. Besides, it would kill my damaged ribs. After mulling it over while he waits in suspense, my decision is made. I need information. He can stay as long as he proves useful.

His left hand is extended, his fingers splayed, just as he'd done when he snuck into my hospital room. He's so strange he could be capable of anything. My gut tightens.

It doesn't make sense to safeguard a hallucination,

but I nonetheless step in front of the sofa where Helice is sitting. Who knows what this psycho is capable of doing in this world or any other. I spread my feet and square my shoulders in a defensive posture in case he acts up.

I growl, "Tell me what you know."

Roman scratches his head. "The police kept certain facts under wraps. I talked to the Channel Five reporter. Tobey Vallencourt. He found the truth." He stops to scratch again. "It's not a kidnapping. Analeese walked out of her house. She never came back."

My mouth is wide open. My jaw had dropped when the licker started to speak. The licker who hasn't said more than five or ten words to me is suddenly chatty?

Helice is squirming and waving, trying to get my attention. By subtly shifting my eyes her way without moving my head, I see her nodding in agreement. She'd just told me the same thing before he showed up. How would an imaginary Mud Eater character in a made up world possibly know this before it ever happened?

I've got to throw the guy a bone so he gets a curt, "Okay. Tell me the latest."

"The little girl has special physical needs. She uses her disability against other kids. That makes for poor social skills." He drones on, "That morning the mom drove her husband to the train station as usual. Told Analeese she'd be right back to take her to school. There was a traffic jam. The mom got back late and Analeese was gone. She assumed her daughter walked to school so she left for work."

He stops to inhale. "The school called her office, asking where Analeese was. No signs of a break in or struggle at the house. No unidentified footprints in the front or back yards. Tobey says the police need a new strategy. They should recheck the neighborhood. I would like to interview the parents. I'm sure they have more insight than they realize."

"Uh huh." No cop would let this freak near her parents. In fact, I can't believe he really spoke with that reporter.

Roman has been fiddling with his hands the entire time but now, he extends his left one. Fanning five fingers, he walks around the area acting like he's measuring radioactivity. He soon zeroes in on the sofa. He points out exactly where Helice is sitting.

My imaginary character is grinning like the whistle blower she is.

Roman exhales. He's got all ten of his fingers in knots again. No reason to be surprised at this, considering where he and I are currently residing. Since he's no longer revealing pertinent information about the case, I decide to gather up my young character and exit the art room.

But Roman has more to say. "You've been a suspect. That's why you stayed. Different than a typical 5150, right? After your brain surgery."

"How do you know that?"

"Tobey Vallencourt. He's been researching you."

My hands clench. "What are you talking about?"

"Ah, ah," Roman stutters, "h-he's done several reports on how you were caught burning your manuscript along with children's clothes and toys. He cited a teacher of yours who said you seemed suspicious the last time she saw—"

"Bethany Moraga, is that who it was? Damn it. I'm gonna kill that bitch."

"Ah...uh." Roman's eyes widen. "I don't think you should say that in a mental health facility, if you know what I mean."

"Oh. Yeah. That makes sense. Hey, how'd you start talking to that guy? Tobey?"

"He comes here a lot. Most days since you were admitted. They won't let him in. He stays outside, tries to talk to people who might know you."

Roman pauses to scratch his head. "He suspects you're hiding out here."

"Oh he does, does he?" It creeps me out that the press is onto me.

Roman speaks faster, "The police don't have much on you now. You can leave here. This facility, I'm pretty sure, a lot sooner. But I'm wondering if...if..."

Now I'm the one worrying my hands, gesturing with my chin for this weirdo to get to his point.

"Sooo?" I wait. "What do you want, Roman?" He doesn't answer. "Not talking? Bye-bye."

Turning on my heel, I send a thought message to Helice that we're leaving. What'd she say? Oh, that little rascal. She won't move from her spot on the couch.

Roman calls after me, "You've been focused on someone. A young female, I'm pretty sure she's prepubescent. She's not *here* if you know what I mean."

Although Helice is grinning and clapping, I rush him. I tower over the guy, yelling, "You don't *know* shit. You licked me for chrissakes, you God damn pervert." I embellish my sentiments with choice f-word cussing.

Helice's eyes bug out. Her hands fly up to cover her ears.

Damn it. I really shouldn't swear around her.

Roman hangs his head. With his shoulders drooping, his body compacts until he's as short as ten-year-old Helice.

"I'm sorry," he wails. "I'm sorry."

"You should be mortified," I hiss. "Do you have any idea how it felt to be licked? I was strapped down on a gurney, completely vulnerable. It made me feel like a total victim. You understand that, right? Roman? Do you?"

Grabbing him by his neck, I swing him around with one hand he's such a lightweight. It hurts my ribs, though.

He'll rue the day he messed with Trez Evans. Hah, he looks ready to pee his pants. Trouble is, my chest feels ready to burst. I release my hold. He gets far away from me.

Hmm. The first time we met, he wore a hospital issued two-piece uniform like all the patients in this place. It was blue, signifying a voluntary stay. Come to think of it, I haven't seen Roman around lately, even though I have hunted down the entire area searching for my dreamboat boyfriend-in-the-making, New Man.

Tonight Roman is wearing neatly pressed khaki pants, a white knit polo shirt (rumpled now, thanks to me), and brown loafers. The loony bin doesn't allow belts. His braided belt is tan, with a black beeper case on his hip.

I decide to give Roman one more chance. "What the hell is going on with you?"

First, he scratches his head. He clears his throat. "My name is Dr. Roman Gillespie. I'm a..." He takes a breath. "I'm a neuroscientist with the Institute for Psychic Understanding."

"What? Are you kidding me? No way, you're a patient here. You bribed Virgil so you could lick me, you little creep."

"No, never," he fidgets. "Virgil's by the book, he wouldn't allow it."

I am on a roll. "No way you're a doctor of anything. Freaking liar."

"It's true," he says. "Actually, I'm the Institute's director.

I burst out laughing. "Yeah, and I'm the Queen of Sheba."

He looks so pained I say, "Okay, let's explore *your* fantasy, *Doctor* Gillespie. You target innocent, drugged-out women like me who can't fight back?"

"I'm so sorry. What I did was unconscionable. I was in the middle of a psychotic break. I love my work but..." He gives me a sheepish shrug. "It's awfully stressful."

I don't make a move towards him so he goes on. "We'd been working on an experimental drug. When it came time for a clinical trial, I took the first dose." He offers a wan smile. "I ended up here. As a patient."

My eyes narrow. "How many women have you licked?"

"None." Roman's face turns an odd, dusky beet color but his discomfort won't deter me. "What happened to you was an...an isolated incident."

I dig deeper, "Unless you go haywire again?"

"I admit it wasn't the first time I've ended up here. With my particular brain chemistry, I've always walked a narrow line between compos mentis and...the great beyond. It's why I became a neuroscientist. I specialize in parapsychology."

"Para?" Rolling my good eye, I let out a groan. "That's great. A new age witch doctor."

Roman smiles. "I'm used to being teased. By the way, 'new age' is an eons old human potential movement. Anyway, whenever I need to take mental health breaks I come here. I'm familiar with the therapies they offer. The staff has come to know me."

"And that's how you bribed Virgil?"

"I never did that! Only the director is aware of my connections to IPU, it's what we call the company. Confidentiality reasons. All the staff knows is that I'm a schzoid personality with a dissociative disorder who goes off my block once in a while." His smile indicates embarrassment, but his eyes light up. "But I'm good at what I do, so they...well, humor me, I suppose."

Helice gets off the couch to come stand by us. Is it for my moral support, or is she afraid I'll beat him up some more?

I must be scowling, for Roman nervously adds, "I was in no shape to talk to anyone that day. I was in such a stupor. But here's the thing. I sensed your presence. I was drawn to you as soon as you were admitted."

I can't let him off that easily so I snipe, "'Drawn to me?' You just wanted to start licking."

"Fair enough," Roman replies. "But hear me out. The drug I was telling you about affected me in a way I never expected. It made me absolutely psychotic, the most I've ever been. It also opened me to psychical insights I never thought possible, and—"

"Give me a break."

He continues, "I understand. I really do. Above all else, I am a scientist."

I press him, "What's the bottom line?"

"Ah, all r-r-right," he stammers, "here it is. I wasn't trying to lick you. Uh, well, yes, I did run my tongue along your face. But, but, it wasn't for sexual gratification. I was sensing you, digesting your story."

I'm practically doubling over in laughter at the absurdity. Then it dawns on me. "Hey wait a minute. You said the staff respects your confidentiality. What about mine? Who gave you the right to read my file?"

"Don't worry. All of your records are off-limits." He goes on, "I know nothing about you. Your inner story is what drew me."

Helice is jumping up and down to get my attention. Ignoring her, I present my argument to Roman with the flair of an actress playing to a rapt audience. "How the hell would you know about my writing, *Doctor*? You must have heard me complaining about being dragged to this place just because I burned my manuscript."

"No. Well, yes, I did hear you. Everyone did. But it's deeper than that. I felt an intense vibrancy around you. I could sense you had a story to tell, it was practically oozing out of you. I believe in that exact moment, you and I were actively engaging the entanglement theory."

"Huh, what?"

"Quantum entanglement. The correlations between two particles that interact and then separate. When we came together in Dr. Lively's exam room, it was...it was..." He's clearly hunting for the right way to explain it. "It was like setting off a bomb."

My expression must be vivid since he adds, "A good bomb. People who fall instantly in love talk about the jolt they feel, the instant connection between two people. That jolt helped me to sense the energy, the 'pulse' of your story."

"So you're saying we're soul mates? What a load of crap."

He puts his hands together as if in prayer. "Please, listen. This 'entanglement' happened before I heard you talking about your manuscript. That's why I had to investigate. Eavesdropping is rude but it validated what I'd sensed about you. I had to get closer, even if it meant getting into trouble."

He scratches at his hairline. "I was in no shape that day. But I couldn't lose such a unique opportunity. I used psychotronics, the study of electromagnetic energy fields. I wasn't in my lab, obviously, so I went a little primal. I had to resort to my animal senses."

He stops to inhale, then he lets it out with a big huff. "I needed to taste you, as the author, to get to your core."

I exclaim, "Taste me? TASTE ME? Yet *I'm* the one who's stuck in the nut house? We're done here." I move towards the door even though Helice shakes her head.

Helice and Roman both follow behind. He calls out, "I'm a voluntary patient here." I turn to see him smoothing his collar. "I just got back from the Institute. That's the agreement I have with this facility. I taught a two day symposium and then I returned here."

He's prattling on, "Even without my equipment, I could tell your brain syntaxes were operating full force. They were magnificent." Roman gets a dreamy look on his face. "I picked up on your energy because ours are entirely compatible. So much so, they drew me to you like a magnet. That's entanglement." He looks at me. "In all my years I've never felt such an intense connection."

Jeez. If this is the geeky scientist's best pick up line, his lineage is sure to go extinct.

He eagerly adds, "The use of biofeedback machines can train subjects to have voluntary control over their psychological and bodily functions. We've worked with Viet Nam vets on their post-traumatic stress."

He's just getting started. "But you, oh, you don't need machines. You're a natural, Trez. A true phenomenon."

This science stuff makes sense to me in a weird way, but he doesn't need to know that. I have an attitude to uphold.

I sniff, "Maybe all this science mumbo jumbo is just

a convenient excuse for you to be a peeping—I mean a 'licking'— Tom.'"

It pleases me that he seems so uncomfortable. I'm about to dig into him again when Helice tells me I'm being mean.

I twist her way to snap, "No, I'm not."

Shoot, that was supposed to be a nonverbal retort. Now Roman is on high alert. It's damn near impossible to have a fight with a hallucination while attempting to act nonchalant.

Roman looks to be tracking my every move while I argue with Helice. It's impossible not to look Helice in the imaginary eye while informing her that I am the adult. I want to physically throw the darn kid over my knee and spank her.

Roman announces, "You're definitely communicating with a female. I can feel her."

Oh, hell no. Roman is not going to 'connect' with either Helice or me. Time to kick this weasel to the curb.

But Helice steps right in front of me. Her face flushes as she tells me to "evaluate" if he can help find Analeese.

That's a pretty big word for a ten year old. Is Magdalena orchestrating this? I act casual while looking around the room for the Mud Eater's presence. I open my heart, inviting her to align with me. I mentally implore my favorite character to clarify the situation.

What I get instead is a fictional ten year old's idiosyncratic point of view: *Maggalena told me to let you figure things out but you're too slow and cranky.*

I burst out, "I am *not* cranky."

Helice continues her mental blast. *Maggalena gave me permission to take charge if I had to. I babysit my sisters and brothers. Karl Junior is a bully but I know how to get him to do what I want.*

Helice positions herself close to Roman and tugs on his pants leg. By his shocked expression he must feel it. He leans over and looks her way. Now that Helice has his attention, she shouts at him. *Roman, you need to help Trez!*

Roman tilts his head. Oh, there he goes again. He's got his left hand raised, fanning his fingers like a metal detector all around the area where she is standing.

He mumbles, "Yes, I need to help."

I snap, "Help what?"

He turns and says to me, "I can help you find Analeese Loveland."

CHAPTER 17

For Better or for Worse

Day 6 —

IT'S ALMOST MORNING but I have not slept at all thanks to my roommate's perpetual snoring. She's the human equivalent of a sawmill what with the buzzing and rasping, whirring, snorting and grrring sounds coming out of her. After lying awake in a lumpy bed, it's a relief to spring to my feet when the 7:00 wakeup call blares over the PA system. I turn to see Helice grinning at me.

My roommate does not stir. Leaving Helice to her own devices, I make it to the cafeteria with one minute to spare. The lady in charge checks my ID bracelet and hands me a tray. A server behind a glass divider dishes me a plate of bright yellow scrambled eggs that have turned to rubber under the buffet warming lights. No sense choking down the coffee, it's decaf.

Despite my vigilant neck-twisting surveillance of the cafeteria, there is no sign of my soon to be lover New Man. My heart sinks, my breath expels. Where could he be? Maybe he comes one or two days a week. What day did we first lay eyes on one another? Our kismet day. It's hard to keep track of time and people in this upside-down land of cuckoos.

There are only a few moments before my kitchen work shift begins. As luck would have it, Dr. Watson happens to pass by the nurses' station while I'm begging for an immediate appointment. His clinic hours don't begin until 9:00 but he must hear the urgency in my voice. He motions me into his office and closes the door behind us.

"What can I do for you, Trez?" No time for banal pleasantries this morning. In order for my Mission to Nab New Man to be executed, I need to look my best.

I blurt, "Doctor, please, can you remove this bag off my head? Like right now?"

"You seem agitated. And your eye looks swollen. Have you been crying?"

"God, no, crying is for wimps." My forehead wrinkles, a moist snort escapes my nostrils at the notion. But then I catch his expression. "Ah, what I mean to say, I've got a snoring roommate. This one is so heavily medicated, it's a wonder her snoring hasn't woken up the entire section."

He chuckles, "That's no fun, is it?" He seems to have forgotten he busted me for faking my aphasia, thank goodness. He reaches into a lower desk drawer and pulls out a couple packages of earplugs. My exasperated expression induces him to add, "Oh. So, what else is on your mind?"

I lean forward to emphasize my plea. "I'm trying to make a new start, form some friendships." This is so not true but he doesn't need to know that.

I continue with a brave timbre to my voice, "I wouldn't want to hang out with someone like me. Seriously, it's hard to overlook a disgusting drainage bag taped to my head." I sigh. "A bag that's filled with sludge from a brain surgery. Not to mention an eye patch." I fake a laugh. "I'm not a pirate, matie."

After thinking it over, he removes the bandage over my right eye. My vision is still a bit blurry. The light is bright, it makes me blink but this feels so much better. He gets out his exam tool thing to peer into my eye. He's so close I sniff out the coffee on his breath. It makes me want to swoon it smells so good but I must contain myself.

He takes a step back and tells me, "I think we can keep the bandage off. Your vision is readjusting, that's why it's still blurry. Let me know if it gets itchy or watery, or you develop eye strain." He walks back to his desk and riffles through some paperwork. Is he trying to tell me our visit is over?

"Dr. Watson. What about this stupid bag on my head?"

He tries to justify my serious surgery and post-op circumstances, but I persist, "Seriously, it's affecting my self-esteem so much, I want to..."

He isn't looking convinced, so it's time to give him some of the shrink lingo I've learned.

Offering a winsome smile I say, "I, ah, feel like isolating myself rather than facing my challenges. It's hindering my ability to forgive myself for my actions and to move forward. Every day I wake up and have to deal with *this*."

For emphasis, I yank at the bag. It hurts more than expected but considering his hands are raising up in alarm, it's making an impact on the surgeon who planted it there.

He pauses to think it over, and my instinct is to stay low and quiet. After a few moments he says, "It really should stay in place at least another week, or even two."

My scowl makes him reconsider.

"Well, I have to say, you came in here with such a high alcohol toxicity we assumed you'd go through the DTs. We had added concerns with the morphine and other post-op medications we gave you. Other than a couple of seizures that we'd expected, you have done remarkably well."

I can't help but smile. The alcohol and drugs helped me reconnect with Helice. It hasn't been the same since they weaned me off the big guns stuff, darn it.

He says, "I have to warn you, without the tube you'll feel more pain and pressure from fluid buildup in your skull. I've kept you on anticonvulsant meds as a precaution. He scratches his chin. "Well, I have to say, you've proven you don't have an addictive personality."

The good doctor is correct. After living through the 60s and 70s—oh, hell—all of my decades of "self-exploration," the only substance I crave is the highest caliber chocolate.

He gives me a compassionate wink. "Let's agree to try this. I'll remove the drainage system later today. But, if there are any complications at all, I'll reinstall it so fast you won't know what hit you. Agreed?"

My impulse is to kiss him I'm so happy but it might not go over well. He could file an "unseemly sexuality" report, which could screw up my eventual release from Crazy Town.

So, instead, I start grinning and nodding like a fool.

JACKSON CATCHES ME coming out of the office. "They said you might be here," he says. He puts a hand on my shoulder and leads me down a hall. "Come on. We need to talk."

This could be good. It could be bad. It's hard to tell with my poker-faced lawyer. He directs me into a consult room that is so sparsely furnished it's depressing.

He shuts the door. He comes right to the point, "Analeese Loveland wasn't kidnapped. She—"

"Walked out of her house and vanished. That means this case shouldn't be considered a kidnapping." I give him a slight victory smile.

He's looking perplexed, not a typical expression for him. "I just found out," he mutters. "How would you know that?"

"Oh. Um, word gets around. Can I go home now?"

He stares me down with an intensity that could wilt an orchid. "First off," he briskly informs me, "until that child returns home unharmed the cops will continue to have a list of suspects. There's no telling if she was influenced by someone to run away. Someone like *you*."

He reacts to my rapid succession of protests. "Hold

on, Trez. You're not going anywhere. You are still top dog on that list. The cops would love to nail you, by the way. Officer O'Doul is still on sick leave. You gave him a heart attack. And someone in this facility has a broken hip, another has a broken nose. All because of you." I am stunned to silence. In his best three-piece-suit voice, he whispers, "Cops never forget."

I watch the hairs on my arms snap to attention.

He fills me in on some facts the police had not released. "Analeese has an above average IQ but she's enrolled in Special Needs classes. Her leg was mangled when she was hit by a car about four years ago. She limps and needs a cane."

I say, "That could explain her lack of social skills."

Jackson nods, "She's a total outcast, not so much for her disability, but her attitude is awful. If she thinks kids are laughing at her she'll swing her cane and try to whack them."

I'm thinking good for her but it's best not to advocate violence in a nut house.

Jackson continues, "Her nose is always in a book. Nonfiction mostly. Her main focus is on nature, and how natives live off the land. I'm told she memorizes entire passages of how-to-books. When she does interact with kids, she tends to lecture."

"Yeah, they probably can't relate to her."

"That's why she dropped out of the Girl Scouts." He picks at a cracked cuticle before continuing. "She thought she knew more than the troop leader. Too bad, too, they all said she has a real command of nature studies."

For some reason, I feel the need to take in a breath. It calms me. I take another, close my eyes, and open myself to possibilities. Hmm, he's not telling me everything. I take a third breath. That's when I "see" a fort hidden in some bushes where there are books and a flashlight, water, and tins of crackers. "Jackson, what else did the police find at her house? I mean, did she have a secret place set up?"

He flashes me another look. "Turns out she fashioned an elaborate hiding place in the backyard. Her parents hadn't noticed anything until the cops pointed it out to them."

My stomach practically flips over. I've never felt this attuned to what Phin calls an "inner guidance system."

Jackson goes on, "Teachers say she's pretty well behaved, but she's had various "flights of fantasy" where she seems pretty out of it. She sees a psychiatric counselor regularly."

He checks out his now perfect cuticle. His nail care completed, Jackson says, "Speaking of flights of fantasy, Trez." He opens his brief case, thumbing through papers until he finds what he wants. "Here they are."

He holds up several sheets of yellow legal lined paper filled with chicken scratch. "My notes. After you told me about your book character, I spoke to Ross and Phin. They've been filling me in on what they claim is an alternate method to find the missing kid." He shakes his head. "Phineas I could understand. He's a nutter from way back. But your brother? Oh well, maybe he's so lovesick he can't think straight."

"What?" Gossip perks me up. "Tell me everything." He hesitates. I add a caveat he'd never refuse, "You can even bill me I'm so starved for news. So, Ross is in love?"

Grinning like a friend instead of my by-the-quarter-hour-lawyer, Jackson leans forward with his elbows on the scratched wooden table.

"Hell yeah, he's in love big time. I've hardly ever seen Ross like this." Pausing, he adds, "Cheryl's a nice girl."

Hmm, his expression says otherwise. "Out with it, Jackson. What's wrong?"

"You know Ross. He sabotages all his relationships, no matter how great the girls are."

"Of course he does," I laugh. "I'm surprised Cheryl's lasted so long. Must be her guns."

He smiles. "Yeah, probably."

Judging by the change coming over him, our gossip fest is over. He sighs. "All this *Helice* nonsense. Do you know how crazy it sounds? Ross is halfway convinced it's true. He's been hanging out with Phin, though. I suspect McCool's infected his mind. But I have to ask. Do you honestly believe your fictional character is speaking to you?"

"Hold on to your hat, Johnny. This has gotten a whole lot more complicated." Jackson grimaces at my use of his former name, but doesn't comment.

First off, I tell him not to count Phin out. "There's more to Phin than you realize." My throat catches. "He's a real sweetheart." Then, I describe meeting Dr. Roman Gillespie, how he's convinced my brain synapses perfectly correlate with his own. "He even communicated directly with Helice."

That's when Jackson bursts out laughing. "What a load of crap. This guy takes the cake. And of course, you believed him. God, you are so gullible."

"Oh, yeah? Then how come Helice knew Analeese wasn't kidnapped *before* Roman told me?"

"Huh," he stalls. "Not sure why." He runs a hand through his hair, mumbling, "That's pretty damn amazing." Then the left-brained Jackson Milan takes over. "Don't you get it? Helice is *you*. Your unconscious, or, subconscious mind, however it works. You must have heard it somewhere—I don't know how—I just heard it myself. But Helice Polansky's *you*. You've been talking to yourself, that's all."

His superb logic makes me feel stupid. It's true. I am too trusting by nature. Roman took advantage of my kindness. It's his title. Doctor. Yeah, he has an advanced degree, all right. A Doctor of BS.

His work done, Jackson prepares to pack it up. "Don't worry, Trez. Everything you say is confidential. No one will hear about it."

He looks around the drab room with its mismatched institutional furniture. "It's this place. I'd probably go a little crackers myself."

"So please, get me out of here."

"No can do. Things could turn on a dime. I can't risk your name coming up again. Even though it's all circumstantial, they'd drag your ass to jail for sure."

He points to my head before lowering his gaze. "Stay here, recuperate. Hey, that's another reason you're not thinking right. You had freaking brain surgery. Don't think I won't pull the brain damage card."

Jackson stands, and sneaks another peek at me before turning away. "By the way. Go to the nurses station and get some alcohol wipes. You've got adhesive tape marks over half your face. Makes you look like one of those cartoon pit bulls with a ring around its eye."

"Sure thing," I tell him. "See you later."

He stops to give me another one of his professional lawyer looks. He seems suspicious and looks ready to say something, but then he checks his watch. He mutters, "Damn. Got to go. Don't get into any trouble. You hear me?"

After he leaves, I make a beeline for the public payphone. We're allowed one five minute call per day. I've never used it, and don't care when others yell at me for hogging the phone.

There's important business to discuss with Marciano. Jackson laughed Roman off as a quack, but the rookie might want to interview him, get his professional take on this case. And for godsakes, what if Roman himself is a suspect?

Marciano brushes off my offer to help, even after I gush that my brain pouch will be removed. He's probably choking up; it must be why he hangs up so fast. No guy wants to be reminded that his girlfriend is brain damaged.

SO, THE DRAINAGE TUBE and its bag has been removed. Dr. Watson will pull out the staples in about a week and he just put in a couple of stitches where the tube was removed. Blue thread. Metal staples. Old bruises. Young scars. Oh, I'm a cutie all right. Now the headaches are back.

Aside from a fading tricolored bruise that runs across my blurry right eye, down my still swollen nose and along my cheek that's a result from my run in with a wall, I'm still having trouble with double vision.

What's worse, Helice has turned into a never-ending hallucination. She never fades away. What's even worse, my visual perception of her has doubled! That's the worst of all—watching *two* ten year olds cartwheeling at the same time makes me want to throw up.

It might be a side-effect from new medications, but I've decided not to mention it to my surgeon or the staff. Reason being, the meds give me lots of energy.

However, now the brain gunk is squeezing out of my facial pores like white head zits. Dr. Watson warned me of this, but I, the eternal optimist, chose to trade the tube and pouch set-up for a real face. And if I get pimples like an acne-prone teenager, I'll pop the brain sludge out of them and tell myself that I'm that much closer to a new life with the dreamboat I've designated as my fiancé.

Speaking of my soon-to-be husband, he is nowhere to be found. I've looked everywhere for him. Rather than ask around, it's best not to publicize my intentions with New Man prematurely. This place is infested with gossips.

Some hussy could try to steal him away.

NURSE HARBINE CATCHES UP with me in the general area. "Trez, here you are." She's breathless. Come with me."

I give her a questioning look but it's best not to say anything that could bite me in the ass later. I've learned a new set of skills in this land of the loonies.

She leads me to Hannah Harrison's office. "No, you must have the wrong patient. I've already had my personal therapy for the day." Harbine opens the door.

I exclaim, "Ross? What are you doing here?" The nurse then closes the door behind her. I stress to the therapist, "But I'm only supposed to have one private session a day with you and—." Harrison cuts me off.

"Don't you remember I'd specified several sessions with your brother?" Damn. Her agreement to transfer me out of the locked ward included Ross in my therapy to get to the bottom of my "family of origin issues." I was so desperate to escape the crazies, I would have agreed to anything. I ask him, "Did you have to come back early from your vacation for this?" He nods curtly.

Uh oh, something doesn't feel right. Ross would never give up one second of his trip away with Cheryl, the gun toting security guard. Unless he had to.

She gets us down to business pretty quick. We are supposed to each take a turn and talk (prompted by the therapist's questions) until the timer goes off. I make sure to schedule my twenty minutes at the beginning of this session. Not only will I get it over with, I figure Hannah Harrison will be fresher and more likely to pay attention. Besides, I feel a killer migraine on my horizon

After a few minutes into my turn, she says to me, "You're speaking so much better now. It must be a big relief to be able to communicate again."

Oh, crap. I could have faked aphasia just now.

We never have much to discuss other than my typical young adult's concerns: where to find a great guy and then, of course, how to make him adore me; or ways to defeat whacked-out women in control like Bethany Moraga.

There's nothing bizarre in my history to delve into, except in her mind, marrying a man older than my father, my disastrous second marriage, and then my almost third. That means she has to stir up some family shit now that Ross is here.

She has the nerve to ask me my age, and doesn't

react in shock when I tell her thirty-three. Hmm, she must have my birth date right in front of her. She's probably doing this just to insult me. Doesn't she know everyone insists I don't look one minute older than twenty-five?

"Hell," I tell her, "Ross is five years younger and I think he looks more like thirty-five."

Ross cracks up at that dig, but she doesn't. Then she has the nerve to compare my physical age versus my "emotional maturity." That's a double insult. The hell with her, she'll never hear any juicy details about my fantastic voyages into the world of men.

She wisely moves on to Ross' turn.

I'm spending most of his time gazing out the window at the tops of trees and the bay beyond. The trees remind me that Analeese is probably somewhere deep in a forest. How the hell is anyone going to find her? Oh, crap. Hannah is looking at me, I should pay attention to Ross in case she asks me any questions. By the way, my younger brother has an entirely different spin on our family life.

He sniffles, "I was a head taller than other boys in my class." He swallows hard. "Everyone assumed I was older. They expected me to be more mature. It caused problems people wouldn't realize."

He's forgetting the upsides of his early development, such as when a cheerleader took Ross to her senior prom. He was a freshman. His friends had a shit fit, they were so jealous.

We writers know a strong story depends upon presenting a character's point of view. POV as we call it. Ross clearly has his side. I'm just not interested in hearing all about it when I should be figuring how to find Analeese. His lamentations sound like "Blah, blah, blah" to me.

Stifling a yawn, I check out Hannah's shoes. They go perfectly with her royal blue jacket, but I've learned not to compliment a therapist on her latest fashions. Therapists consider that "inappropriate." Gawd, they are so boring.

Hannah still doesn't look interested in my brother's story. Neither does Helice. She's catnapping on a plush area rug near Hannah's desk. Being a hallucination, Helice is usually more animated, constantly gyrating or nailing her perfect cartwheels.

Anyways, back to Ross' whine-fest therapy session.

I suddenly have a love for Helice I've never felt before. It's so deep it's palpable. She's awake and nodding, as if she can read my mind. As if? Of course, she knows my thoughts.

Oh, crap. It looks like Hannah is on full alert. I divert my eyes from where Helice is now standing, although not quickly enough. The therapist scans the area. Helice dives back down on the floor—as though that would solve anything.

"What's going on, Trez?" Hannah gets up from her desk and moves to the area rug. The therapist edges so close she would probably knock her over, if Helice were a real girl.

"I, um...aw crap." I start blubbering. Hannah's asking what's wrong. I shrug my shoulders. "It's...it's that a girl is missing and I feel guilty that I can't find her," I say between hiccups. "I keep thinking I could find her if I did that remote viewing thing, but just as I get a glimpse of where she might be, I go blank."

Ross leans forward, obviously wanting to be engaged in this new conversation.

So, Hannah the top banana says, "Do you think you had anything to do with her disappearance?" Then she blinks like Betty Boop.

This is so unfair. I want to throw things at her. I start to cry again, which probably is convincing her that I did it.

"No, of course not," I manage to answer. Vivid images flood my mind. "The Red Eden," I mutter. "That might be where Analeese is."

Ross is quick to ask, "So, the Red Eden is a real place or what?"

I don't answer.

Ross thinks a minute. "As I understand, you created it as Helice's other world so she could escape being paralyzed in an iron lung."

Hannah is all over this. "He-lice? Is that one of your characters?"

I have to respond. "Yeah, you could say that."

Ross the idiot goes on talking as if he hasn't just detonated a bomb. "I gotta say, you described a place I used to know in perfect detail. It can't be a coincidence. You were there with me. We explored it one summer when we were kids."

"W-what?" It feels like he just kicked me in the chest. "Wait. Why, how would you know?"

"Phin gave me his copy of your manuscript. I've been going over the most recent version."

I carp, "First off, he had no right to give you that."

Ross twists his mouth, hunches one shoulder. "I found a lot of correlations, like the red soil."

My eyes narrow. "C'mon, Ross, don't be so literal. My other world was based on research: the Old Testament, Dante's Inferno, the Torah, things like that. I took the best parts from a bunch of accounts, that's all."

He prompts, "And Magdalena eats mud because...?"

He can't know my story without reading every bit of every version. It's best to give him a generic answer. "I was fascinated with the ancient tale of the Adamah, a female Adam formed out of red clay. The Red Eden, get it?"

Ross folds his arms as if he's just won the debate. "Yes, but *why* does she eat it? Focus on the mud. It's got to be an important clue. No one eats mud. So why does she?"

Hannah is blinking like she has an eye disorder. The only sound is the ticking clock on her desk. Tick-fricking-tock. As soon as I think about my story, Helice perks up. She points to the noisy windup clock. *Time is running out for that girl.*

193

"Trez?" It's Ross again. "Why does Magdalena eat mud?"

"Goddamnit. I don't know why!"

I hear Hannah's saccharine voice. "Does this have something to do with the disappearance of that little girl?"

After bursting into tears, I need a short break. How embarrassing is that. An alpha female does not show weakness in front of its pack. Now we're back to therapy.

I'm gulping in bunches of air to get through this session.

"Trez," Hannah says with her sweet girl persona. "Let's get back to that character who eats mud. Let's figure out the relationship between her and your other character. He-lice, is it?" She mutters, "Unusual name. Anyway, let's work on why this upsets you so much."

"Yeah," my brother replies. "I have questions."

Damn. Ross is tearing into me like a mosquito that just found an arm.

Here he goes. "You said you don't know why Magdalena eats mud, but I think I can give you some answers. Hopefully that will help."

"Oh, really? You know my story after one short read?"

"I recognized the location you described. Don't you remember?" He turns to Hannah. "Every year at our dad's work, there were picnics for employees and their families. That's when we met one of his friends. He, I think his name was Mike, had a couple of acres in an unincorporated area down here on the Peninsula. He kept two horses."

He goes on, "Once Trez found out, she begged to go there, she was crazy about horses. Mike invited her to come down and spend a few days. Mom didn't like the idea. He was a nice guy but he was a bachelor. Mom said it wouldn't look right. Dad had to agree."

He smiles at the memory. "Trez wouldn't stop bugging them. It was all about the horses. Dad gave in.

He decided to help Mike repair his deck and took me along to help. But really, Dad told me to watch out for Trez." His eyes glint as he quips to Hannah, "She's always been a handful, heh, heh."

My brother leans back, folds his hands behind his head. "I played my role well, a chaperone for my older sister. Never let her out of my sight." He grins like an egg eating dog.

"Trez? How do you feel about your brother's memory

Helice is urging me to remember. Remember what? Oh. My. God. The bohemian!

CHAPTER 18

Turning Point

Day 7 —

I'M STARVING HERE in the cafeteria, poking a fork at "meat loaf" with mashed potatoes. The lumpy mash is concocted from white flakes mixed with water. I can't tell what the loaf is. It sure as hell isn't meat. The server had dished me a double dose of gravy, despite my protest, so my slice of white bread slathered with margarine is floating like a boat. It's one more reason I want to leave this dump.

When I entered the cafeteria, Phin was there as usual waiting for me. Such a loyal guy, he's come every day since they transferred me to the voluntary population. Then Ross showed up with Jackson. The first thing out of my mouth when I saw Ross was if we had another family session. He and Milan had given one another a weird look, never a good sign. Then Ross said, "Can't I visit my sister without a reason?"

My immediate thought was hell no, but I decided to take the higher road so my brother got a hug instead.

As soon as Ross throws down his fork with a frown, Phin nibbles from Ross' plate. I snap, "For chrissakes, Phin. You're not a dog. Go back in line and get a second helping."

Ross is quick to point out, "You're super bitchy today."

196

I stick out my tongue *and* flip him the finger.

He retorts, "Oh, that's real mature."

Truth is, I am pissy. Marciano finally got back to me after my many phone messages. He brushed me off, even though I told him I knew things no one else did, which is kind of bullshit but also kind of true. Apparently, the police don't feel like playing ball.

I gasp, "There he is." My heart flutters as I push my chair back and stand on my tiptoes. My gaze upon my New Man must be so intense it prompts Ross and Phin to follow it.

"Uh, Trez?" Ross looks pained. "Ah, what's happening?"

"Are you talking about *him?*" Phin points at the orange-vested man.

New Man is walking through the cafeteria with a straight-ahead gaze and his arms flat against his thighs.

I tell him, "Yes, if you must know. Isn't he gorgeous? He looks just like a young Paul Newman."

Phin lets out a low whistle. "Man oh man. You sure got it wrong this time." He must be jealous so I ignore his protests.

Ross is not nearly as subtle, nor kind. "That guy there? In the orange vest? For crying out loud. Are you that horny you'd go for a retard? This is a new low, even for you, Trez."

My love-struck eyes flash with rage. "How dare you!"

Ross shrugs. "Heh, heh, just look at him. You're a fool if you can't tell he's a retard."

"Knock it off, Ross," hisses Phin. "That word is offensive. The orange vest means he belongs to an autistic men's group. They're outpatients who come here for special services. They don't get down to the cafeteria very often."

Helice comes to me, her eyes wide with misgiving. *Trez? What's happening?* What with my double vision, I'm seeing two of her. They're both pointing judgmental fingers at me. I sigh. She's just a kid, she has no concept of sexual attraction.

I return my attention to my true love. New Man autistic? No way. I get up from the table and march over to the sandy-haired man. Emboldened by my brother's insult, I flutter my eyelashes and use my best come on voice.

"Hi, my name is Trez. Trez Evans."

He immediately diverts his turquoise eyes down to his immaculate white sneakers. Both of his shoelaces are untied. New Man rocks back and forth while making soft, whirring noises with his wet, perfectly formed movie star lips. I notice the skin around his mouth is red and chapped.

His shoulders stiffen when I break down crying.

It's not my fault scores of people are gawking at us. But I refuse to hold back my grief over being widowed before New Man and I could ever wed. Obviously he's still alive, but since our love can never be, our future together is dead. Society can be so cruel when one is deemed *different*.

My brother and lawyer turn their seats away, pretending not to know me. Phin rushes to where I've been left standing in the middle of the cafeteria. Welcoming his kindness, I bury my head into his fold. He is a genuine sweetheart.

Although, I feel compelled to look up, as if sensing a faraway heat source missile in the midst of an ice storm.

Be still my heart. Officer Ron Marciano has shown up and he looks dashing in his police blues. I've been crying so hard my eyes are red and swollen. It is the worst time for him to show up.

Yet, he's coming towards me. Rubbing my runny nose along Phin's T-shirt, I step forward. I wipe away my tears and put on my best Trez Evans smile to greet my beefcake rookie.

A gasp escapes me when Marciano gets so close his arm brushes mine. "Hi, Ms. Evans."

I detect a flirty undertone but he's in uniform so we have to be cool. "Please, Officer, I told you to call me

Trez."

His soulful brown eyes penetrate me as he says, "What's wrong, are you okay?"

Phin starts in, "She's been crying over some guy and—" I stomp on his sandaled foot. Phin yelps, "Ow!"

I glare at Phin before saying, "It's this place, Ron. I can call you Ron, right? It's really getting to me." My lips form a convincing pout. "Can you pull some strings, get me out?"

His perfectly sculpted body tenses. "Err, no, I'm not here for that. I need to ask you more questions about September 21st, the day Analeese Loveland disappeared. I'm worried about her. Aren't you, *Trez*?"

My lawyer has come over, my brother too. Jackson leads us back to our table in a quiet corner, then says, "What's the problem? My client has already fully cooperated."

Marciano the lover boy turns into a steely cop. "Perhaps not, Mr. Milan. An eye witness can place Trez Evans in her vehicle at a Woodside gas station at approximately 7:35 a.m."

Cocking his head, Jackson goes into his lawyer mode, showing his palms, acting breezy. "So what, she needed gas."

It seems Marciano is no pushover. I'll have to remember that when we bed for the first time. He pounds on. "Ms. Evans, you have two vehicles, is that correct?"

"I own four cars. Or, actually, it's three cars and a truck."

"Duly noted. We have you on record stating you drove a black 1981 Jeep Wrangler hard top with tinted windows to the hardware store in Woodside two different times that morning, roughly between 6:35 to 7:20."

"Yeah, so?"

"Do you also own an orange 1958 MGA sports car?"

"Uh huh."

"Our source identified the MGA as the car at the gas

station and that the person in question, Trez Evans, stayed in the vehicle. Her male companion pumped the gas."

I glance at Ross, who is chewing on his cheek.

Jackson is about to object but Marciano isn't finished, "The top was down on her sports car and she was clearly visible."

For once, Jackson Milan appears to be speechless.

Marciano turns to me. "Trez Evans, let me ask you again. Were you alone, as you previously indicated, on Wednesday, September 21, 1983, between the hours of 6:45 to 8:30 am?"

Oh, crap. "Um, I, well, you see, ahh, this is so awkward."

The cop's eye color is turning from sweet puppy brown to coyote shit. I pull out the big guns with my best diva attitude.

"Jesus, do I have to go into this? I'm a consenting adult."

Jackson mutters through clenched jaws, "Answer him."

"Um, okay. You see, a male lover spent the night in my home. In my bed, if you must know. He was there when I decided to burn my manuscript."

Marciano mumbles so I cock my head with a cute over the shoulder emphasis to reply, "Huh? What'd you say?"

He doesn't think it's cute so I say, "He didn't come with me to buy the fire pits, he was cooking breakfast. He didn't help with the burn; in fact, he tried to talk me out of it. We argued. I told him to leave but he didn't have his car so I took him home. I had to stop at the gas station first. He got out to pump the gas. End of story."

The rookie says, "I need his name and number."

I counter, taking a swipe at any brain sludge that might be dripping down my face. "No way. I'm taking the Fifth."

Marciano shakes his head. "You don't want me to take you down to the station. It'd be unpleasant for you."

Ross has remained uncharacteristically quiet. Now he is frowning, "C'mon, Trez. They'll find out anyway."

Hell no. This is my Alamo. I will die on this mountain, or wherever that cowboy and Indian war took place. I state with the utmost conviction, "You'll have to arrest me, Officer."

Oh, shit. The cop is taking out his handcuffs, he looks ready to read me my rights.

All of a sudden we hear a screeching confession, "It was me." What'ya know? Phineas McCool is being a gentleman.

His eyes widening, Ross gags as if his throat's been slashed. I can barely discern his sputtering attempts to yell at me. Oh, now, here it comes, he's groaning, *"Phineas?* This joker?" Ross lets out a barrage of swear words.

Helice's eyes crisscross at his use of the F word, but it's not the time to console a hallucination.

Ross glares at Phin. "She's my *sister,* man." He covers his eyes with clenched hands. But then, he lifts up one hand to glare at me, to cast judgment by saying, "You and *him*...?"

Phin makes a full confession, defending me with a caveat that I was totally stressed out and not my usual upright self.

Ross refuses to look at Phin. It's no riddle. Theirs is a complex relationship. They love each other as brothers, yet the manic Phin drives the reserved Ross to the point of physically flinching, as if he's dodging a prizefighter's punch.

Marciano decides to take Phin in for questioning. He's not under arrest, at least for now. Jackson needs to fly to Los Angeles for a case later today, so he's making arrangements for one of his law partners to meet Phin at the police station while glaring at me for screwing up his day.

Ross may be royally pissed but he's accompanying Phin to the station just in case.

Truth be told, I am proud of Phineas. Too bad Ross is not speaking to me. My brother is avoiding me as if I am a toxic waste dump. As for me, I can't look Marciano in the eye.

CHAPTER 19

Down, Down the Rabbit Hole

Nurse Harbine comes into my room right as the 7:00 wake up bell rings to say we have "business to attend." I barely have time to get dressed before following her to one of the small meeting rooms. Jackson and Marciano are waiting for me. From their expressions, it appears that I'm in the hot seat again.

I guess it was bound to come out. Once Phineas was put into the police interrogation room, the kind with two-way mirrors, his dam broke. In defending his actions, he'd revealed mine. At least they're letting him go this morning. Ross will pick him up at the station.

Jackson is supposed to be a stone-cold attorney but he's firing burning glowers at me. I stifle a chuckle. He reminds me of a poshly dressed dragon who's inhaled lighter fluid.

He's probably pissy because I didn't tell the truth, the whole truth, and nothing but the truth. Plus, after rescheduling his flight, and missing it yesterday, he had to book an even later one. Only to fly back right back on the red eye for me this morning. They won't tell me why.

Marciano presses, "Mr. McCool said after you dropped him off the day Analeese Loveland disappeared, you were headed to a woman's home office in Pacific Heights. On Clay Street. Is this correct, Ms. Evans?"

I fidget, scratch my prickly head. Anticipating his

line of questioning, I take a breath but remain silent.

He goes on, "You'd dropped McCool off at 8:10 am, more or less. That's within the projected timeline of Analeese Loveland's disappearance. You could have circled back to her house, and absconded with her to a secluded hiding place."

"No way, Ron. Can I call you Ron?"

My rookie's all business as he shakes his well-shaped head. "No, that's not appropriate."

"Oh. Anyways, your timeline's too tight. I'd have to drive a zillion miles an hour. Traffic sucks going in and out of the City. The bottom line is I wasn't anywhere near that kid."

He again asks about the woman. I'm forced to reveal, "Her name is Paloma Del Mar. She was my husband's um, ah...his *friend*. My late first ex-husband, Lawton Pennalton."

Milan winces, "You still see her after the palimony suit?"

He hates that she won a settlement against Lawton, her longtime lover before and after me. Convinced her case was a slam dunk, I actually testified on her behalf, after all, I *am* an honest person. The estate paid for her Victorian manse but Jackson took it so personally, he's never forgiven himself and...oh yeah...me.

I stress, "Paloma is still my friend. Don't worry, she wasn't home. She's in Italy...or...is it Israel? Oh, I don't know, she's visiting one of those *I* countries."

Marciano urges, "Did you talk to a neighbor? Did anyone see you, maybe a passerby, to corroborate you were there?"

I shrug. Jackson squeezes his brow, lets out a groan. I try to explain, "I'd just gotten fired. I needed her advice."

It's best not to mention I'd wanted Paloma to ask her crystal ball to predict my future. That thing is fabulous.

I plead my case to Marciano. "I needed to figure out what to do with my life. I always consult with Paloma

Del Mar. She's the most sought after psychic for the rich and famous."

"Who cares about that?" Jackson's lip curls and his voice squeaks like a rusty gate. *"You don't have an alibi."*

Marciano reminds me the girl's been missing six whole days. He confides that he is worried sick. Aw, how sweet is this? Brings us closer, for sure.

He asks how I feel about it. Comforting him, I say, "It hurts my heart too. All of us want Analeese Loveland back safe and sound."

He leans across the table to ask me, "Ms. Evans, do you remember our telephone conversation?"

How could I forget, it felt deliciously like pillow talk, only while standing up at the public payphone.

He goes on, "I'm still wondering what you meant about your book character helping you with this case."

I don't need to look at my lawyer to know he's dying a slow death inside. I tell Marciano, "That's right. It's how I know things before they're revealed to the public. Like the girl's hair."

Jackson alerts. "Wait, what are you saying?"

"It's how I know Analeese cut her hair into really short chunks before she walked out of her house, alone, without anyone harassing her." I smile victoriously.

Marciano wipes his brow. "We haven't released that information to the public. Yet."

He turns to Jackson. "Mr. Milan, we need to talk." The two men leave the room. I creep over to the door and press my ear against it but can't make out anything. Jackson almost bangs my head when he opens the door to come back in. Marciano isn't with him.

Jackson is playing his lawyer role and won't tell me anything. His mouth is clamped so tight it's like he has lockjaw.

There's a knock on the door. It's my rookie. They whisper at the doorway, all the while staring at me. Jackson leaves the room for a while, comes back alone, and says that they are going to check me out of Crazy

Town. Just like that. All I have to do is complete a ton of paperwork.

They're letting me out with a few caveats. For one, they strap a tracking device on my ankle. It chafes.

Plus, I have to return for therapy sessions six days a week with Hannah Harrison, and some of them will involve my brother. She wouldn't sign off when Jackson asked last time. This must mean I'm now "cured."

Dr. Watson still won't let me drive, which sucks. I also must return in a few days for him to remove the staples.

Best of all, Marciano is my court assigned babysitter. We'll see one other every day. I'm gonna get lots of Italian.

Despite my glee at getting sprung, I feel a deep impotence. I thought Phin and I would find the girl. I thought Helice would lead me to her. Like every goal in my life, my words and actions have proven meaningless.

Now, realistically, my worry is that time has run out. It's been six days. Even if the Bay Area is currently enjoying the best weather of the year, temperatures drop at night. From what the police gathered, the kid did not pack proper clothing, not to mention enough food and water.

There is no physical evidence to link Analeese with Helice. At this point, I must assume hallucinating a fictional character is the result of my brain trauma. There's nothing else to go on. Still, I have a niggling feeling that there is something I'm overlooking.

Helice looks as sad as I feel. Concentrating on my mental communication with her, I ask these pertinent questions one more time: *Did maybe you forget part of Magdalena's message? Is there anything, anything at all you need to tell me? Helice, do you know how to find that missing girl?*

She smiles. *It's up to you. It always has been.*

I'm practically screaming in my mind. *Damn it, Helice, you always say that. What's it supposed to mean?*

She's grinning now. *Maggalena says we have answers inside of us, we just gotta trust ourselves to figure 'em out. You should hurry, don't you think? Analeese has been out there a week. I mean, think hard.*

I throw up my hands. *I've been thinking this entire time. All it's done is land me in Crazy Town. With you. This...* I wave my arm around the general area. *This is all your fault.*

Nope. You got here all on your own. I just followed you.

Grrr. It'd feel good to throw this pint-sized figment of my imagination over my knee and paddle her. But I. resist whacking the air like Don Quixote.

Nurse Harbine interrupts my daydream of me winning the argument with my punky hallucination. "Did you get breakfast?" I nod, after deciding not to complain about my last meal in the loony bin: oatmeal that looks and tastes like thick globs of gray glue. She hands me a paper bag with my red high heels. This is what you were wearing when they admitted you."

"Hey, I wasn't naked when they brought me here. I had some leggings and a loose top. Plus a sexy bra and my favorite thong panties."

She coughs. "Oh honey, they were very, very spoiled with urine, vomit—lots of vomit—and blood from your...uh...unfortunate head injury."

Oh, yeah, I forgot about that.

"I gave the clothing to your brother for cleaning but I think he threw everything away as he left the ward."

That makes me smile. "Sounds like him, he's such a neat freak. I liked that top, though."

"Time to go shopping!" She pauses. "Obviously, I can't send you back out into the world in just shoes."

Hmm, I'm thinking that seeing me in my birthday suit with the stilettos just might seal the deal with Marciano, but Harbine goes on.

"You can wear the facility uniform home." She giggles, "Think of it as our parting gift."

Glancing down at the boxy blue cotton top, pull on pants, and used white sneakers with orange soles, not to mention scratchy institutional underwear underneath, I tell her, "Sure, it'd be fun to burn this crap." My eyes bug out at her reaction. "No, please, it was just a joke, an inappropriate one since I learned positive behavior here that I'll carry forever, please, I didn't mean it."

"See, I'll make this outfit work." I roll up the oversized pants to my knees to make them into Capri pants. " Grinning, I jut out my right foot."

Nurse Harbine laughs, "You look just like a runway model." She slides over the last document for me to sign.

I do it.

"It's official. Go home, Trez."

I'm ready to exit the facility.

I can barely contain my excitement after Harbine tells me that my hunk rookie will drive me home. "He is required to make a home visit report so please allow him full access to your property, and make sure to answer any questions he might have."

I reply in my most polite manner, "Oh, of course. Thank you," but I'm practically tap dancing out of the place I'm so excited.

Spotting his cruiser I shout, "I call shotgun."

A lot of good that does. Marciano says, "Against regulations." He makes me sit in the back. I settle in, and cross my legs for him to notice my sexy red heels. But we're separated by a security grille behind the front seat, not the best way to touch off our post-5150 love affair.

To lighten the mood, I joke how this makes me his moll. He doesn't laugh. Is he too young to know a moll is a tough yet lovable cookie circa the 1930-50s gangster film noir?

"So, Officer, did you grow up around here?"

He says no.

Helice is giggling about riding in a patrol car. He's going faster than the freeway's speed limit. Perks of the job. As a treat for her, I ask Marciano to put on his siren.

He says no.

She frowns, but I respect Marciano's strong silent style.

She asks me if he knows about her. I bust out laughing. Why not, she asks. As if I'd jeopardize a budding romance by introducing my soon-to-be lover to my hallucination.

Ron turns round to check me out. I flash him a perfect Trez Evans smile, not too cheeky but still enticing.

"Are you seeing things at the moment, Ms. Evans?"

I put on a pout. "Why would you ask that, Ron?"

"Ah, you're laughing at nothing."

"How do *you* know?" Oops, not the best move. It appears my rookie does not have a sense of humor. We both shut up.

I relax the moment he exits for Kings Mountain.

"Hey Ron, ah, I mean Officer. Check out that view." He whistles.

He follows my directions and soon pulls into my long winding driveway. It's such a relief to be welcomed home by comforting crunch-crunch sounds of gravel beneath car tires. I chuckle at Mary's barks warning *Keep Out* to anything who would dare invade her territory. I can't wait to see her.

Helice is jumping on the backseat she's so excited. I feel like jumping too, but someone has to be the grownup. A flash of black with tan tells me Mary is near. As the rookie opens my rear passenger door he is pushed aside by the force of a hundred and forty pound dog fixed on reaching me first. It's the first time I hear my straight arrow rookie laugh. Pure joy.

A juicy tongue slides along my face and shaved head. After climbing all the way into the cruiser, Mary pins me with a gigantic paw to position maximum globs of wet kisses.

I giggle so hard her tongue slips down my throat.

Yuck.

She gets turned around in the patrol car, so that her stubby tail is wagging fast as a whirlybird against my cheek.

Mary slobbers Helice, who is shrieking hilariously. Best homecoming ever.

If Marciano wonders why a dog is intensely licking thin air, he doesn't let on. He's focused on my sprawling Victorian estate but it's the land itself that makes me sing out loud.

Sol Green, my latest ex-boss, told me that the land alone, without the 5,000 square foot lodge with its European millwork and the guesthouse behind it, is worth millions.

Is that why Sol said I had potential? Too bad I'm just not good at any of the dozens of my short-lived "careers." I may be a trust fund heiress, but I need to work. My bottom line: I can't—I won't—live anywhere else but here.

Scarlet O'Hara had her Tara. I have Pennalton Lodge. I yearn to sink my bare toes into its rich loam but that must wait. My rookie cop needs to inspect my home prison.

We enter into my front parlor. He whistles softly at the high vaulted ceilings with wood beams. He notes the original Tiffany lamps, Navajo weavings, and antique Turkish rugs.

Ross greets us. He looks aghast at my uniform with the rolled up pant legs and the stilettos but wisely keeps any comments to himself. He hands us both cups of coffee. Oh, Lordy, it's real caffeine. Slurping contentedly, I can't stop grinning over my homecoming. Ross says he dropped Phin at his North Beach flat; the police didn't have anything to hold him. Good.

After downing my first cup of java, Officer Marciano interrupts my story of spending time in a nut house, which I think is pretty rude because I've been embellishing how my roommate spoke to me in tongues and it's damn funny, but business is business.

He opens the file he carried in and asks me to show him around the house. He doesn't say it, but I know he intends to snoop. Let him, he won't find anything.

I say, "If you don't mind, I am dying to get out of these awful clothes. Can I change first?"

"No, I guess that'd be all right."

I smile. "Want to come with me?"

He blushes. "Yes, ma'am, I'll need to inspect the room before you, ah..."

Hmm, this could provide lovely opportunities. With Mary at my red heels, I lead him down the hallway to my suite of rooms, which is really its own wing with bed, bath, and my office. He looks around, opens the drawers (unfortunately he doesn't linger over my extensive lingerie collection). I take him into my office, the alleged scene of my crime. It's a shock, I must say, to see ten years of my life's efforts burned to a crisp. "As you can see, Ron, there are no corpses of little girls in here." We loop around and then walk into my bathroom. He stares at the shower, which is probably the biggest one he's ever been in other than a group wash at a gym.

I invite him into my walk-in closet. It's twelve by fifteen feet, the size of an average master bedroom. Pennalton Lodge is far from average. He takes in my extensive wardrobe that is meticulously color-coordinated by seasons. He's had enough and backs out.

As soon as he leaves I stand in front of the six-foot mirror and stare at myself. Shaved scalp with a horseshoe scar covering half of my head. Fighting back tears, I tell myself never mind, all is well now. I have a handsome rookie to attend to.

First things first. I tear off that awful institutional uniform and kick it into the corner. The scratchy underwear is next. Hmm, there's always hope Marciano will show me his manly side so I dig into my lingerie cabinet and pull out my favorite black Victoria Secrets. The four-inch stilettos will have to wait for his libido to overcome his by-the-book professionalism.

Now, what to wear? My rosy red dress is a

showstopper but it's taffeta, perhaps not the best outfit to begin my courtship with a straight arrow policeman. I settle on my favorite pair of jeans, the ones that define my butt just right, with black boots that make my long legs go on forever. Helice shows up to nag me about my boots. She points to a well-worn pair of Nikes. Fine, I snort, changing shoes is easier than arguing with her. I pull on a tight T-shirt that accentuates my breasts.

There's nothing much to do about my hair; the bits left on my head are still wet and sticky from Mary's exuberant welcome. Since one side is shaved and my remaining hair on the other side touches below my shoulder, I pin that part onto the bald side of my head to even it out. A quick dash of foundation, powder, lipstick, eye shadow, liner, and mascara finish me off.

I return to the main area to find that Ross has already led the rookie around my first floor. They're in the kitchen nibbling on fresh baked cookies. I insist Ron inspect the second level and make sure to take the stairs ahead of him so he can take in what a former lover described as "the finest ass this side of the Mississippi."

I let Ron do his thing. He's checked every one of my four fireplaces. Other than poking through the ashes to uncover my burnt writing dreams, he finds nothing. Once he's satisfied with his interior home inspection, he closes the file and we go back downstairs. I claim my favorite spot on the sofa and so does my dog. She climbs onto my lap, she's so happy.

I wonder how long Marciano will stay. Shouldn't he be getting back to the station? He must like it here. I want him to like me. Or is he breeding familiarity so I'll say something he can use against me?

I watch Marciano examine the grizzly bear Lawton's great-great-grandfather purchased from a local hunter who killed it a hundred and twenty five years ago. He had it stuffed and here we are, staring up at a fury friend.

I explain, "Folks were allowed to hunt bears back then, there were so many of them around. It makes me sad they were wiped out, but this is a fact of California history."

Ron asks astute questions. He'll make captain for sure.

I tell him, "He came from the Bear Gulch stream here in Woodside. The hunter lost half an ear in the fight. Lawton's great-great-grandma wouldn't allow her husband to shoot big game. But he'd built this place as a hunting lodge so he bought the bear and had it mounted out of spite for his naggy wife. In any case, I feel a deep responsibility for 'Bernie.'"

I don't mention Lawton asked a native American shaman to bless Bernie so its potent bear spirit wouldn't go awry.

I go on, "If I got rid of this bear, he could end up in a far worse place. So instead, he's been an honored member of the family. Besides, Mary thinks Bernie's her father."

He adjusts Bernie's tweed newsboy cap. "Is that why you dressed him up?" The cap had slid over the bear's left eye while he was investigating the seven-foot tall showstopper.

I laugh, "Humor is a great camouflage." He chuckles.

Hmm, wonder how he'd react if he could see Helice climbing up Bernie's leg. Would he run away screaming or, would he play with her? He's lightened up now that he's out of his cop realm; he's showing the nice guy side of himself. A solid first step in our relationship. I enjoy a cozy notion of us parenting the girl together. And Mary too. A happy family.

Wandering over to the massive stone fireplace, he runs his fingers along the hand carved mantle. Uh oh, he's spotted the pickle jar with my two ovaries floating in formaldehyde. My reproductive organs have been on display since 1978, as a daily reminder of what cannot happen for me.

He's younger than me, he'll probably want kids. I mean, real live children. Not a problem. We'll take a nice cruise overseas and adopt some.

Speaking of the mantle, the layer of dust covering it is easy to spot even from my vantage point across the room. I glare at my housekeeper/cook Esmeralda.

Considering the estate pays her for a sixteen hour week and it appears that she's skipped the last two sessions, the mouse must have had a field day without the cat. And Ross, who was supposed to supervise the help in my absence, obviously flew the coop.

Whatever. I've been having delightful fantasizes of consuming hot and spicy Italian sausage, so it surprises me when Mary abruptly jumps off my lap. My rookie blanches at her bellowing growls. Ah ha. The doorbell rings. Mary is ready to investigate who would dare cross her threshold.

Ross answers the door. "Hey, Trez, you have visitors."

OH MY GOD! Roman the face licker is standing on my doorstep.

"How'd you get my address?" I snap. "Phineas told you, right?" That's before I see he's with a handsome young man. Behind Handsome is a smiling older guy who's supporting a TV camera on his shoulder.

The young hunk bends to scratch my dog's rump before introducing himself. "I'm Tobey Vallencourt, Channel Five News." He extends his right hand.

I shake it and can't help but flash on the night of Bethany Moraga's book launch and the way Vallencourt fawned all over her. What's he want with me?

Mary grants them passage into my house. Esmeralda brings a tray of fresh coffee and cookies. Gawking at Tobey, she swoons over the star reporter like a backstage groupie.

I'm annoyed at Roman's audacity for showing up at my home, for crying out loud. Tobey Vallencourt is another story. Not only is he leading man drop-dead gorgeous, he's a take-charge kind of guy. Before I know it, he's pitching me his vision of how my tale of a wrongful 5150 charge will unfold to his "core audience," a significant number of Bay Area viewers who regularly watch his broadcasts. Then he says that Dr. Gillespie told him about remote viewing and my psychic abilities.

I don't know about disclosing that, especially considering a police officer is listening to every word we say. Will it end up in his report? That's a lot of pressure, but I can't help thinking that when people learn about my novel-burning, they'll be curious about *The Mud Eater's Apprentice* and want to read it! I'll get a publisher! Have my own book launch! Vallencourt is still smiling. Hey, Bethany Moraga—eat your heart out.

Tobey outlines how Dr. Roman Gillespie will act as the scientific authority. Tobey's plan is for Roman to introduce his remote viewing mental processing protocol utilizing extrasensory perception. I'm apparently the conduit. Oh, dear, how will Ron react to that, would he want his woman to be that different? Tobey goes on to say Roman will lay out the steps of how he would find the missing Analeese Loveland through me. I glance over at the rookie, who looks to be inhaling Tobey's every word. Well, I can't control that. Roman has been busy and Vallencourt bought into it.

Tobey predicts his show will vindicate me as a suspect. Plus, it'll launch the tell-all book we'll quickly co-write. He swears finding Analeese this way will make me a local celebrity. My fifteen minutes of fame! I begin to dream about my publishing contract for *The Mud Eater's Apprentice.*

He flashes me an infectious grin that seems to say *just sign on the bottom line.*

GOLDEN SUNLIGHT IS STREAMING through the French doors overlooking my estate, landscaped to perfection.

My troubles are behind me. My rookie is here. I can visualize us living together. I look over at Helice, who has been following him around. Her first crush. I'm thinking it's nice to have a kid in the house.

Marciano is patting Mary's blocky head, a picture of domestic bliss. He looks up and sends me a smile. Even Ross is nice to me.

Hmm. A new chapter in my life, perhaps?

Marciano snaps me back to reality. He needs to inspect the property. "All twenty acres, Officer?" I tell my man in blue that I'm glad he's staying around, using the excuse that I'm feeling nervous about my abrupt homecoming.

"My release happened so fast," I cunningly say to Marciano, "I wasn't able to process it...and now..." My eyes flick to the roomful of strangers.

"That's perfectly understandable, ma'am."

With a playfully dramatic hand over my heart, I scold, "Oh, please, don't ever call me ma'am again." He blushes a lovely shade of cabernet.

Tobey is coming along. He wants his cameraman Kirk to take "B-roll" footage of Mary, the grizzly bear, and my property to propel the story.

Mary runs out to the back yard through her plus-sized doggie door. Helice follows. I'm too distracted to notice if she uses the door or simply passes through the wall. I'll pay more attention next time.

We all step outside for a tour of my property. I can tell Marciano's watching me as I pose amid various areas of interest. Tobey gushes. Kirk swears the camera loves me. Of course it does.

Ross is adamant I should clear this TV interview with my lawyer first, before the entire Bay Area judges me. No big deal, I tell Ross, don't worry about it.

Marciano refuses to be filmed, he's putting up a hand along with a growly, "No."

With everyone distracted in the rose garden, Roman the licker asks for a moment alone. We step away from the group. He makes the edges my mouth pucker like sucking a lemon but what the hell, he's about to become a media star and me along with him.

He starts up. "I thought of a method for Helice to answer specific questions. Since she's part of your imaginative process, she can only parrot whatever you wrote for any of the novel's scenes."

"God, Roman. Let's get one thing straight. I don't want people to know that any of my literary characters talk to me. Got that?"

"I, ah, I haven't read your novel. But I just thought *if* you wanted to communicate something that's not in your story, you could write a new scene where Helice is directly involved. Then, she'd know more about it later if you chose to question her."

Wow. What a great idea. I can hardly wait to try it.

I give him a blasé shrug. "Whatever."

Back with the group, I grill Tobey about the vapid gossip tome writer Bethany Moraga. We blather about her latest drunk driving arrest and he promises more juicy nuggets if we work together. Marciano won't answer when Tobey asks if he knows about her case but he's chuckling. I'm thinking he's fitting in nicely. Even Ross has warmed up to him.

Hey, all right. I'm ready for my close-up.

That is, until Helice begins to dig a huge hole. I'm squinting, wondering how she's turning over my grassy field so fast without a shovel. I gather my thoughts and mentally order her to stop. She's too focused.

It forces me to shout out loud, "Helice, knock it off."

All eyes are on me. I'm waving, calling to the gardener nearby, "Take care of that, please." He pivots to where I'm pointing. He turns back to give me a puzzled look.

Staring at him I shout, "Oh, my God, it's you." Realizing all eyes are on me, I motion Ross to come closer to tell him, "It's the guy I saw in my dream, or OBE out of body thing, whatever it was. It's him. The kidnapper."

Everyone rushes to surround the gardener, especially Marciano. Kirk the cameraman is filming us.

I'm about ready to make a citizen's arrest when

Ross says for all to hear, "Hi'ya, Chris. How was your trip to Greece?"

Glancing at me and the cameraman, Chris replies, "Great, best three weeks of my life." As if fearing for his job, he points to the garden, "I've made up for lost time since I got back."

I take a better look at the man. Oh, now I know who he is. It *is* Chris. Damn. The mole on his cheek is real noticeable.

Hmm. I recall straining to "see" the alleged kidnapper during a vivid dream. Then Ross said the cops had a facial clue. Looks like my imagination conveniently provided Gus' big black mole and I filled in the blanks. So much for my psychic ability. I can't do anything right.

I feel my face blazing as the cameraman moves in for a tight shot of what is most likely my scarlet-hued expression.

At least Helice stops digging. She's talking to me now, insisting Roman doesn't care about anything but his career. *But I'm going to write a tell-all book with Tobey!* I envision myself autographing hundreds of copies for admiring fans...Take that, Bethany Moraga.

Helice interrupts with a tart order. *Get rid of 'em, Trez.*

"Uh, what?" I suddenly can't fathom life without Tobey and the guy with the shoulder-held camera.

The tenacious ten year old kicks Roman in the shin. He does not react. At all.

After all of his claims of scientific perception success and how he "feels" our two energies are cosmically compatible, he has no clue if Helice is actually here or not. He *is* a sham.

That's it. I'm done. Screw my fifteen minutes of fame. I tell Tobey and his guys to scram. They don't go easy. The camera is running. Ross asserts his alpha male attributes to run them off. So does the tall, dark, and oh-so-handsome police officer who stands strong next to Ross while resting a hand on his gun holster. Be still my heart.

It's a shock when my sweet rookie blurts, "Trez, what have we here?"

I answer, "Huh? What?" That's when I notice Mary running up to me with a muddy object in her mouth.

It's what the cops call a vital piece of evidence. Mary's carrying the black and white saddle shoe.

THERE'S MAYHEM AT MY PLACE, what with cops digging up my beautifully tended back field. Not to mention the K-9 presence. Bully dog Mary was not amused when they show up. Barking incessantly, nipping at their heels like the little lambs she used to herd in my fields, she shows two professionally trained German shepherds who's boss in about three minutes. We hear Mary expressing her outrage over being locked up in the caretaker's cottage even though it's on the far side of my land.

This is all happening because Mary has not only brought back the missing saddle shoe, Marciano found my dog's chewed up Hello Kitty pillow in an empty horse stall.

Now he's asking me, "Ms. Evans, are you aware that Analeese Loveland owns this exact pillow? Could this be *her* pillow, Ms. Evans?"

He keeps asking me this over and over. Jeese, I hope he's not obsessive compulsive. Could I live with an OCD man?

I sigh. "Thousands, hell, millions of kids must have this same dumb pillow. Dogs, too. I bought it at a pet store."

Hmm, I think it was a pet store. All I know is Mary spotted it and wouldn't leave the shop without it. I caved in and bought the damn thing. Big freaking deal.

He's all business. "Ms. Evans, do you have a receipt for this particular pillow you say you purchased?"

"Why would I, Ron? Look at it, it's so old."

"Kindly refer to me as Officer Marciano."

"Excuse me, Ron, I mean Officer." I can't help

batting my eyelashes at him, he's so serious.

His forehead is covered with a thin film of sweat and it's all crinkled up in a perplexed, albeit sexy, way. That tells me he's privately on my side, although I must admit, his words are harsh. It would hurt me if I hadn't figured out his secret code of grimacing and arching his left eyebrow whenever he says Analeese's name. That peculiarity tells me not to worry. Deep down, my by-the-book rookie is totally rooting for me.

All in all, I'm proud of how he's taken over the search with such command. He's sure to make captain in record time. Of course, with all the police around, there's been quite a commotion going on.

Uh oh, seems the dog cops have dug up something. Bones of some type. Oh, crap.

Damn those gypsies! I speak up, "I was on vacation when my friend Phin McCool met a caravan of Bulgarians. He felt sorry for them so he gave them the go ahead to camp on my land. They dug a pit and cooked a goat for some Romany holiday. These are goat bones," I assure the cops.

"Trust me, just ask Phin," I tell them. "Ask Ron, I mean Officer Marciano." I point to Ron. His face is an odd shade of fuchsia. Wonder if he's overheated?

"Hey, Ron, tell them it's all Phin's fault. Guys, once you meet Phin, you'll know what I mean. He's *cray-zee*." They're not laughing. "Bottom line is I wasn't home so end of story."

Marciano frowns. "That's a big stretch. How many gypsies show up asking to barbeque a goat?"

Laughing, I throw up my hands. "I know, right? Leave it to Phin, he has a knack for attracting stuff like this."

They're not buying my alibi so I ask, "Is this payback for O'Doul?" Several cops titter. "Guys, I didn't cause his heart attack. He's old, thirty, forty pounds overweight. You should have seen it coming, so really, it was a blessing in disguise. Maybe now he won't eat so many donuts and fries."

Marciano tells me with steely resolve, "Ms. Evans, our investigators suspect they've found the bones of the missing Redwood City girl on your property."

My mouth pops. "Oh, come on. Seriously? These aren't human bones for crying out loud. Plus, it'd take a hell of a lot longer than six days for any kind of body to turn to bones."

One of the cops snickers, "Unless you boiled them clean."

"Eww, that's sick, even from a disgusting pig like you."

He snipes, "So, how many fire pits did ya buy?"

"How about I boil *you*, Officer?"

The cop makes a move but Marciano steps between us.

"Take this psycho bitch to the station and book her," the cop orders. Marciano nods.

Oh, crap. There doesn't seem to be any argument, they all must think I'm guilty. Does my sweet rookie?

Marciano tells the canine unit, "Listen, you're done here, might as well take off." He points to the snarling, growling German shepherds. "The homeowner's dog is cordoned off on the other side of the property but it's so pissed off, your dogs are going ballistic."

When the dog cops leave, Marciano asks Ross to break Mary out of her prison. He's quick to oblige. After the nonstop racket she's been making, we're all grateful for her reprieve.

Marciano turns to the rest of the police who'd assembled on my property. "Forensics gathered all the evidence. You guys can go too."

Nasty cop says, "You sure?" He points a finger at me. "This one's a nut case."

Marciano laughs. "Dealing with her is like herding cats, but I can handle it."

Wow, that barb cuts me to the core. I don't know if I can love him quite as much anymore.

He goes hard on me, just not the way I'd like. "I'm taking you in, Ms Evans."

The cops cheer, "Go, rookie!"

NOW THAT THE POLICEMEN have left and Ross has come back with Mary, Marciano asks to speak to me privately. I lead him to the gazebo but he doesn't want to relax and enjoy the view. I'm thinking he'll apologize for being so mean to me in front of his burly cop buddies but he doesn't fulfill my fantasy. He breaks my horny heart when he says, "Sorry, Trez, here's nothing I can do. I have to arrest you. I can't wait until forensics gets the info because you're a flight risk."

"Seriously?" My throat closes tight when he gets out his handcuffs. He looks ready to read me my rights. I can't believe my cutie pie rookie is arresting me.

What's worse, Tobey's cameraman has caught this entire fiasco. I demand that Marciano confiscate Kirk the jerk's video equipment but apparently, I'd already agreed to being filmed.

Officer Marciano is all business, but I ask, "Can you wait a minute? Before we go, I have to use the bathroom." He nods. He's so accommodating, I push, "And can I please spend a few minutes with Mary? I just got home, there's no telling when we'll see one another again." That gets him. He leans down to pat her head as he agrees. I say, "Thanks for being so considerate. Let's go back inside through the kitchen. Standing by the massive island, I use my best hostess voice, "Ron, why don't you sit down and have another cup of coffee? Esmeralda just made a fresh pot." I flash him my best Trez Evans smile. He sits.

With Mary following close behind, I rush to my master bedroom. I pull back the thick black-out drapes that Ron didn't think to check, and slowly, carefully open the sliding glass door so it won't make noise. My heart is thumping as I step onto my private deck. I quietly close the door behind me so no one will be the wiser. Holding Mary's collar, I coax her to the far side where there are steps to some utility buildings.

Helice appears. I tell her, "No more games, kid. I'm sneaking away from getting arrested."

Her face flushes, she clutches my arm. *Analeese is in danger and you have to save her. Right now.*

"What? It's her fault I'm in so much trouble."

There's no time. I'll tell you in the car.

I'm running so fast I huff, "To go where?"

"Up all those big red hills, just like in your story. You know where."

"No, I don't. At least tell me what's happening."

There's a big fire brewing. She'll die if you don't save her in time. Let's go!

It's not like me to simply obey, especially from a juvenile apparition. We sneak across the gravel driveway and into the car barn. It's dark and cool in here, and smells of rough-hewn cedar. We pass the other vehicles and rush to my four-wheel drive Jeep Wrangler hardtop. Mary jumps in, expecting a joy ride.

I yank on her collar, yelling at her to get out but Helice insists the dog should go too; she could be a help to us. Mary barks, as if to agree. I shush her. The dog reluctantly moves to the rear. Helice is riding shotgun.

Who am I to argue with the team efforts of my imagined literary character and her hundred forty pound canine sidekick?

With my fight or flight hormones surging through my system, surely nothing can go wrong. I do force myself to stop a moment to ask what woman in her right mind would intentionally head straight into danger?

Well...given my recent history, there are a number of people who would swear I am not in my right mind.

What the hell. I climb into the driver's seat and pull down the visor. The keys fall into my lap. Turning on the ignition I exclaim, "Let's go, girls."

CHAPTER 20

Truth or Dare

MY TEMPLES ARE POUNDING I'm gritting my teeth so tight. My spine feels prickly, as if it's been taken over by porcupines. It appears all the macho adrenaline that fired me up to risk my life just a few minutes ago has leaked out of my system. Helice is uncharacteristically quiet but it's not the time to go maternal on her. This is all about me.

I start blathering, "I'm not a detective. I don't write crime novels, I don't even read them. What the hell will happen to me? I can't figure this out on my own."

Well, you gotta.

She's gotten awfully moody. "Listen, missy, now's not the time to throw an attitude. What do we do now?"

That's for me to know and you to find out.

I snort, "Are you kidding? Your purpose, your very existence, has been to warn me about this missing girl." I turn to her and mock, "It's time, *Trez*, pay attention, 'Maggalena' wants you to find her."

Yeah, you've done such a great job so far.

"What? You little brat. Everything has gone wrong for me since you showed up." I rub my bare scalp. "Brain surgery! 5150 in a nut house! I'm running away, right fricking now. It's called resisting arrest! You're not real, you're not gonna get in trouble. I'm the one, Helice, I'm the one going to jail!" Saying that out loud freaks me out. I let loose with a barrage of heavy duty profanities.

Hey. She cups her hands over her ears. *Phineas told you not to swear around me.*

"Where is this coming from?" I want to reach over and pull her freckles off her face one by fricking one, but it's too damn hard to fight and speed at the same time.

It feels like I'm doing a hundred miles on the back roads from Woodside to Redwood City. It's really more like forty, still way too fast for around here. I keep checking the rear view mirror. So far, there are no signs of any cops. This doesn't mean we can slow down. It's been almost ten minutes since my escape. Marciano may be an untried rookie but he's not stupid. He'll figure out my ploy.

You can't do anything right, Trez, this is all your fault.

Now is not the time to get distracted. At the crossroads I can't slow down in time and take the turn on two wheels with a loud squeal. Driving and talking at the same time is not my forte on a good day. Fighting *and* speeding? I am surely driving towards my certain demise. It must be primal.

I'm so worked up I'm hyperventilating. It hurts my ribs so I force myself to take in a deep breath, just like I show my characters doing. It makes me calm so I breathe in again. Third time's the charm.

"Helice, let's start over. You need to let me in on Magdalena's plan. I'm risking my life for a kid I don't even know. What am I supposed to do?"

She's slow to answer. *Well, Maggalena figured you'd work out the plot. She says everybody wants a happy ending. You had to want the end of the story bad enough to go out and find it for yourself. That's what an author does.*

I can't describe how rewarding it is for Helice to grasp my intention. She gets my storyteller ambitions. But somehow, Analeese Loveland has become one of my characters, even though she's real flesh and blood.

"Yeah, well, that's great but I'm done playing games. What's in it for you?"

I want to live with you. Wouldn't it be fun to have me all the time? Like a little sister? She waits. *Trez?*

"Aww, Gawd."

Her eyes widen. *I just mean you created me, so you must like some stuff about me.*

"You said you came into my life so I could help Analeese; you stressed how important it was for me to find her. Now, you're telling me that you need a place to crash. Permanently? I didn't sign up for this."

You ruined the Red Eden. It isn't safe for me and I don't have any place else to go.

"Listen up. You're right about one thing. I have to find that girl for my own sake. My good name deserves to be cleared. If her case isn't solved, people will gossip, they'll point and stare at me like I'm the perv ogre under the bridge who made off with her. And, and, if we never find out if she's alive or dead, the uncertainty will kill my reputation. Who's gonna hire me? Who's gonna buy my book? Worst of all, who's gonna date me?"

Me, me, me, Helice singsongs. *You'd be nowhere without me. I'm saving you.*

"You have got to be kidding! Saving me, my ass."

Hearing a siren, I check the rear view mirror. "Oh, my God, I am so screwed." It's a lone police cruiser, probably Marciano. "How'd he find me so easily?"

Gee, maybe it's the tracking device on your ankle.

Oh, yeah, I forgot about that thing. I push as far down on the pedal as possible and floor it.

My jeep lunges forward. It's groaning as if it's coming apart, rattling and jerking so much I can barely control the vibrating steering wheel. Despite the odds, we continue to keep a good distance ahead of Marciano. We climb uphill, past neighborhoods of suburban tract houses, then more remote spreads with barns and horse pastures. Now higher into the hills, we whiz through land that's more open.

Checking the mirror for the patrol car that's hot in pursuit, I can't help gazing at Mary's broad head; it's blocking most of my visibility. Her tan polka dot eyebrows are dancing up and down; she's expecting fun on this fast bumpy ride.

Now higher up the mountain where Analeese Loveland is supposedly hiding, we're at a good vantage point to spy on my pursuer. "Shit, I see Ross' car behind Ron." I squint. "Uh oh, behind him is a van with a model of a camera on its roof."

The siren has been relentless. Now I'm hearing horns. And a loud crash? I slow, downshift to neutral. Ross is pulling over his BMW; the van also tries to do that but there's smoke blowing out of the crushed front end. They all get out. What the hell? Keith is filming Tobey socking Ross in the nose. Ross lands a gut punch and wrestles Tobey to the ground. Marciano has to pull the two guys apart.

"Lucky break!" I switch gears and we're off. Oh, damn, the rookie's already back in the chase. Jeez, he's relentless, like a terrier digging for a gopher.

Trez, go to your right up there. She's pointing to a narrow footpath up the side of a grassy hilltop.

I barely have time to downshift before making the sharp turn. Mary rolls off the back seat; she lands with a growl and a thump. Damn, the cop car is gaining on us.

We continue climbing upward but it's slow going even in four-wheel drive. I think there's a thin wisp of smoke curling in the far distance, what I hope is a zillion miles away. Where we are this high up, there are no structures to burn, thank goodness, but the area is covered with trees, shrubs, and high dry grasses. No sign of fire trucks.

Hearing the squeal of tires I turn my head to watch the cruiser roll into a ditch. Ron gets out, he seems fine so I keep going. But after navigating along the narrow rutted trail with the brakes screeching like a jilted wife, I realize we've reached as far as the jeep can go.

Helice and I get out and hike uphill. The police car is nowhere to be seen but we can't risk dawdling. Before long, I'm wet with sweat and berating myself for not thinking ahead. We have no water or protective clothing, not even a shovel in case we have to ward off burning brush.

I'm so busy delighting myself with the last lost remnants of my story coming to light, I almost walk past a significant landmark. I stop in my tracks. "Helice, is that it? Is that the weirdly shaped tree branch?"

Her grin is my answer. She'd pointed it out while we were in the Red Eden and told me to remember it. She'd insisted, actually. Yeah, yeah, sure kid, I'd said. Now here it is in the real world.

I look around. Ross was right! This has to be at the farthest reaches of the hobby farm we'd visited decades before. Dad surely didn't take this route in his brand new 1960 Chevy Impala, but I'm pretty positive this is the place. We've probably come onto the property backwards. The house and barn were way on the other side from where a creek widens into a pond but I think an old hay shed was somewhere around here. Oh, it's true, I can spot a few rotted fence posts from where they pastured horses on hot summer days.

I wonder if the ditzy bohemian is still around. How old would she be? Gotta be at least seventy-five. Eww, I don't want to imagine her naked old lady body. The sky has turned hazy. Sniffing the air tickles my nostrils. Although there appears to be smoke farther north, the air has a slight scent of burnt charcoal.

Moving on, we come across a creek lined with blackberry bushes. There is a reddish boulder the shape of an alligator head that juts into the water. Ah hah. Now I'm certain this is the same creek where Ross and I ate so many berries our lips and tongues turned a bluish black.

Mary trots alongside us as we follow creek. Up ahead, there is a shallow pond in the middle of high pampas grasses that are waving in the mild breeze. Over to one side is a small grove of shade trees.

I tell Helice, "This is it, the pond where I first saw the naked lady with long black hair. She was taking a mud bath."

The girl graces me with a smile but doesn't add to the conversation. Whatever.

After years of doubting myself, this pond is physical proof I really did lay claim to my personal Red Eden. Vindication has never tasted sweeter. Without slowing my pace, I marvel over the realistic details incorporated into my novel, considering I'd only spent a few days here in 1960 when I was ten years old. I must be a fricking genius. It's true. We writers really do write what we know.

I barely pay attention when Mary dives into the underbrush. It is way too much fun looking around.

True, I jazzed things up for my story, designing magenta and lavender patterns for tree barks, geometric leaves and enhanced shades of the sky and mountains. Too bad there's no waterfall here, the one I made up for my book is glorious.

One element remains true to life as I race to the top crest. The red clay. It looks so rich I want to eat it, same as Magdalena. I can soak up the nuance and model my future works on this actual paradise. There'll be no more struggling to conceive fresh concepts of my very own version of heaven on earth. I envision at least one sequel, more even. I can picture my book covers. Blood red earth and lilac skies. I'll create an entire series!

But Helice is still so snarky, she's bumming me out. Instead of being happy for me, she's glaring.

"Helice, what's wrong? Are you scared, maybe? Don't worry, we'll find Analeese."

Trez? I did a bad thing. I prompt her to go on. *I made up a bunch of stuff so I could live with you.*

"Huh, what?" I'm practically choking on my heart, it's climbing so far up my throat.

Maggalena didn't send me here. I figured out how to get here on my own. I needed to be so important to you, you wouldn't want me to leave.

My voice goes dry and raspy. "But...why?"

It's true, the Red Eden was ruined by your fire. Pria does want to get me. But, but, I made it sound so horrible, you'd feel bad about sending me back.

Clenching my hands, I can feel my nails digging into my palms. "I'm getting arrested, Helice, any time now. Do you understand what that means? Unless I can find her, they will blame me for everything."

Crossing her arms tight, she juts out her hip. *Duh. I'm not stupid like you.*

"You little liar." Suddenly it hits me. "Oh, my God. Is Magdalena even real?"

What does it matter now?

I scan her face; it looks as bland as a vanilla wafer. Hmm. She is just a character. She served her purpose. Why does she still need to be alive in any realm?

I lunge at her. Grabbing air feels surprisingly solid, it's empowering to knock down my character. Ow. She's not a lightweight, though, this kid is giving me the once-over. I can feel her pent up frustration through her blows. And she's not even a real girl. Well, I am flesh and blood and I am pissed!

I'm now spread-eagled on the ground, with the kid beneath me. I wrap my fingers around what seems to be a pretty solid neck. Her eyes bug, just like a real girl. It's a terrific sensation, so I keep doing it. It feels right. What the hell, I'm going for it, I'm going to finally kill this damn kid.

Mary is barking off in the distance so I lose focus for a second or two. In that brief flash of time, Helice flips me. Now she's on top. She twists my head so I'm face down in the dirt. I attempt to do a death roll like a crocodile I once saw, but she pushes my mouth down harder.

You love the red dirt so much, eat it!

It tastes surprisingly good but she's forcing me to eat way too much, too fast. I'm gagging as I spit out dirt. "Mary! Where are you? Help me!"

Helice lets go of my head, sighing. *Trez, you're doing it again. You always expect someone to do your work for you.* She rolls off of me and I sit up.

She gets to her feet and brushes herself off. *You*

know you can't kill me, right?

I snap, "Yeah, yeah, I know, but it sure felt damn good to try." I stand up. I have to reach inside the back of my jeans and adjust my thong pantie that's wedged deep into my butt. These skimpy strips of string were not designed to do anything but make my buns look hot.

"What was that all about? You were a little bitch."

She grins, as if she knows something I don't.

All of a sudden I'm watching the dense shrubbery move and shake and then, Mary pops out of the bushes. Following my dog is a boy around Helice's age.

I think it's Tigiran, my character who ran off with Helice that day we came to the Red Eden. Wait. This kid has black hair that looks to have been shorn with a weed whacker. Oh my god... Is this Analeese Loveland?

CHAPTER 21

Here I Come to Save the Day!

I CRY, "ANALEESE, I'm here to help you."

Mary bounds to join me. Analeese, who's using a cane, limps a few yards forward, then stops. She's keeping her distance but this kid isn't quaking like a frightened bunny.

Although her skin is caked with mud, she doesn't appear to be starved or dehydrated. Her clothes are surprisingly clean; she's wearing a sleeveless T-shirt and athletic shorts, with a plaid flannel shirt tied around her waist. Her sandals are shot, though, and a bandage torn from yellow flowery fabric is wrapped around her left foot.

"You sure were makin' a racket." She puts a hand up to her eyes to block the sun and stares at me. "You're weird. You got no hair but leave-ths and twig-ths are th-sticking to your head." She makes such an ugly face at me, I'm second-guessing my selfless rescue mission.

"Who are you?"

"You must be so confused by all this."

Filled with a sudden raw emotion, I extend my arms to her. "Don't be scared, sweetheart." My voice cracks. "I'm here to save you."

Tilting her head, stiffening her shoulders, she studies me. I'm figuring she's gone batty from the ordeal of her isolation, but she's not acting like a damsel in distress. All the way up the mountain, I'd envisioned myself swooping up a frail, grateful child and carrying

232

her out of a firestorm to safety. A modern day Mighty Mouse. His victim lady mice swooned when he swooped down from the sky and rescued them.

This kid doesn't look or act like a victim. She and Helice are the same age. Compared to my petite novel character, she's an Amazon who's six inches taller with a good ten, fifteen pounds more muscle than Helice. This kid's cheeks are round as apples. There is a granola bar peeking out of her pants pocket.

Analeese Loveland may only be ten years old, but she is sending me some fierce vibes. Ah, she's on the move.

Oh, crap, she's fast.

Her left foot is bandaged, so she injured it sometime this week. Although she relies on a cane, she's approaching with both strength and purpose. The loosened soles of her worn scandals are flapping with each determined step.

She stops short, leaving scant personal space between us. She's panting, reminding me of a pissed off bull guarding its territory. Her head is so close beneath my nose I can't help sniffing her scalp. It smells like Eucalyptus, remarkably fresh for camping out these past seven days. Our close proximity allows me to examine the missing girl I'd feared was dead. This kid is anything but.

She may be coated with a layer of mud but it is so evenly applied it appears intentional. I detect a few scratches along her arms and knees. Her right third knuckle is pretty scraped up, yet the earth-darkened flesh around it looks clean.

I zero in on her left leg. There's a good-sized divot missing from her thigh and her shin is crooked from the accident. No wonder she has an attitude.

Now she's repositioning herself, standing too close to me for my comfort. From the smirk spreading across her face, she knows she's invading my personal space. Little brat.

She does not back off. Neither do I.

Shifting my eyes, I seek out Helice. She's nowhere that I can see. I mentally implore her to help me with this kid. There's not a peep from Helice. Where the hell is she?

Mary nuzzles the girl's deformed thigh. Analeese wraps an arm around the dog's broad neck. Mary licks her hand, a sure sign of familiarity.

Grabbing Mary's collar, I force my dog closer to me. Not an easy feat, considering the Rotti's bulk. "Her name's Mary. She doesn't take to just anyone."

"Tha'th *your* dog? She like'ths me."

"Huh, what'd you say?" This bold, assertive runaway not only lisps but has a high, squeaky voice to boot.

She's boring holes in me with her eyes. I tilt my head down and ask, "Did anyone come with my dog?"

She looks confused so I prompt, "A little girl around your age. Red sweater."

Analeese's brows furrow. She twists herself around as if looking for something. Or someone.

Before I can react, she pouts, "I don't wanna go home, it'th not time yet. Ya can leave now." As if remembering her Ps and Qs, the girl adds a saccharine, "Pleaseth."

"Listen, kid, you don't have a choice. There's a fire coming this way. We have to get out of here. Right now."

She sniffs, scans the sky. "Nah uh, there'th no fire. The sky isn't smokey."

She's got a point. Was Helice wrong? Or, it could have already burned out. I tell her, "Well, ah, maybe not at this moment, but trust me, a fire is coming our way. If the wind shifts..." I spread out my hands. "Better safe than sorry."

Analeese shoots me a look of intentional intimidation. Her voice deepens to a growly, "You're not the boss-th of me."

"Excuse me?" Her brows lower when I snap, "Knock it off, missy. It's not safe." She doesn't look convinced so I add, "I risked my life for you."

Apparently, she doesn't care.

"Look, kid, I'll give you a minute to get your stuff together and then we'll go."

She studies me. "Are ya the polic'th? Show me your badge."

This child is such a pain, but I have to be the grownup. Smiling, I soften my tone. "Okay, let's start over. Hi. I'm Trez Evans." I hold out my hand but let it drop when she doesn't shake. "I'm a concerned citizen, one of dozens of people who have been out searching for you."

Analeese yawns. A power move to be sure.

I stand up straighter. "You've been missing for seven days, Analeese. A whole week. Surely, you can understand everyone's concerns."

She hesitates. "But, but, I'm fine. Go back and tell them that. Pleaseth."

As a writer, I'm fascinated by her lisp. It's fun to flick my tongue against my front teeth every time her words end with S sounds. I'm wondering how to realistically portray her lisp in dialect. A literary challenge for when I get back home.

Okay, enough of that. It's time to get serious. I tell her, "Your mom and dad are worried sick."

"Naw, they know I can take care of myselth."

Jeez, Analeese is one tough nut. I need to ask Helice why this kid won't listen, but my hallucination isn't cooperating. It appears that I am on my own.

I manage a smile. "Tell you what. I'll drive you home so you can tell them yourself. You can show them you're fine."

Analeese looks around. "I don't see a car."

"That's because I had to pull over and hike in. It's not far, promise." I make a move towards the downward path.

"No! You're a stranger."

"You got it all wrong. I'm your rescuer. I'm saving you. Did you ever see a Mighty Mouse cartoon?"

A thin smile stretches across her face. "Thankth,

but I don't need help. I'm out here earning meritsth. I fill out a worksheet for all the requirementh. I'll get a bunch of badgeths. Wilderness survival, of courseth."

I ask, "Do you know an Eagle Scout? Did he fill your head with all this?" I stop short of saying *this nonsense*.

"Nope. Did it all on my own." She counts on her fingers. "It means badgeths for camping, physical fitnessth, bird study, and I fished, studied plants, I hiked and climbed." She points to her bandaged foot. "And firsth aid, too."

There are strands of plant fiber sticking out of the bandage. It looks exactly like the poultice Helice used to treat my bleeding head in the Red Eden. I gesture to Analeese's foot and ask, "Who taught you about plant healing?"

She flushes. "Some lady. I dunno know her name."

Cocking my head, I wonder who that was. Magdalena? Or, more likely, could the ditzy bohemian still be around doing her thing? I'd love to delve into her backstory, but this isn't the time.

I say, "Um, I hate to tell you this, but you got it wrong. Eagle Scout's only for boys a lot older than you."

I can't recall, was Helice ever a scout? There are so many versions, who has time to memorize a made up life?

Analeese is going on about her accomplishments.

I clear my throat a couple of times to shut her up. "Tell you what. I'll vouch for your nature skills. You could get lots of Girl Scout badges, enough for an entire sash. Wouldn't that be great?"

"Already got 'em." Her expression sours. "Besides'th, the dumb troop leader'th just a mom. I know tons more. Too bad nobody believed me." Her mood perks up. "That'th why I left home. Ta prove I can be an Eagle Scout."

She points to a grove of trees nestled along a pond. "That'th where I set up camp. C'mon, I'll show ya."

I frown. "I need to get you out of here."

The girl persists, "Pleaseth? Just for a minute?"

I check the sky. It's clear. Maybe the fire's out already? Whatever. I still need to get the kid home so I tell her with firm, adult authority, "One minute. Then we've got to go."

Mary and I walk behind the girl. I compare this setting to my made-up world. With trees shading the southern slope of the pond, I've depicted this land well. Especially the red soil.

When Analeese tucks her cane and ducks under a briar bush, I balk. "I'm not doing that." She pokes her head out to tell me another route in. It doesn't take long before I'm scratched and itchy, convinced she's directed me through a maze of poisonous plants on purpose.

I find my way to her camp. There is a small pup tent not far from a round fire pit of river rock with ample supplies of tinder, kindling, and a large pile of thicker branches for firewood. Thick rope is neatly coiled. A small combination ax and shovel is propped against the pit, along with an oversized tin of long wooden matches. I see a tidy cooking setup with a dented pot, a hefty cutting blade, as well as a vintage Swiss Army knife, an aqua melamine cup and plate, plus a bent fork and a spoon.

Stacked nearby are three six pack quarts of bottled water, about a dozen packages of jerky sticks, and an oversized carton of granola bars. The carton's close-up image of grains, nuts, and raisins looks delicious.

I push my eagerly sniffing dog away from the food.

Analeese points to her cache. "I still have plenty."

"Yeah, I can see that. Um...do you mind giving me one of your granola bars? You see, I haven't eaten and..."

She leans down, grabs one, and tosses it to me.

I wolf half of it down before realizing she's watching me intensely. Whatever. I'm too busy eating while scratching the red bumps popping up along my arms and legs.

She says, "Told ya I was fine. I made a plan. I saved my allowance for month'sh to buy supplies. I laid out my campsite just like the book show'sh, and I brought stuff here little by little." She nods at a child's red wagon.

"Wait." She limps into her tent and comes back with a few thin workbooks. "Wanna check 'em out?"

"Ah, let's bring them with us." A startling burst of white light goes off. "Hey, what are you doing?" I'm blinking my eyes after a flashbulb practically blinds me.

"To prove you're here. So they'll believe me." She holds up a Polaroid camera, pulls out a photo, and shows me.

Great, I look like a serial killer. The leaves stuck on my sweaty head add a realistic homicidal attitude. No wonder she doesn't trust me. A little flattery won't hurt so I enthuse, "Wow. Your camp sure is cool." She smirks, a good sign. It's time to close the deal so I say, "Obviously, you've done great by yourself, but I need to bring you down out of these hills."

She barrages me with protests. I wave her off. "No more stalling. We're in danger."

She's still resisting so I inform her, "You're the one who ran away. I've found you. Let's go." When she doesn't follow my lead, I snap, "Listen up. I'm taking you out of here one way or another, so you better get with the program."

"Help, stranger danger! Somebody help me!"

I'm about ready to tackle the kid when Mary wedges herself between us. With one hundred forty pounds of insistent canine plowing through our legs, we both get out of Mary's way. Now that she has Analeese to herself, Mary licks the mud off the girl's face with loud, wet abandon. The girl reacts to the tongue bath with a lilting childish laugh.

Within another blink of my eye, Helice manifests. She's ready to play. I can't be sure, but it seems Analeese sees her. I squint, studying Analeese's movements. Yes, she is definitely communicating with Helice.

I observe the two girls acting like new best friends.

Analeese towers over Helice, is heavier and more muscular, yet she's clumsy. Helice lands a perfect cartwheel. Analeese drops her cane and tries her best but her leg isn't stable enough to execute it, which is understandable. She's wearing casual athletic gear whereas Helice looks old fashioned in her '50s pedal pushers and saddle shoes. I'd designed Helice as a mid-century parochial school kid whose Catholic school nuns didn't tolerate slang or improper diction. She speaks in proper English, versus Analeese's coarser "wanna and gonna" talk. Most of all, my character doesn't sass adults like this kid. Other than that, they're typical ten year olds giggling and whispering secrets.

Helice is laughing so it's difficult to "hear" her mental communication. The gist seems to be that all is well.

Seriously? I look up at the sky. Ah hah, it's not my imagination after all. The sky looks darker than it was five minutes ago. I'm sweating the air is so thick. I don't care what Analeese the wannabe "Eagle Scout" says. The fire has got to be moving closer.

Uh oh. Analeese's expressions are morphing from delight at playing with a friend, to distrust. Pivoting away from me, she leans down to grab her cane. She sidles up to Helice and whispers. They both turn to look at me. Little conspirators.

Oh, great. Helice is marching over to me. From the looks of her, she's ready to scold me. She has some nerve, I'm her creator. I'm too pissed to even try using my inner voice.

"Helice, what the hell have you gotten me into?" That stops her. "From the moment I first saw you, you've been nothing but trouble."

Helice's eyes go wide. I wag a finger at Analeese. "I'm a major suspect in this kid's disappearance. And now?" I stop to clear my raspy throat. "I'm risking my life for *her*. This kid I've never met clearly doesn't give a shit I'm here. At least she explained her reasons up front. Not like you, Helice."

It's time to confront my gap-toothed literary character. But first, I must cough. Aggggh, my throat is sore.

I croak at Helice, "You already told me Magdalena wants you to live with me. I get it, it's your motive for being here. But why do you care so much about this girl? Huh?"

She doesn't give me anything to go on.

"Helice, listen up. I'll ask you one more time. You brought me and Analeese together. What's *that* motive? Why are you haunting me for her?"

Analeese pipes up. "Haunting? What'th she talking about?"

Helice sighs. *Okay, guess I have to tell both of you. Analeese is part of your story now.*

My mouth pops open. My character knows me well enough to keep talking. Or, rather, telepathically. Whatever.

Maggalena said Analeese will need you when she's older. That's why you had to meet.

I stammer, "Ah ha, so now I'm supposed to put up with two kids? No way."

Analeese is clearly "hearing" Helice. Cocking her head, Analeese growls, "What if I don't wanna? Thisth lady can't make me." She stomps her cane for emphasis.

I shout, "Fine!" It's a bit over the top, admittedly, but I want to make a show of wiping my hands. A literal, definitive gesture. "Stay if you want, Analeese. I'll go back and tell your parents where you are. Let them deal with you."

Now I'm the one pivoting away. Analeese has joined Helice. Hunching their shoulders, the two of them seem diminished, like marionettes with their strings cut. Even Mary is contrite, as she hesitantly moves over to my side.

"Hah." With a sniff and an exaggerated head toss, I make my climactic exit. There's a nice breeze blowing off the heat that has been steadily building. Edging along the pond's muddy banks to the trail at a fast clip, I stop so short, Mary plows into me.

"What the...?" Stooping to investigate I dig my finger into the mud. "No way. No bloody way." I put it to my lips.

I scramble back to Analeese. "Tell me who visited you."

"No, no one," she stammers. "You're the only one. I, I mean, your little girl came to play a bunch of times but she's not really here."

"Stop lying to me. I saw footprints in the mud. Let me look at your feet."

Letting go of her cane, Analeese plops down and removes her right sandal. Her foot is pudgy, childlike. The tracks I saw look to be that of a full-grown woman, judging from the length of the instep. A woman who's barefoot.

"Put your shoe back on, there are stickers everywhere."

As the girl buckles her sandal, I can't resist saying, "By the way, I don't believe you."

Analeese gives me a shrug.

Helice intervenes but I'm sick of her at the moment. I want a real-live girl to speak out loud in plain English, preferably one who doesn't lisp.

"Analeese, you need to tell me every—Awk, son of a bitch." A gust of wind blows dirt into my eyes. I make a scene rubbing them. I've had it with these girls, real or otherwise.

Analeese sucks in air. "She'th a lady, but she'th like your little girl. They're not real, you know. I can kinda make them out if I wrinkle my eyesth."

Her cheeks redden. "The lady was naked. I'm not sure why. I asked where her clothes were at. It's hard ta talk. Ya gotta con-cin, con-cin-trate, um, I mean ya gotta think real hard to understand." At my urging Analeese continues. "She rolled around in the mud, she said it was her nature time."

Where have I heard that? My throat goes so dry I sound like a screech owl when I say, "W-What did she tell you?"

"She told me to rub mud all over myselfth. It protect'th the skin." She smiles, pointing at my red welts. She also said it was good to eat, so I did."

Helice joins in. *That's what Maggalena told me, too.* The girls share giggles over comparing eating mud to cookies.

I sigh, "Hey, you two, this isn't a slumber party. What else did the woman say?"

Analeese gets serious. "I, um, one night I heard loud howling, like a coyote, I'm not sure. But it was scary and I think she said I was a brave girl, just like her daughter who died. She buried her in the pond. That'th why she eats the—"

"She eats the mud! I practically fall over, this is so monumental. "How would you know that?"

Analeese's face creases in thought. "She called it her com, her commune—?" She looks at me. "You know this'th?"

My mind is racing back to when I was ten and met the bohemian caretaker. Oh, wow, I suddenly remember everything. She was grieving her lost daughter and had scattered her ashes in this very pond. She showed me how she partook of the body and blood every day.

"We ate the mud together," I murmur. "Communion."

I'm deep in thought when Analeese lets out a shout.

Turning to see a fiery blaze in the far distance, I yell, "It'll hit the ridge soon. We have to get off this mountain!"

Analeese shouts, "I can do this'th, I know this'th! Firsth, jump in the pond. Get th-sopping wet, then roll around in the mud. Cover every bit of yourselfth. Eyelidsth, earsth, lipsth."

Grabbing her cane, she limps to her tent and unzips it. Before going inside she twirls around and orders, "Hurry!"

I obey. Mary follows me into the pond. She's enjoying her mud bath while I'm shaking all over. Helice counsels me to take deep breaths to calm down. She's been doing that for me all this week and it pisses me off that she's telling me what I already know. So why should I be surprised that it works?

Analeese returns with a satchel over her shoulder and a pile of clothes in her arms. "Soak 'em. Don't squeezeth the water out. They'll help protect us if the fire gets too closeth."

She tosses her cane aside and kneels to stuff water bottles into the satchel. She grabs the combo ax/shovel. She goes to stand but loses her balance, just as I realize she never finished buckling the strap on her right sandal. Down she goes. We all hear the odd snapping sound.

Now she can't get up and she's crying for her mother.

I run to her. Bending down to investigate, I shudder. There is a bone sticking out through her flesh. "Oh, God, kid, you broke your ankle. It's bad, this break is really bad."

That outburst wasn't very smart of me because now she's freaking out. Who knew an ankle could snap as easily as a twig? The fracture punctured her skin as if it were thin parchment. The wound reminds me of the canyon surrounding us: its chasm is deep and a color blend of red to purple. Will she bleed out, should I use a tourniquet? Could one wrong move kill her?

I screech, "Oh, shit, oh, shit!" Bending over the panicked girl sprawled on the dirt makes me dizzy. Feeling like a top spinning out of control, I drop to the ground alongside Analeese.

Curling up tight as a hedgehog, I wail, "I can't do this by myself."

Helice is telling me something but it sounds like a hive of berserk bees. I cover my ears.

I groan, "We should wait for the fire fighters, they'll know what to do. Why aren't they here by now? Marciano must have called it in, don't you think?" I squint at the horizon. "The fire's moving closer. We're screwed!"

Analeese won't stop screaming. Helice wants to help but a figment of my imagination can't carry her. Helice can't even talk. She's useless. It's up to me. I break down, sobbing.

I'm on the ground thrashing, my face buried in dried leaves. It's not enough of a release so I pound the red earth.

Teresa Rose Evans!

"Huh?" I twist my head. Analeese looks up so quickly, she's clearly picking up on it too.

I squint at my character. Rubbing my eyes, I wipe the sweat and dirt off my face. "Huh...you're acting a lot older all of a sudden."

Helice scowls at me. *I had to take charge. Don't worry. You're the one who designed every bit of me.*

Uh oh, I forgot her character lives to an extended old age. In that book, her nickname is Bruja and she is a force to be reckoned with. I flip over into a sitting position. "What's happening?"

I won't let you to fall apart. You're selfish and super annoying but—

"Hey, now, hold on. You can't talk to me like that."

She continues as if I hadn't spoken. *You talk big but you never do anything. Deep down, though, you've always wanted to help people. You just never figured out how. Now's your chance.*

Helping people. How does she know that? It's not like I go around disclosing my innermost thoughts. I keep my aspirations to myself, the way it should be. Phineas is the only one who knows my secret desire to be a real life super hero.

The bottom line is running smack through a forest fire with my hallucination to rescue one little brat. This is NOT my idea of saving the world. The fire is coming. We're screwed, we're screwed, we're screwed!

Trez! Helice gets my attention with a shrill call for action. *This is the moment you've been waiting for your whole life. Stand up now!*

"Ahh, I, um…" I'm not responding fast enough so she raises a fist. "All right, all right." I spring to my feet. "Jeez, don't overact. I just don't see how you can help."

She jeers. *That's what I've been doing since day one.*

"Seriously?" I burst out laughing. You have a funny way of solving situations. Oh, unless you count endless cartwheels."

She snorts. *Blah, blah, blah.*

There's no question Analeese is listening. The girl asks Helice, "How can this'th lady resth-cue me? She'th so dumb she'th arguing with a ghost-th. No offenseth, Helice'th."

Helice'th? This must mean the poor kid can't even say her own name properly. "Analees'th" needs speech therapy.

Helice snaps at me. *Pay attention, Trez. Your future is tied with Analeese no matter what.*

Analeese sticks out her tongue. "No. I don't like Trez'th."

Through sheer adrenaline, I make a run for the tent and tear it down within seconds. I grab the poles, the tent's nylon fabric, her sleeping bag, and the large coil of rope, which is surprisingly heavy. I run back and spread out large loops of the rope before laying down the girl's mummy-style sleeping bag.

"Roll over onto it." She obeys. So far so good.

The rope is long, thick, and cumbersome; it takes time and effort to wrap up the kid. Oh, here it comes, now she's complaining, telling me I'm stupid.

"I'll just wrap you up like a cocoon, little girl." Leaving only her face free, I chinch the mummy bag tight around her face. She can hardly grit her teeth at me it's so snug.

"Come here, Mary. Be a real good girl for me." I pat her rump and tell her to stay.

I take the tent poles, and, forming them into a triangle, I bind them with the tent lacings. It's awkward fashioning a harness to wrap around Mary's broad chest and back with the long stretch of rope but I'm able to connect Mary to Analeese's "sled." Sled. It reminds me of the western movies where a cowboy gets wounded. His partner always drags him back to civilization. No one should ever underestimate the indomitable will power of Teresa Rose Evans.

In short order, I have Analeese Loveland hooked up to my Rotti. Helice is by my side. With the fire rolling in from the east, we begin our descent off the mountain.

CHAPTER 22

Thanks a Lot

ANALEESE HAS BEEN COMPLAINING our entire trek down the mountain. I've tuned her out, but her shrill voice does serve a purpose, booming as loud as a public address system. If fire crews are nearby, they'll track the sound decibels.

Mary's a trooper. She could easily take a quick turn and disconnect herself from the ungracious girl she's been dragging. Truth be told, I think Mary's enjoying her primal flashback to the days when Rottweilers were used to haul heavy wooden carts.

Helice is doing a much better job of comforting her, which makes it easier for me to figure the fastest route away from the fire. Once we reach the jeep, I realize how hard it'll be to disentangle Analeese from the sled and hoist her up and into the vehicle. Besides, it's a tight fitting four-seater and we need to lay her out flat.

We instead stick to my primitive hauling system and follow the rutted trail on foot. It's tough going for Mary. I find a grassy slope so we are half hiking, half sliding downhill. Oh, this does not delight the kid at all. She's wailing like we're killing her so I close up her mummy bag face hole with the kid's stash of duct tape. She really did think of everything. But that really pisses her off. It's not my fault we encounter sharp rocks along the way down.

The fire is following us from a distance. The air is thick and it's hard to breathe, but so far we aren't in eminent danger. As long as the wind doesn't shift, we should be fine. *If* the rescue team gets here soon. If Marciano had merely humored me and never called it in, then we are royally fuc—.

Trez! Helice instantly interrupts. *No bad language.*

I twist around. Helice glaring at me. So is Analeese.

My mouth pops open to argue that it was only in my mind, I wasn't even talking out loud. But I give up. Two against one. I begin to feel sorry for duct-taped Analeese.

I lean over the sled. "Lookit. I'm rescuing you. Get it? You chose to come up on this mountain. Suck it up, nature girl."

For once, she looks cowed, maybe even regretful.

"Will you stop screaming?"

Analeese nods. I rip off the tape.

"Ow-ow-ow."

I feel bad when Analeese begins to snivel, but the fire is at our heels and the show must go on. I grab Mary's collar and lead her forward.

I call back over my shoulder, "Maybe you can get a Wounded In Action Badge. Wouldn't that be nice?"

In a few minutes, we round a bend. "What's that?" I stop and hold up a hand to listen. Mary's ears cock. She lets out a low growl.

A rescue team comes into view. Seven hunky fire fighters resplendent in their field uniforms. We all let out hoots of joy—human, canine, and hallucination alike. I allow myself to collapse into the capable arms of a blond Adonis.

He struggles to use the walky-talky, but to his credit, he doesn't drop me. An alpha male in his prime, he radios in.

"Calling all units, this is unit four. Two females located, one adult, one child, one dog. All clear. Repeat, we found the missing party. We're bringing them to base."

They make swift work of disentangling the kid and placing her on a real stretcher. Meanwhile, I nestle my head into my blond Adonis' chest as he carries me to safety, where a rescue operation is set up. He hands me off to darling paramedics who sit me down, check my vitals, wrap me in blankets, and give me water.

Helice's mood is heavy as she sidles up to me. *Trez, am I really a ghost?* She responds to my puzzled expression. *Analeese called me a ghost. It hurt my feelings.*

I hesitate, trying to think of a good answer. *Ah, well, you see. Um, look, Helice, she doesn't know you. She doesn't realize how important you are to her story. She was mad and in pain so she—*

She called me a ghost. Helice sighs. *Am I dead?*

This I can answer. *No. You were in a coma in a different world, but no, you are not dead.*

She cheers up. *So, I'm alive. Just like Analeese.*

Not exactly. As a book character, you weren't born into the physical. You're not alive the same way she and I are.

Her face darkens. *Analeese is mean, don't you think?*

I nod my head. *She is definitely mean. The good news is you can't die like we can. It should make you feel special.*

Helice groans. *Yeah. A special ghost.*

Analeese is snapping at the rescue team, she's bragging that she could have done such a better first aid job, she's complaining that the rocks hurt her back and she'll probably be paralyzed for life, that I captured her and duct-taped her mouth, that I'm a mean lady. Her complaints never stop.

I turn back to Helice and a wave of inspiration comes over me. *I think of you as an angel, Helice. A lovely, special angel in my life.*

Helice grins. *I'm an angel!* She's practically glowing she's so pleased. *I'm an angel and Analeese isn't!*

I'm laughing as I spot him. *Helice, there he is!* My heart goes pitter-patter as my delicious rookie comes into view.

I can't wait for Marciano to reach me, I call out, "Oh, Ron, I did it! I found Analeese!"

He tips his police hat to me. "That's good news."

I stop myself from embracing him. He would probably say it's improper.

I plop into a nearby folding camp chair. Sighing for extra attention, I tell him, "She broke her ankle but she's alive and well due to *me*. Now I know what being a true hero means. Rescuing her makes me feel so alive!"

He's standing before me now. "Ms. Teresa Evans?"

He's so straight and formal I play along. "Yes, Officer Marciano?" I smile, bat my eyelashes.

"You're under arrest." He handcuffs me. "You have the right to remain—"

"Wait a minute. I saved this kid. I should be given a hero's welcome." He doesn't respond the way I want so I shake my head. "It's been a long, taxing day. Let's start over." I force a smile. "Ron, you're still learning the ropes so I'll overlook this unfortunate misstep." I stop talking to squint at two men approaching. "Hey look, here comes Tobey Vallencourt. "

Marciano reacts to Tobey by muttering under his breath, but I grin as the reporter moves into position with his cameraman. Mm, Tobey looks dashing in a bush jacket.

We're live. Smiling, I look into the camera and say, "I'm delighted to announce I found the missing girl Analeese Loveland. I used grit and determination to locate her after seven—or is it eight now?—gut-wrenching days when everyone else failed, notably all the San Mateo County Police Departments."

Tobey's puts a mic under my chin. I keep it short and snappy. Plus, the cameraman is moving in for my close up. Girls don't look great being filmed with open mouths. I tilt my head to feature my best side, the side with hair. I widen my eyes and offer a closed lip, albeit benevolent smile.

Marciano orders them to turn off the camera. He says to me, "As I was saying, you have the right to remain silent."

"Oh, look, Roman's here." I call for him to come closer, after noticing the camera light is back on.

"Dr. Roman Gillespie, tell our audience how I remote viewed the girl's hiding place. That's how I knew where to find her. In the nick of time, by the way. That fire would have killed her. This nice officer needs to hear this for his report."

Roman puffs out his scrawny chest and mugs for the camera. "Ah, I wasn't there," he says out of the side of his mealy mouth. "I can't verify what you did or didn't do. Let the police weigh the evidence."

Tobey explains Roman's paranormal protocol to the audience while my rookie recites my Miranda Rights.

Marciano and I are having a private conversation. "I *found* her, Ron; you have no grounds for arrest."

"I'll let the D.A. figure out all the charges but for one, you broke the law the minute you stepped off your property."

I argue. He counters, "I warned you. Remember?"

I give a curt toss of my head. "Not to my knowledge."

"No problem. I recorded our conversation with your lawyer before you left the facility."

Oh, crap. "Hey, is that legal? Whatever, Officer, I plead innocent."

He chuckles, "Tell that to the judge." As an aside, he says, "You're killing me, Trez. You know that, right?"

The long hot Indian Summer day has morphed into evening, with dark purple and reddish orange streaks. Nice night for a walk together. Too bad it's to his squad car. I notice the chatter of birds has ceased and the first stars are breaking through the early night sky. Despite the warm glow of being so close to my rookie, I shudder in my lightweight shirt. He peels off his Police jacket and slips it around my shoulders. So fanciful, just like a Fabio cover of a romance novel.

We pass Analeese Loveland, who's on a gurney waiting to be loaded into an ambulance. Her parents are huddling around her.

I say, "'Bye, Analeese. I hope your ankle heals fast."

Her mom spins around faster than a whirling dervish. "Don't you dare speak to her." Her dad fists both his hands.

I say, "Jeez, have a little compassion for her savior."

Mr. Loveland jeers, "See you in court."

This is not a hero's reception I'd expected. *Here I Come to Save the Day* is not applicable. I hum it anyway.

Ron helps me into the back seat of his patrol car. I think his hand lingers as he adjusts my seatbelt. His silent message of our solidarity? He's a rookie, after all, he has to act tough around his peers. Maybe we'll have a good laugh about it. Someday.

I turn to see Helice sitting next to me. She smiles. *Good job, Trez. Analeese is safe. It's all that matters.*

"Yeah, well, I just got arrested. I could go to prison."

Marciano is in the driver's seat but he quickly jerks around to peer at me. "What? Who are you talking to?"

Making a show of looking around, I snort, "No one, duh."

Helice pats my hand. *I'll be with you wherever you go. I love you, Trez.*

Her sweet naiveté sucker punches me. I softly weep in triumph as Marciano puts on his siren to drive me to hell.

EPILOGUE

Everyone Has a Story

The Legion of Honor
San Francisco
Sunday, November 11, 1984

TV REPORTER TOBEY VILLENCOURT makes his way to the podium. His professionally trained voice sounds even smoother as he speaks into the microphone, "Ladies and gentlemen, thanks for attending this much heralded book launch." He waves a hand around the pinky marbled room that is bathed in the soft glow of candlelight.

"I gotta tell you folks, this launch has got to be *the* party of the year. Trez Evans has an amazing story to tell and she's written a terrific book so all of us can know her story too." He holds up a copy of my book, *The Mud Eater's Apprentice*. "And she really did burn her manuscript!" The crowd erupts in laughter. "Trez, come on up here and say a few words."

I'd lingered by one of the ornate columns nearby. Feeling as if my red stilettos are suddenly glued to the floor, it's a miracle I can make it to the podium. My knees are knocking together so loud I'm sure every one of the two hundred guests will laugh but they don't. They're too busy applauding me!

Tobey plants a kiss on my cheek and steps aside. I gaze up at the towering vaulted ceiling waiting for my heart to stop pounding. My voice is raspy as I announce, "This is the happiest day of my life. My book launch for *The Mud Eater's Apprentice*." Now I'm the one waving my book for all to see.

Yes, my published novel by a legitimate, well, fairly reputable New York press. New Jersey, precisely, but no one's going to spot-check the location. Tobey introduced me to his people in exchange for exclusive interview rights from my prison cell. I have an honest-to-god publisher *and* a literary agent. Who knew my psychic to the stars Paloma Del Mar was also a shrewd contract negotiator? She's working on getting me a sequel publishing deal. She swears she sees this and more for me in her crystal ball. As long as I can play superhero, I'm in.

This portion of my launch is airing live to Tobey's multitudes of fans. I'm an old media hand by now. Talk about fifteen minutes of fame, I've already plugged my work on our local *People Are Talking* program in September, '84. Making it onto *The Phil Donahue Show* can't be that far off. My other career goals continue to be lofty: win a Pulitzer and make the cover of *Time Magazine*.

We'd decided beforehand that I shouldn't talk. Tobey said to let the book speak for itself. So, after giving me a hug and holding up *The Mud Eater's Apprentice* one last time, Tobey concludes this program by promoting the tell-all book we wrote together after I rescued Analeese Loveland.

I Found Her! The Saga of a Missing Disabled Girl and the Woman Determined to Rescue Her by Trez Evans with Tobey Vallencourt sold pretty well around the Bay Area. That book deal was our initial commitment, then Tobey extended the contract to include my novel, so here we are.

Here comes Roman the weasel to finagle two minutes of my launch to tout his new ESP book. He can't steal my thunder. He doesn't know Tobey cued the cameraman to stop filming plus he cut the microphone.

I'm the only media darling today. Sidestepping Roman, Tobey takes my arm and escorts me off the stage to greet my adoring fans.

Speaking of reporters, they threw me under the bus and convicted me in the press after I heroically rescued the missing girl. The paparazzi dug up fifteen years of nasty dirt about me, most of which I'd forgotten and was mostly true.

Is it any wonder Analeese Loveland's parents swore their revenge and didn't stop with my arrest? Good thing Tobey is so well established. They couldn't get a thing from our book deal. After my lawyer Jackson Milan wangled me a hearing and knocked down the sentence to time served, he blocked their civil suit so my estate is intact. He diffused their bogus dispute against my novel dedication. *To the special girl who showed me the way* was not my covert message to Analeese.

The Lovelands won't stop haranguing me. The day I was released from confinement, they filed a restraining order. As if I'd want to see that brat. I read an article about her. Her photo wasn't that flattering. Her hair's grown out but she still reminds me of the "boy" in my Red Eden dream. She didn't put me on her acknowledgement page or thank me for saving her life or inspiring her kid's how-to book *Do Your Own Thing No Matter What*. She hit the library and club circuit hard so her book is on the juvenile best-selling list. It earned a coveted Critic's Choice award but I'm the real winner.

Truth be told, I wasn't hauled off to a bird man of Alcatraz prison dungeon. It was a woman's detention center here on the Peninsula with dorms, not cells, but my seven days of incarceration were intense enough for me to want to toe the legal line from now on.

These days, bimonthly out-patient sessions with art therapist Hannah Harrison keep me in mental check. Even though I'd resisted arrest from day one, I've come to recognize that my captivity instilled the discipline to birth my novel. I'm into metaphors these days. After all,

I'm a published author.

My jaws ache from posing. Now that the Channel Five live feed is done, we're finishing up my photo shoot for the January, 1985 spread in *SF City Magazine*, the "it" publication everyone who's anybody must read. It's been voted *the* most influential magazine for 1983 *and* '84.

After my criminal release, I returned to the scene of the fire. Hundreds of acres were destroyed. If anything had remained of the old hobby farm, it was decimated. As for the bohemian caretaker, there are no leads on her whereabouts. I hired the Broadmoor Detective Agency to sniff out clues. Phineas McCool is heading that operation. Considering I don't have the naked woman's name, it could be one of those proverbial needle in the hay hunts. So far, a property search going back thirty five years to 1949 has not revealed the owner of the farm Ross and I visited as kids.

Ross always says to keep a little mystery. It's for that reason I didn't tell the detectives about the stretch of an adult female's footprints in the mudflats along the pond. I counted them, I traced my fingertips along their crisp edges. I even ate of the mud as communion. Funny thing, though. I'd planned to confirm a few things as we were heading down the mountain but those tracks had disappeared.

My agent thinks that's another mystery in the making.

There's a long line of fans waiting for me to autograph their purchases. Real people far outnumber the shills hired to make me look successful. I take my place of honor at the table and sign everyone's books with my trademarked bardic moniker *TreZ*.™ These days it's all about name recognition and marketing. I'm signing so many books my hand is cramping—the real measure of a successful author!

Ross and Danny, Janine and her family from Seattle, Phineas, and a lively bunch of my girl and guy friends are here. Per my request, Jackson is playing nice with Paloma Del Mar even though his lawyer-self is still miffed she won the palimony suit against my late first ex-husband's estate.

Bethany Moraga, size zero skank and *New York Times* best-selling author, won't crash this A-list party. She fled to Mexico after her third D.U.I. It cost me a small fortune, but I one-upped her book launch into *the* social event of the year. Best of all, I beat my goal of being fairly famous by my thirty-fifth birthday by ten whole months. All is right in my world.

My guest of honor is Mary, with a bow on her big head and a sequined fairy skirt around her fat middle. She's on her best behavior motivated by liver treats. The crowd loves her.

My character Helice Polansky is by my side, soaking up the literary nuance. "The special girl" in my life probably doesn't know what a muse is. Helice frowns as I ponder the inscription. I feel a heaviness about her.

She tells me why. *It's my birthday today.*

It's hard to reply nonverbally with hundreds of people around but I try. *Hey, that's great. Happy Birthday, Helice.*

She's still frowning. *That's it? You're nicer to the fans.*

They don't expect anything from me except books.

Without Maggalena and me there'd be no book.

I slam my pen on the table and tell my fans I'll be back in five. They groan good naturedly. I promise a swift return.

I go into the ladies room and peek under stalls to assure we're alone so Helice and I can talk. First, I check my hair. After brain surgery my bald head gave off a depressed Sinead O'Connor vibe. Funny thing, I liked my hair short. Nowadays I'm rocking Pat Benatar's look, spiky with frosted tips.

You forgot my birthday. She poo-poos my excuses of working on this book launch. *You forgot last year too, Trez.*

"I did? I'm sorry." Damn stats. Developing a fleshed

out character profile for her may not have been such a great idea.

Her chin trembles. *When I came to live with you I thought we'd be a real family, like the one I had in Detroit. Maggalena says that part of my life is over and I should get used to it, but it's hard. I miss my parents.* She snivels. *I hoped you'd be my new mother. Or at least a big sister.*

Her tortured face says it all. I tell her, "You're right, I blew it. I'm sorry, Helice. I'll make it up to you, promise."

She brightens. *Can you give me new clothes?* She picks at her red cardigan. *This outfit is so childish.*

"But you look cute. I love your striped pedal pushers."

You had the same pair back when you were ten. I guess they were in fashion in 1960, or so you say. She sniffs. *Trust me, a twelve year old doesn't want to look 'cute.'*

"Twelve? When did you leapfrog two years older?" She rolls her eyes, an attitude I regret giving her. At least I no longer see two images of her. That side effect of brain trauma went away along with the majority of killer headaches.

Nowadays, migraines mostly plague me when Helice and I disagree. It's not easy living with a child, let alone a phantom one. The headaches typically subside when I admit the argument is my fault.

Helice isn't finished. *You need to give me breasts.*

"Hold on. You're a kid, don't rush growing up."

Her eyes narrow. *You can't stop time. My body is going to change whether you like it or not.*

"Ah hah. You said there is no time in the Red Eden."

A smile creeps across her face. *We live in California.*

"Fine," I sigh. "We'll talk about it. Later."

Her lower lip juts out. *You always say that. Promise?*

I nod my head. "Yes, tonight. I promise."

Oh crap. All of a sudden it dawns on me. That won't work. I have a date.

So I tell her, "Let's make it tomorrow morning okay?"

But then I'm thinking what if he spends the night.

I hold up a hand. "Um, Helice, let's schedule it late afternoon. It'll give us more time to chat."

Her eyes narrow as she mulls it over. *Talking is not enough, Trez. I'm not some sweet midcentury girl from the Red Eden anymore. I'm a modern teenager living in the here and now. You need to write new stories to show I'm maturing. Including a new wardrobe. Can we go to Paris?*

My breath expels slowly, gaining me a few seconds to think. There are no books on parenting an hallucination.

Helice hangs out in my guest house and keeps to herself during my more personal, intimate moments. She's a great listener even if I don't always take her advice. I've realized she is my voice of reason whether I want one or not.

Helice wants me to give her breasts. She'll probably expect a period too. Oh, Lord, kissing a boy isn't that far off. My saving grace as her "parent" is that she's not aware of her three husbands from past book versions. At least not yet.

Thank goodness a woman walks into the bathroom. Helice knows better than to engage me in such a small space. She leaves me with a cryptic shot: *Analeese is very unhappy.*

"HEY TREZ, YOU MADE a huge haul today." Ross loves to count money. Janine and her husband rave about my book sales, embarrassing their son Matthew. He's not much older than Helice, come to think of it. I'm cool in his eyes. I think...

Everyone's ready to head out to dinner at Stars, the

latest San Francisco hotspot. Danny asks me to join them but Phin doesn't know about my date. I don't want to hurt Phin. He's a dear friend but that's all, no matter how hard he wishes.

I'm bent down fussing with Mary's bow when I detect a manly scent. Before getting up, I sneak a wink at my hallucination. When Helice recognizes who my escort is her expression is priceless.

My heart skips as he says, "Hi Trez. You ready?"

"Why, yes I am, Officer Marciano."

From the looks of her, Helice is expecting to come along.

I give her a cheery grin. *This is my happy ending so butt out.*

I'm standing now, ready to face the man of my dreams.

My dashing rookie takes my hand.

Ron and I set off on our very first date.

The End

Acknowledgements

No one truly creates alone, even if we might crawl into a dark writerly cave and refuse to emerge from time to time. My writing and editing skills have flourished since the year 2000 from attending San Bruno's weekly critique group, The Crystal Springs Creative Writers. However, it proved laborious to present three or four pages a week of The Mud Eater's Apprentice, my then 500 page novel-in-progress, to a short story group.

One hapless day, I burned that manuscript and scores of its versions in a fit of literary rage. Out of the fire, a new story emerged: *Novelmania, My Ticket to Crazy Town*. Fiction follows fact, sometimes. Yes, I did indeed burn the bloody thing. No, I was never hauled off to the loony bin. In search of a new novel writing group, I discovered Lazy Laid Back Writers. My fellow LLBW members were with me when I first held up a Mason jar filled with the ashes of my work, and all the way through to the home stretch of this publication. Lisa Meltzer Penn, Ann Foster, James Hanna, Tory Hartmann and Christopher Wachlin will be lifelong recipients of my heartfelt gratitude for their suggestions, at times sharp criticisms, and laugh out loud moments as Trez Evans, my alter ego, run amuck, and crept out from some place deep within me.

Tory Hartmann has been more than an avid LLBW member. She is my colleague on the San Mateo County Fair Literary Stage, and publisher of the fair's annual Carry the Light anthology, as well as this book. We have a soul sister connection, sharing an almost supernatural kinship with the zany female protagonists in our respective novels.

SHRP
Sand Hill Review Press

Made in the USA
Lexington, KY
23 June 2017